Walking the Dog

Contents

Acknowledgments *vii*

Aubade *1*
Maternity *6*
Paterson's Flats *13*
Candlebark *22*
Fragment *29*
The Sea *39*
A Family Story *57*
Together *63*
Adult Education *70*
Nuclear *86*
Chanson d'Automne *97*
Cream Sponge on Sunday *101*
Nature *109*
Flight *119*
Interior *126*
The Ringbarker's Daughter *132*
Antique *155*
Wayside *167*
Selling Out *184*
Solitaire *193*
Walking the Dog *210*

Acknowledgments

These stories have appeared, with some differences, in the following publications: "Aubade" in the *Canberra Times, Australian Voices: Poetry and Prose of the 1970s,* ed. Rosemary Dobson (Canberra Fellowship of Australian Writers in association with the Australian National University Press, 1975), *The True Life Story of . . . ,* ed. Jan Craney and Esther Caldwell (University of Queensland Press, 1981); "Maternity" and "Fragment" in *Westerly*; "Paterson's Flats" in *Westerly, Coast to Coast 1967–1968,* ed. A.A. Phillips (Angus and Robertson); "Candlebark" in *The Sun, Festival and Other Stories,* ed. Brian Buckley and Jim Hamilton (Wren, 1974); "Cream Sponge on Sunday" and "A Family Story" (under the title "A Family Picture") in *The Sun*; "Together" in *Luna,* read over 5UV (Adelaide) 1980; "Nuclear" and "Nature" in *Muse*; "Adult Education" in *Paper Children: McGregor Literary Competition Anthology*, ed. Alan Lawson (Darling Downs Institute Press, 1982); "Flight" in the *Canberra Times*, read over 2XX (Canberra) 1982; "Selling Out" in The *Dandenong Journal* Short Story Supplement, "Interior" and "Chanson d'Automne" in *The Bulletin.*

The half-dozen lines of poetry quoted in "The Sea" are from Matthew Arnold's "The Forsaken Merman".

Aubade

When Alvie Skerritt woke, the kids Trish and Billy were squabbling in the next room and the wind was howling in the snowball tree and making kinky shadows on the curtains. Two people, fat round heads swaying on stalky bodies, short arms outstretched, kept coming at her across the curtains, stroking the windowpane, whispering *Alvie! Alvie!* . . . Herbie Mason and Butch Gilbert. She'd sat next to Herbie Mason that period Miss Lamb had handed back their maths tests — and just as she'd expected he'd slid his hand along her leg, over her knee until she'd shot her knee up hard against the desk and bruised his stupid knuckles for him. But Herbie Mason tried that on with all the girls. Real creep. What had she sat next to him for in the first place, then? . . . Alvie jumped out of bed and twitched the curtains apart and of course it was only that massy green shrub with the great white flowers that the wind was tossing against the window, but it unnerved her. Well, goodbye today. The kids were making such a racket by now that she guessed her mother hadn't got up again, which meant *she* would have to see to breakfast and cut all the lunches and plait Trish's hair — and then push her bike to school against a headwind. You couldn't win.

She thumped her feet all the way down the passage so that her father actually put down his paper and said, "Alvie, your mother has a *headache* . . . " So what, she thought, whose fault is that, eh? If there wasn't another kid on the way we could have carpet like other people . . . Of course he didn't have a reply to these savage, silent thoughts, oh no, he never did, just hid behind his paper and when he'd swallowed his tea he skipped off to work — stayed overtime — coward! She jerked her thumb at him behind his paper so that the kids giggled and she slapped Trish and slammed peanut butter onto everyone's sandwiches. They hated peanut butter.

. . . He was always on about things like pollution and smoking and H-bombs and trail bikes (Butch Gilbert had one, lucky dog), so that after awhile you couldn't do anything without wondering what *he'd* think . . . Like screwing up the bread wrapping and aiming it plunk! into the tidy. You told yourself you were a dill but all the same you made yourself retrieve it and smooth out the creases and then you used it to wrap the sandwiches. Where was the fun in that? Everyone else had their lunches in neat little plastic bags. If she had a job now, say on a cash register, she could please herself and buy what she wanted instead of always listening to *him* . . .

"Can I leave school, Dad?"

"No, you cannot." And then the usual spiel about all the opportunities for kids these days, his generation never had anything like it . . . Alvie switched off. Soon he'd be asking her about the result of her maths test and she'd have to tell him . . . and he wouldn't believe her. No wonder. Could anyone really be *so* dumb? After all those months of Miss Lamb banging away with her knuckle on Alvie's skull, crying "You stupid, stupid girl!" Miss Lamb had one red ear and one white ear and a mouth that sprang like a mousetrap. "It seems you don't even know your own name, child!" Miss Lamb took Alvie's test paper and walked out to the front of the class and crossed her legs. Miss Lamb always stood with her legs crossed, like someone who needed to go in a hurry and had to hold on. "Do you know what this stupid girl has written at the top of her test? Algebra Skerritt."

Algebra Skerritt . . . Alvie wanted to scream out against the ugliness of it all, the silly grinning class, Miss Lamb with her red ear and white ear, the creeping fingers of Herbie Mason. Against her father who was against all the fun things and sat there talking about the importance of education while Billy poked his fingers in the toaster and dilly Trish asked if God was everywhere and her father answered "Yes dear" so mechanically that Alvie knew he hadn't heard a word.

"Inside this room?"

"Yes."

"In my weeties?"

"Yes yes."

"On my spoon? In my mouth? Then I — AM — GOD!"

"Oh Dad stop her!" shouted Alvie. "She doesn't know what she's saying! That's just nonsense — it's blasphemous — how do we know there is a God anyway? You weren't even *listening*!"

"What's all the excitement?" said Ray Skerritt, rising, pushing in his chair, reaching for his lunch with one hand and his "Work Safely" overall with the other. "So long, everyone. I might make it in time for dinner. Look after your mother."

Alvie flung away to her room which she had once shared with Trish but had to herself now that she was growing up. Staying up to study and arguing about bras and staring at herself in the mirror. Sometimes she felt a big goof, alone in the solid quiet with the pop stars and footballers that she and all the other girls collected to pin up on the walls. Then she would turn up her tranny full blast. Or she'd tear down the posters and call in Trish and Billy and they'd have a cushion fight, or she'd jump out at them from the wardrobe.

She called Trish now, and the little kid wandered in as though the room were still hers, dabbing at her eye shadow and quizzing her about the safety razor. "What you got in that jar, Alvie?"

"Never you mind. Come here, I've got to do your hair."

Trish dodged, and snatched up the jar. "*Grasshoppers,*" she said, looking disgusted. "What for, Alv?"

"Oh belt up, Trish!" Alvie seized her hairbrush and began to bang away at Trish's scalp. Serve her right if it hurt. That jar of grasshoppers had been a secret. They gave Alvie a funny feeling still, like that time she'd sat next to Herbie Mason. She'd caught them a week ago and released them into an old coffee jar with holes punched in the lid. She hadn't bothered about food or water. She wanted to watch them mating. There were plenty in pairs out amongst the vegetables and on the nature strip, but she had caught only single ones because *she* wanted to be the one who ran things. Like God. Or Miss Lamb. Only they hadn't mated. They hadn't done anything except creep around in the bottom of the jar and stare back at her hugely. And then they'd begun to eat each other. First a front leg had disappeared, then a hunk out of a thigh, then half a head.

Trish pulled a sick face. "Throw them out."

Alvie nodded. She didn't want to look at them again. "You. And then get off to school. I've got to see Mum."

But in her mother's room she stood twisting her bangles, not knowing what it was she wanted to say. And her mother didn't seem to hear those struggling thoughts. She held up the maternity smock she had just finished hemming. "I'd love a cup of tea, Alv," she said, in a weary, pleading voice that Alvie thought was a bit put-on. "Has everyone gone? Sorry I wasn't up. I think I could stagger to the kitchen now. Oh I'll be glad when this baby's here." And she stretched, smiling that slow, absent smile that Alvie hated.

She set about making a fresh pot of tea, one eye on

the clock. Her mother, wearing her pretty new smock, padded into the kitchen. If she's well enough to dress up and do her hair, why does she leave everything to me? thought Alvie angrily. She watched her mother sit down and put her feet up on another chair. Her legs were knotted with veins. That's what having kids does to you, thought Alvie. We're cannibals. Like those things in the jar.

"And on your way home," Joan Skerritt was saying, "I want you to call in here — and here. I've made a list. Whatever would I do without you, Alvie?"

Well at least I'm good for something, thought Alvie. And felt trapped. She kept glancing at her mother's belly. What did it feel like, growing a baby inside you? What if it turned out . . . well, stupid, even after you'd given it all the opportunities you never had? What if . . .

"What's the matter, Alvie?" asked Joan Skerritt irritably. "Is my smock funny?"

Alvie guessed wildly at the amount of tea she was shaking out of the caddy. "I'm never going to have children," she said. "All the bother — the headaches — "

Joan Skerritt laughed. "Now don't you worry your head about things. We're all right. We'll manage. You're looking too glum so early in the morning. Is anything the matter?"

Alvie shook her head. There was nothing, really. Or everything. Just . . . living. It was all too big to explain. And it was time she went to school. She had just seen Butch Gilbert and Herbie Mason ride past the house, and circle around and ride past again. If she hurried, she could catch up. She wouldn't speak to them, of course, oh no, the creeps! Just toss her head and sail past. But hurry!

Maternity

Pillows of cloud lolled in the sky. There was a wind — far below in the nature strips trees woke and stirred. A child ran. Mrs Girvan's glance slid over him and stopped. Teddy! It wasn't, of course, but she watched from her bed until he ran into one of the houses. Did Teddy miss her? Joe never said.

She followed a rag of sunlight drifting over the town. In hospital where the temperature never changed the day outside was whatever you made it . . . warm, windy, just enough to put a bit of life into the wash and make it easy to fold. Being in hospital was like waiting to be born, she mused. "Ten days' holiday for you now, Betty," said the doctor when he delivered the baby. She smiled . . . someone else to think up meals, herd the boys to the table, bolt after the cows when they came tangling their horns in her sheets and towels, someone else to be alert always for the patter of raindrops, the squall of tears . . . She drifted across a sky of sleep.

"What are you doing" — Teddy crying, the cows trampling Joe's lettuce, Joe in for dinner — "lolling in bed like this, Mrs Girvan?" Guilt jolted her. Sister Daniel, straight and cool as a thermometer, stood by the bed. "You must either lie flat on your tummy, arms by your side, one pillow under your hips — or sit bolt upright. Otherwise you'll *go bad inside*!" She slapped the hard pillows, tweaked the bedspread into order. "Now rest while you can."

Mrs Girvan's body tingled. Rest! As Sister Daniel hurried out Sister Darcy ran in to slap and straighten all over again because Matron was on her round. Then Maisie, clinging like a roughrider to her polisher, "This machine's the very devil! *Sorry*, Mrs Girvan!" as it cracked and jarred the bed. "Sleeping?"

Rest . . . She'd heard of spirit drinkers begging for a smell of the cork, just a smell of the cork . . . "Gee you're cranky, Mum!" grumbled Joe and the six boys as she dragged herself through the dreary months with a nightmare sitting on her head. "Get something from the chemist . . . Use a knitting needle," advised her girl friends when it was clear poor Bet had fallen in again. She watched a stray pumpkin swelling amongst her sweet peas, her sweet william and sweet alice. "I didn't root you out," she bargained. *"Be a girl."*

"Just one more push, dear. You're doing very well, dear. *Now* — one last — good — push!" But it was no use. Her body wouldn't obey. "I'm too tired. I can't — " The mask was clamped over her face, the gas machine roared. She struggled faster! faster! to escape the spinning lights, the mask, the pain . . .

"Mrs Girvan! Here's your darling baby, Mrs Girvan!" cried the mothercraft nurse, Celia, the pretty one who could have been her own daughter. Her eyes fluttered open and she wondered at the red old man's face, the elongated head, the instrument bruises on each temple. "There now — wasn't it all worthwhile?" bubbled Celia. "Isn't he beautiful?"

He . . . She closed her eyes and wept.

"Awake, Mrs Girvan?" Sister Daniel prodded her stomach and wrote something in her book. "Awake, Mrs Frost?"

"She says me fungus has gone right down. Whatever does she mean?" giggled Mrs Frost who was seventeen. "I'm going to be a grandma at thirty-four so I can hop around on the floor with me grandchildren," she boasted. "I reckon it's a real shame the way some women run to seed."

I'm just a dried-out thistle, thought Mrs Girvan as Mrs Frost changed into yet another new nylon bed-jacket. She glanced down at her own poor old nightie pulled together with a pin, pink once or blue or cream and now a sad grey like her teatowels and tablecloths and especially her hands — everything that once had been pastel and pretty. That was bore water for you. A slow flush burned along her cheekbones as she recalled something one of the aides had said. The girl had washed and dressed and trollied her from the delivery room into the ward and was unpacking her case. "These nursing bras look pretty tatty," she pounced, holding them up. "Are they *clean*?"

"Yes." The water . . . she was too tired to explain. But as soon as Joe came in she insisted that he go into "Madame's" and buy her two new brassieres. "Aw struth! Couldn't one of the nurses — "

"*No,* Joe." And then she hardly wore them. Her milk just fizzled out.

"I never had trouble before, Doctor, I gushed everywhere. I don't know, I'm drinking jugs and jugs of water, maybe he's just a hungry baby, maybe the milk's slow coming — "

"You fed all the others, you say?"

"Oh yes!"

"Well then, don't you feel you've done your share? Give yourself a rest, Betty. Plenty of milk on your dairy farm, isn't there?"

"Yes but — yes. All right, Doctor."

"That's the idea. Don't want to let these little things get us down, do we?"

He smiled — she smiled . . . but when he had gone she

fell to thinking about that brindle heifer Joe had sold in disgust to the butcher because all the molasses and grain and grass hay he poured into it went straight to its back while its calf bawled and butted in vain for a drink.

"I've had to wean the baby, Joe."

"Plenty of good cows at home," said Joe.

He was leaning on the heart table over her bed, turning the pages of one of the magazines her girl friends had brought her. "You must get awfully sick of yourself," they'd said, "with nothing to do all day." He hadn't kissed her, in fact he hadn't even said hello but had filtered in with his eyes lowered and a silly little half-smile on his mouth and a nod at her before he hid himself in her true romance. Thrusts of laughter from the other wards hurt her — what *did* husbands and wives find to say to one another? Mrs Frost was telling Mr Frost how he'd love changing the baby, she'd done it twice already and tomorrow —

Just then Joe spoke. "Sow had piglets last night. Thirteen."

"Oh good! Thought she was getting close. Are they sows or boars? Thirteen's a good lot. Are you pleased? Did you tell Teddy? What else, Joe?"

"Nothing else. Just thirteen."

"I mean — the boys."

He took another magazine. "Harry went to a dance last night. Never got in till three."

"Till *three*!" Her heart died. "What on earth was he doing out till — "

"Look don't fuss, Bet. He's tough. He was up again at five for the cows."

"But out till *three*, Joe!"

"I tell you, Betty — stop worrying! Teddy dropped his sandwiches in a puddle and never had any lunch today."

Teddy — her baby! "But he's got a plastic box for his sandwiches. They shouldn't have got wet."

"Yes but he lost it."

"How? How come he lost it, Joe? What happened? Tell me, Joe."

"A maggie nesting down by the dam dived at him he says so he threw his lunch box at it and it fell in the dam out of reach."

She felt quite helpless. Dragging things out of Joe was like milking that brindle heifer. "By the dam! But he never goes that way to school. What if he'd — Why weren't Danny and Colin looking after him? Colin's old enough, he's got some sense. Where were they, Joe?"

She saw those big boys Colin and Danny running fast, running away from little Teddy as he struggled across great tussocks and stumbled into wheel ruts, clutching his scrap of lunch until out of the sky a monstrous bird menaced him, swooping and snapping.

"Colin dipped out on school today. Reckons he's got a crook throat. Nothing much. Took him to the doctor this morning. Got him some honey balsam. He's okay."

She fell back against the pillows. Her throat was shaking. To stop the tears she stared very hard at Mr Frost as he bounced out of the ward clutching his baby-viewing card. He looked no older than Harry.

Mrs Frost raised her voice. "Mr Girvan! Aren't you going along with all the dads to look at baby Girvan *today*?" she teased. It was her daily joke with them. Joe grinned, turning his magazine.

"Not him, not Joe!" laughed Mrs Girvan, making herself laugh, rushing in to explain once more. "Joe never was one for babies. Saw Harry just ten minutes after he was born and that was enough for him. Soon enough when he gets the baby home, he reckons. He'd rather look at a new calf or a piglet, wouldn't you, Joe? And as for a nurse of the baby — not him! Wait till kids are interesting, round about a year, he says. You won't catch Joe near a baby!" — bruising herself with the joke. Joe grinned.

"Colin's sick, Joe says you've seen him — Is he bad?" she babbled as soon as the doctor appeared on his round. "He wouldn't be getting — It isn't like Colin — "

"Listen, Betty." Her blood stood still. "I examined young Colin thoroughly and apart from a bit of a cough there's not a thing wrong with him." She lived again. "He could be missing his mum. Which reminds me — you must be wondering when I'll let you go home. I thought all the mothers started asking from about the third day, Sister?" Sister Daniel, who waited with her notebook and heard without listening, smiled an aseptic little smile. "Time marches on, as they say, Betty." He consulted the notebook. "Saturday then?"

"All right, Doctor. And Doctor — "

"Yes?"

"This baby wasn't a girl — "

"The chances of having a girl were pretty slim, Betty. Not at your age, not after six boys."

"Oh well — nothing like trying again!" But at the awful prospect the words trembled in her throat and turned into tears. "Seven's enough, *no more*," she muttered.

"We can certainly help you there, Betty," said the doctor, so mercifully that she couldn't stop, the tears simply gushed. "Seven's the final score, right? You discuss it with Joe, and we'll talk about it again in a few weeks, okay? And listen to me, before you face up to them on Saturday — "

Face Saturday? Face Joe perched for dinner the baby howling the cows at the washing again while sleep rasped her eyelids and scattered her wits like chickens? Face Saturday? "Doctor, I *can't* — "

"Try and relax. Have a good rest. You deserve it." He smiled at her until she smiled in return. "Right, now who's next, Sister?"

As she sagged, invoking the rest they said she deserved, Sister Daniel returned with a medicine glass. "Doctor said to take these," she said. "For your headache."

"But I haven't got a headache." She stared with rising despair at the two little white tablets lying in the medicine glass. "I know what these are — tranquillizers!"

Automatically Sister Daniel began to straighten the pillows. "Only for a day or two, dear," soothing and smoothing the pillows. "You're just a bit homesick, missing your family — "

Paterson's Flats

"Then if you won't lean on my shoulder, Pa, at least take your stick!"

Paterson ignored his daughter-in-law, conscious in the back of his scalp of her disapproval as unaided he drove one foot after the other out of his room and down the passage. Like sheep his feet huddled and jammed together, ready to bolt in all directions should his will-power falter. He heard Margaret, busy with clean linen for his bed, thumping obedience into his pillows. Her voice running after him snapped at his heels. "Remember, Pa dear, only to the bathroom and then straight back to bed!" He made a little rush at the bathroom door and shut it against her, locking himself in the bathroom's neat suburban safety. Women!

Breathing heavily, he clutched the chrome taps over the clean pink hand-basin, and saw his liver-spotted, swollen hands grown straight and strong as a boy's again, and black from bagging potatoes with his father all morning. He wanted to rinse his hot wrists, splash his face, gulp from his cupped hands. As he reached towards the brass tap that ran rainwater from the tank outside into the crazed porcelain sink (on the wood stove hot water simmered continuously in the heavy black kettle), *her* voice stung him like droplets of steam: "Waste not want not! Mark my words, son, it won't rain tomorrow!"

Women! His shoulders sagged under a hundredweight of provisos. Deliberately the old man avoided the plug in Margaret's pink hand-basin, poking his fingers one by one under the gushing tap. "We'll do just what the doctor says, Pa, and we'll be back on our feet in a flash." Soapsuds trembled through his fingers. On his feet, she said! Didn't she know he'd been trying his whole damned life? If at first . . . He sucked his gums with excitement as a scheme suddenly suggested itself. Steadying himself against the hand-basin, he thrust out his jaw at his enlarged image in the shaving-mirror. Today he would beat that bed.

But hurry! Teeth — he fumbled them from their beaker, wiping them across his lapel before plunging them into his gums. He grinned. *She* would have approved . . . eat with your teeth in . . . shave every day — shave! He glanced uneasily at his razor. If he hung around any longer Margaret would have finished his bed and his scheme would be ruined. Hang shaving!

In his haste to escape he brushed against the passage walls and the doorway of his bedroom. "Sit down, Pa!" panicked Margaret, dropping a heap of bedding and pushing him into the chair by the window. "I'm sorry — you *were* quick today!"

"Beat you, did I?" Paterson grinned, easing his old bones into the comfort of the chair. Its foam cushions sighed with success. This was the life, here by the window. Above the high brick wall that his son Colin had built to shut out the roar and thrust of the traffic, Paterson could just glimpse the sky. It was a sky white with stones. Stones were a sign of good soil, they said, if you waited long enough. Not an acre of sky could he ever see from that coffin his bed. When Margaret turned around and saw how much happier he was out of it, the dear kind girl would gladly let him stay up for his Akta-Vite and — his chest hurt with cunning — by drinking the foul stuff slowly he would have all the morning to sit watching that old dog the wind at work. "He'd a'been a champion only I never got round to training him right," he muttered. Margaret looked at him kindly. There was such a bustle and bleating in his ears that her voice grew distant, like Kate's thin shout from the house to the yards when she'd wanted something — "I'm out of wood!" or "Dinner time!"

"Bother, I've forgotten your Akta-Vite," Margaret was saying. Akta-Vite! Why couldn't she let him be? "But I've brought you a surprise, Pa. Look." On his plate with his pink pill, his white pill and his red pill was a slice of orange cake instead of the usual dry biscuit. The dear kind girl. His jaw trembled greedily. He wished she would go away so that he could take out his teeth to eat it.

Something held her, however. "You didn't manage your shave this morning, Pa," she pursued him. "Listen dear, I have a plan. Why don't I shave you each morning after breakfast?"

Paterson's eyes bulged. Let a woman shave him! "I — I — I — " He began to cough.

Margaret made a little rush at him. "Dear, now I've tired you keeping you out of bed. Lean on my shoulder — "

Bed! His bellow came out as a whisper. "What about that — "

"Of course, Pa, right away — but are you sure you can — "

"*Akta-Vite!*"

"Yes, Pa." In the doorway she turned triumphantly. "I told you the taste would grow on you!"

A bus drummed along the street, or in his head. They were forever pushing him, Margaret and that doctor. Bed! He dropped his lip. The pillows sat like a tombstone, the green blankets, with the sheet turned down like a nudge to get in, were as thick and springing as new grass, as — Paterson jerked forward — as Klepl's river flats! The rye grew knee-deep, the clover bloomed. But where were the cattle? He struggled to his feet. He knew — in his grandson Timothy's bedroom, in a box called "Farm Set". Painfully the old man set off on his second long walk that morning. It was a crying shame the way young Klepl understocked those flats of his. Paterson was forever telling him so. Time and again he had put off whatever he was supposed to be doing, planting those bloody poplars in a new washaway, or burying a couple of milkers that had died of bracken poisoning or swallowing stones, in order to stroll over to his neighbour's for a yarn, cornering the boy with his advice until young Klepl was forced to take his foot out of the mounting stirrup and listen. "Never mind what anyone else tells you, Will, *you're* the boss now. Those flats should be carrying twice the stock you've got." "Yes, but it says here — " and Klepl would quote some new-fangled nonsense from *Farm and Home* or *The Weekly Times*.

This stubborn streak in the younger man maddened Paterson: "Now, if *I* was running those river flats — " But Klepl would twitch his long hands, sliding his eyes like tea in a saucer. "Ar, she'll be right, she'll be right." That *she* made Paterson's heart pound his ribs in rage as with fingers thickened like artichokes he grasped what he could of Tim's farm set. Anyone could see it was Mary Klepl who ran the place. What else, when the woman spent her life beside him, riding every inch of the property, going to auctions, planting out seedlings as fast as he turned the garden beds, prodding Paterson about that saffron on their boundary fence? She'd have been a pretty girl, dressed up and silenced, if it had ever struck her to seek Kate Paterson's advice on women's fashions. Of course it was Will Klepl who did the actual talking: "I'll come over and give you a hand with those thistles, Pat. Thursday suit you?" Pinned down, Paterson would agree with a bad grace, fancying he felt *her* influence in the background, like a bloody conscience . . .

. . . "What are you doing hanging about instead of getting on with it I'd like to know? You mark my words — " (She was forever at him to mark her words — but twice down the passage was a fair effort, Mother, and Tim's bed cradled him.) "In *my* day young people didn't moon about under their betters' feet, they hopped in and helped" — glancing at her empty woodbox — "or improved their minds" — flinging her hand towards the cherished old books of her girlhood, those treasures he was always meaning to read — "or they went courting. You mark my words, *the world mirrors a man's face.* Have you washed yours? Put your work clothes to soak?" He'd forgotten, of course. "Don't polish your shoes on your cuffs! You never think of me cooking and washing for you all these years and you chasing after that Kate what's-her-name every other minute and nothing but a dirt floor in my kitchen! Eh? Eh? Your father would turn in his grave!"

And of course she was right. He could never argue with her. Seizing an axe he would flee into the gully where a small creek ran more swiftly each winter, in order to ringbark a few more of the straggling old gums along its banks that in later years he tried to hold with poplars. Damn her! Damn her! as he gashed the sappy wood. It was his farm, wasn't it? His life? She wasn't the only one who dreamed of the thin stony hills turning themselves into a parkland. As for Kate, let her sit there in her fine room at the schoolhouse with her gloves and her parasol and her best hat! She had no hold over him. And if she fancied that he owed her an explanation — "But of *course* I understand how it is on a farm, Pat dear," cried his dearest Kate. "And my afternoon wasn't wasted a bit — look, I made you a scarf."

Oh wonderful, perfect Kate! She called the road "the

street" till the day she died. He had been lucky. "Of *course* you're too busy to put a floor in the kitchen," she soothed. "Though I do think it's horrid of Will Klepl to insist you and he net your boundary fence when everyone *knows* rabbits are part of a farm. Now I've heard of a carpenter who could do the whole floor one weekend. I'm amazed that your mother — But if he's too expensive — "

"No, of course not," Paterson lied.

"And then I'll repaint the kitchen. And throw out all those old saucepans. Oh, I have such wonderful plans!"

So much energy . . . Memories flew against the old man like moths . . . His boots thrown off in her kitchen. New bread. Kate kneeling in her garden, her hand suspended above the soil and a seedling crisp in her fingers. Himself leaning over the back gate, watching her. He wasn't too keen on gardening himself, fiddling about with seedlings he had to get in before the roots dried out and then chasing after weeds that sprang up thicker and faster than whatever he'd planted, especially after that time he dug in barrow-loads of rich rotted-down sheep manure from under the shearing shed. Poor Kate could hardly bring herself to touch the soil after that.

He smiled wryly at other memories . . . Kate creeping out at daybreak to the cold stove. Himself opening his eyes just as she slipped her nightdress over her head, so that, although he wasn't in the habit of staring at her as she dressed, her gaze held his until he was sure that when she moved she would run to him, falling back into the warm bed as though she had all the morning to give him. And why not, he argued. Why should she come to him only at night, the last thing after setting for breakfast, shutting the stove, chaining the dogs, like some sort of sleeping draught? He stirred impatiently as she hesitated. What was she waiting for? Just as he moved

to fling back the bedclothes, *her* voice startled him:
"You mark my words — you mark my words — " so
that to save Kate from indiscretion he cried harshly
"Get your clothes on, woman! You'll freeze to death!"

For a moment her eyes burned him, then she plunged
into her clothes as though she too felt the presence of a
third person, fleeing into the safety of her kitchen while
he huddled under the warm inertia of blankets. Hang
the overdraft, he would buy her that piano! She deserved that. Hadn't she grown up amongst lovely things?
The kind *she* had wanted — he really would read those
old books, those treasures. He would — Suddenly there
was Kate at his shoulder saying in a perfectly normal
voice, as though he had just woken, "I've brought you
your cup of tea, dear. You work so hard once you're
up, you stay there to drink it." Funny how he never
resented Kate's little domestic tyrannies! Love curled
around him like the steam of his tea. Kate knew how to
look after a man. He lay in bed until the cows'
anguished bellowing at last forced him out to the
milking shed. Damn it, he'd wasted half his morning in
bed! *She* would have prodded him out hours before!

Clutching Tim's farm set, he began his slow return
along the passage. Kate wouldn't like animals in his
room. Swish! swish! with her mop. Hadn't realized
farms were so dirty, she said; couldn't bear the smell of
his boots. Swish! swish! — "Don't walk where I've
mopped, dear!" As though he would dare! . . . But all
the same a floorboard in the passage creaked —

"Is that you, my poppet?" called his daughter-in-law
from her kitchen. "Timothy? What are you doing inside?"

The blood bolted in his ears. Don't let her push you
around, son! But she'd beaten him every time.

"Did my poppet remember his teeth this morning?"
called Margaret.

With dull rage Paterson levered his teeth from pocket to mouth. Always onto a bloke! . . . "Tickey, eh?" Klepl had said, springing upon him as drearily he pulled together two wool-covered strands of barbed wire where his sheep had been scratching themselves. He hadn't got around to dipping them that year. "Listen, Pat, you're fond of advising me. I suppose you've heard those river flats are coming onto the market?"

Paterson shook his head. "No one tells me anything these days."

"You've lived in the district longer than me. What do you reckon the flats are worth? Truth is, I'm thinking seriously of putting in a bid. Crazy, eh? Selling ourselves to the bank. But I look at it this way. It's a kind of promise I made to myself, to farm a bit of good land one of these days. Bloody hills. Cripple a bloke in the end." Paterson nodded. "And take this little bloke," Klepl rushed on, his eyes bright with dreams as he looked down at his small son. "We've got to think of his future."

Paterson felt suddenly angry. Didn't anyone think of *his* future? It hadn't even crossed Klepl's thick head that Paterson himself might be keen to own those river flats. When Klepl, damn him, had at last ridden away, Paterson dropped the broken strands of wire and slowly walked back to Kate, half listening for the piano that often welcomed him home these days. Paterson's river flats. Kate would be pleased. He deserved a bit of good land sometime instead of crippling hills all his life. It would mean selling himself to the bank, of course. He'd had bad luck lately, carrying too much stock through a trusting faith in rain. He would have to be careful. Sell the piano. No more dresses for the girls. And Colin could forget about going away to learn wool-classing. His hands trembled as he pushed the little animals over the thick green blanket. He grinned. The rabbits were as big as the sheep. Soon fat cattle grazed knee-deep. He would cut grass hay in the spring. And put in a new front fence and paint the name over the gate: *Paterson's Flats*! *She* would have liked that. He listened in vain for something appropriate from Kate's piano — "See the Conqu ring Hero Comes". He'd forgotten that it was washing day, that since breakfast time Kate had been boiling clothes in kerosene tins on the kitchen stove and carrying them outside to be rinsed in big tubs on the back verandah. Late in the day though it was, she had just finished, and he watched her as she bailed the last of the greasy water over the brown patch they called the back lawn. She straightened her back when she saw him. Her smile and her voice were tired. "Won't it be wonderful when we put in that hot-water service next autumn? I'm so glad you let me write away to the plumber, dear. You can't imagine how much I've missed a proper laundry and bathroom."

He smiled faintly. He could never argue with her. He was beaten before he started. She came up to him. "You look done in. Have you been working too hard? Sometimes I think I should have learned more about farming, gone out with you and picked up stones and helped you plant poplars — but so much dirt everywhere! I've been scrubbing and polishing for *years* — "

He began to laugh. He put his arms around her and leant his head on her shoulder, fumbling for words. "You're perfect, perfect. You're all I ever wanted of woman — "

Laughing until he was tired. Life was too strong for him. He needed a shoulder to lean on. Wherever was Margaret? Wasting time in her kitchen. She had already forgotten his Akta-Vite once that morning and here he was still out of bed. He stood up. He would have to climb in by himself. Paterson's Flats! He sank into the springing clover, drawing the green blanket right up to his chin. Sapped of energy, he closed his eyes to the truth: great hills and gullies wherever he thrust his legs.

Candlebark

"For me? Just a moment, everyone, please." Miss Coombes came across the classroom to the doorway to take the book. The senior master smiled. It was automatic now, his little knack of making people come to him; it made them aware of him, established authority. And he could see that she would need his guidance in her teaching; she was so young, hardly older than the senior students, and spilling over with airy-fairy idealism he shouldn't wonder. When, for instance, she realized that he was giving her one of last year's exercise books to take her notes from, she tossed back her long hair and announced that her class would make all their own notes from their own reading and research.

Geoffrey smiled down at her from the wisdom of many years. "That's fine in theory, Miss Coombes." He articulated her name very carefully, as though it were a little girl's party bow he was tying. "That's fine in theory, but when it comes to more than two or three students ever getting to the core of things . . . " He shook his head apologetically. Miss Coombes frowned. Her nose was faintly freckled, like a little girl's. Geoffrey felt protective. "That fellow, for instance, Miss Coombes — " nodding at a big red-haired boy slouching in the front desk. Gareth Hobson. For two years Geoffrey had been trying to reach that boy; for two years Gareth Hobson had stared insolently through him. He dropped his voice to a friendly hiss. "Hobson. He simply can't work on his own, you see. He has to be driven all the way. Under the tightest of reins. Tell me, has he given you much trouble so far this morning?"

"Trouble? Gareth?" Her eyes widened. "Absolutely none, Mr Fussell. On the contrary."

"*Really*, Miss Coombes?" She was wearing a perfume as fresh, as delicate as nectarines. Unconsciously he feasted — staring all the while at Gareth Hobson until the boy's ears flared scarlet. Ingratiating wretch, winning her over within two lessons! "In my classes, Miss Coombes, he is always most conspicuous."

Miss Coombes said gently, "Perhaps it's his hair, Mr Fussell?"

Geoffrey sighed. She was making things difficult for herself. Intransigence bred intransigence. She hardly deserved it, but just to make things easier for her he moved the boy into a window seat so that whenever he passed along the corridor he could see what the fellow was up to. Sure enough, ten minutes later his foresight was well and truly rewarded, for what should he discover but the contrary lout scribbling with a texta pencil on the hand of the girl in front of him. So much for Miss Coombes' fancy ideas! Geoffrey flung into the classroom — right in, this time.

"Excuse *me*, Miss Coombes!" Up! up! his hands indicated. The students dragged themselves to their feet with an ugly scraping of chairs and shoes, drowning Miss Coombes in mid-sentence. They stared bemusedly at Geoffrey. His eyes travelled from face to face until there was a breath-bitten silence, upon which he nodded. "Sit down, class." He smiled teacher-to-teacher at Miss Coombes; that's how it's done, the smile said. "Now Helen," he continued, to the girl in front of the red-haired boy. "Would you please tell us exactly how you came by that vandalism on your hand?" Heads craned, faces grinned. He glanced from child to child. Their eyes kindled. "Right, Hobson — that's assault!"

Assault! The class fell very still. Miss Coombes looked

as though he had struck her. He picked up a piece of chalk to stress his words. "You think, Hobson, because you no longer have me in front of you that you are free to do as you please. You are evidently one of those louts who delight in taking advantage of a woman! You think, lad, that because Miss Coombes is new to the school, she is young — inexperienced — young — "

Somebody giggled. He saw Miss Coombes flush, and drop her gaze, so that her long hair swung forward, hiding her face from him. He raised his voice. "You are impervious to reason — inimical to discipline — " The words tumbled out like reels of uncoiling film. Thank God for the recess bell! He left Miss Coombes to dismiss the class and made his way to the staffroom. He still had the piece of chalk, he found. He flung it into the bin. There were times when he almost gave up in despair. But tried again. To reach. To touch. To leave some lasting mark. Wasn't that what dragged him through the classroom day in day out year after year after year?

"The trouble today," he said, taking his cup from the rack over the sink, "is that no one listens any more. No one cares. There's this appalling lack of belief . . . " He saw the others smile, or glance at one another as they moved away. He knew what they were thinking. Old Fussell. Off again. Who's on sport this afternoon? He nearly fell over Miss Coombes as he turned from the tea urn. She said, "Oh I believe in the children, Mr Fussell!" as she lifted a cup airily from the rack.

Geoffrey said, very gently, to discipline her, "I'm afraid, Miss Coombes, that that is Mr Brown's cup. And that's Miss McEntee's. We each bring our own to the staffroom, you see. What a pity the head didn't tell you."

"Then perhaps, Mr Fussell — " He felt her anger sharp as a kiss. "Perhaps, Mr Fussell, you wouldn't mind lending me your saucer?"

With dignity he turned his back. Oh the insolence of it all! At last the final bell released him. Delcia his wife was sometimes a fool but she never flung challenges at him like the arrogant youth of today. He hurried home thankfully. A nod here and there, "Good afternoon" there (to the P.&C. president's wife), a narrowing of his eyes at two first-years mooning home hand in hand. "Good afternoon, Mr Fussell!" He felt the girl was mocking him. No doubt the boy had a packet of cigarettes that he would pull out as soon as Geoffrey was out of sight. To impress the girl. Young fool. Geoffrey's body suddenly ached for a cigarette. Reaching his home, he lingered by the willow at the front gate to smoke. Delcia didn't like cigarette ash in the house; dirty, she said, unhygienic. Inhaling, all at once he breathed Miss Coombes. He saw again the childish freckles, the upthrust breasts, the taut stomach of the woman who has borne no children. She approached through a swirl of smoke and willow fronds, her heels tap-tapping, her firm flesh offered. He stared. The girl came closer, no longer Miss Coombes, he saw, still staring, but some unknown hussy who stared right back at him. Drawing level, she gave an insolent lift of her chin. "Hi, Dad!"

Hi, Dad! He flung away his cigarette and fled indoors. Hi, *Dad!* Anxiously he peered into the hall mirror to see himself as others might . . . veins scribbled faintly on his cheeks, teeth like rocks at low tide.

"Coffee's ready, Geoffrey. Why, whatever's the matter?" From the kitchen doorway his wife Delcia stared. Home from shopping, or bridge, or whatever she did all day, she was dressed for comfort — feet thrust into old orange scuffs, her stomach, ungirdled, sagging against the skirt of her maroon suit.

"Delcia, have I . . . *aged* much lately?" He held his breath.

"No, Geoffrey." She looked at him curiously. "No faster than usual." And stood waiting patiently to pour his coffee, blinking a little, ready to hear about school.

"Delcia! We've been neglecting ourselves lately. We're running to seed. Go and change your shoes. We'll take our coffee out to the river and climb the hill behind the pool."

Delcia began to gobble, like a maroon turkey. "But Geoffrey, you know I'm not one for mountaineering. And I'd planned to write to Laddie this afternoon. And then there's dinner . . . " Under his stern gaze her protests trailed away. "All right, dear, if you really want to. But don't complain at dinner if the peas are out of a packet."

He smiled indulgently. "That's a good girl. Now run and put the coffee into a thermos while I start the car."

The river ran into a pool at the foot of a small steep hill. Fishermen came there, and picnickers, but on this occasion he and Delcia were alone. In the hush of late afternoon, like a breath withheld, he began to feel afraid. His eyes darted like a wagtail in search of solidity. "Look at all this filth, Delcia. Beer cans. Obscenities. Rocks carved with names. You'd hope a place like this might be free of louts."

"Look at something else, dear," Delcia soothed. "Look on the bright side, I always say. Aren't those pretty trees? Nice white trunks."

"They're called candlebarks, Delcia."

"What a nice name. Candlebark. There's a lovely one right at the top of the hill — see? And here's a wee violet. I should think birds might nest here, wouldn't you?"

"For heaven's sake, Delcia, in a moment you'll be quoting nests of robins in her hair!" He laughed good-humouredly. Delcia was so dreadfully trite. But heart of gold, heart of gold.

"I'm sorry, dear, I'm just a silly old chatterbox. You tell me all about school while we drink our coffee. How did the new teacher get on with your old class?"

All at once Miss Coombes returned to walk at his shoulder. "She'll have to watch young Hobson," he said. And gave Delcia his version of the morning's confrontation.

"She sounds like a very nice girl, dear. I mean, to be kind to poor Hobson."

Geoffrey jumped up. School was beyond Delcia. He raised his eyes to the white tree that Delcia had observed at the top of the hill. "Let's climb now," he said.

They edged around rocks, grasping at roots and branches. Delcia's breath sawed in and out. Twigs crackled underfoot, pebbles rattled down the hillside. A solitary bird flew past. Below, the pool was a teacup, the river a scribble. "On the other hand, Delcia, we are growing smaller," he postulated. "How insignificant we are, you and I. Here we are — and who's to know that we ever passed this way — or care?"

"A cairn of stone, perhaps, dear?" Puffing, she offered him two pebbles, one on each palm. Mocking him? Delcia? He glared at her.

"I wish to God Delcia you wouldn't wear that maroon suit! You look like a dried clot of blood!"

She said nothing, simply looked at him curiously as at a stranger, then turned her back so that she merged with the wattles and hissing she-oaks . . . the insolence of creation. His hands began to shake. To reach. To touch. To possess! He raised his eyes to the slender white candlebark. Pale as flesh it gleamed in the long sunlight. From its branches hung shreds of bark like clothing a woman had flung down. To such a woman you brought gifts . . . nectarines, papayas.

"Stand aside, Delcia!" He took out his pocket knife. "Here's substance for you!"

"But Geoffrey — !" Delcia, shocked, plucked at his sleeve. He shrugged her aside. Steadying himself against the tree, he ran his hand over the satin-smooth wood and brutally, sharply, scored his initials. Carefully curved for G, upright for F. Himself. Driving the blade triumphantly into firm white flesh.

Fragment

You may arrange the flowers, Alicia. The words swelled like curtains across her sleep. She woke. The wind ran in the trees. The sun blew across the sky. Her breath crept past the muscle that waited every morning like a watchdog to grip and twist her with cramp. She bent her left leg cautiously, then stretched her right. Slowly she eased herself up in the bed. By doubling the pillows she could see into the rose garden. Mother's roses. Father had planted them for her, planted and watered and pruned under her thorny surveillance. *Charlotte! Alicia! Go downstairs at once and tell your father I DON'T want* . . . Mother's hand was everywhere. The bird-shaped cypress, stretching, pressed its wings. Fly, poor bird! cried Alicia. Her glance ran along a path to the lilypond where fish darted to and fro as though they would leap out of the pond and race princes and princesses across the beds of iris . . . *Young ladies never run, dear, they always walk.* A pulse ticked in her temple. She had lifted her head too quickly. Her fingers scrabbled amongst her treasures on the bedside table, the Copenhagen girl cradling its doll, her heavy silver watch, her cameo, scrabbling, seeking the handbell. In years past its fretful silver voice had drawn one or other of the sisters to Mother's bedside. *Alicia! There you are dressed for tennis and not a soul to read to me . . . Charlotte! I smell tobacco in the house again. You must tell me if your father . . . Charlotte! Alicia! Charlotte!*
. . . The bell, Alicia remembered, sinking back on her pillow, was still in Lottie's room. How thoughtless of

Lottie. She was really quite well again. "A regular see-saw," commented Mrs Wilson who came in once a week. "One up. One down. Just as well it's never both down together, eh, else how'd you get by then?"

Alicia swallowed a nasty taste. "Lottie!" she called thinly . . . Thin as the bread-and-butter Mother had made her offer on rose-patterned Doulton at all those afternoon teas. *Smile, dear* . . . Lottie was always the cheerful one. *Sugar, Mrs Simpkins? Three, is it, or four? . . . Yes, Mother gave her a week's notice, so clumsy with the china . . . Ah well, these days* . . .

The roses on the Royal Doulton trembled. *Lottie! Mother! That poor girl was having a BABY* . . .

Hush, Alicia!

Did Lalla tell you, Mrs Simpkins, we almost had a victory on the tennis court? Instead of mixed doubles last Sunday, just for a lark we challenged your boys to a match. But of course they won, did they tell you? Oh, we simply ADORE tennis . . .

"Lottie!" she protested. Lottie was always so prompt. Sweeping up spilt crumbs. And always said "we" as though Alicia were part of herself, a foot that had gone to sleep, or a sandwich to be gobbled up . . . She held her breath against Lottie's having heard . . .

The bedroom door flung open. "Well dear, how are we this lovely morning? Lalla, you naughty girl, you said you wouldn't move before I came to help you."

Thin yellowing strands shook loose from Alicia's plait. "I'm sorry, dear. I was just thinking . . . the flowers . . . in case someone calls."

"Calls? Why should anyone — "

"But it's such a lovely day, Lottie."

"Unless you were thinking of Mrs Wilson, dear. She'll be here presently to clean."

"There you are then, Lottie! Mrs Wilson."

"Yes, yes. Now do straighten yourself so that I can

give you the tray while everything's still hot. Here's your tea. And your tablet."

Alicia pulled a face at the tablet. "I expect you've forgotten the tea strainer, Lottie. It's a week since *you* did a tray."

"I have not forgotten the tea strainer, Lalla. May I remind you, which of us always did *her* tray?" A tea leaf slopped out of the spout. Alicia turned away. Lottie sighed. Seating herself on the bed, she rested the heavy tray on her knee. Alicia froze at this incredible piece of thoughtlessness. Was one's own sister so stupid that she could not see how the bed jarred one every time she breathed? "And guess what I've brought to tempt you, dear," Lottie coaxed.

Alicia's eyes snapped shut . . . *Don't you wish it were yours, Lalla? It's sharp and it shines and it's just what I want for the top of my mud-cake* . . . Alicia's head turned. Her eyes peeped. They took in with satisfaction Lottie's careful tray . . . tea in Mother's silver teapot, milk in the silver jug, hot water to heat her cup and a bowl to pour it into. And on a plate so dainty that it might have belonged to a child, a round biscuit stamped in the shape of a flower and sprinkled with hundreds and thousands . . . *Isn't it pretty? Isn't it a treasure? The gardener dug it up in the strawberries* . . .

"Give it to me, Lottie." . . . *Only if you run and ask him to help us turn on the tap* . . . Alicia caught Lottie's hand. "Lottie! Do you remember once when we were making mud-cakes and we didn't have any water we mixed the mud with our own — with — "

Lottie pulled her mouth very tight, like a ribbon around Alicia's flyaway hair. "They say living in one's past is a sign of decay, dear."

Offended, Alicia took the tray and turned back to the garden where pear trees hung heavy with fruit and borders were fragrant with rosemary. Amongst the wildly grown prunus that separated garden from street the gate lifted on its hinges.

Alicia shook out her fine lawn table napkin and blew her nose. "Here she is! She's letting that dog in again, Lottie. After all our hints!"

"Hush, Lalla. We must be kind to people like Mrs Wilson."

"She'll talk about the weather. She'll tell us it's going to rain. It isn't going to rain, is it?" The sisters peered at a straggle of cloud. "Why can't she just let the sun shine?"

Mrs Wilson was a youngish, windburned woman with a bouncy step and a chest that tugged at the buttons of her coat. She patted her knee for her dog, a yellow-eyed kelpie the exact colour of her coat. The dog lapped briefly at the lilypond, then lifted its leg on the stone seat.

"You must tell her to wash it, Lottie," said Alicia.

Lottie's hands fluttered. "I couldn't possibly!"

Alicia frowned. "Remember a saying of Mother's? *Where's your broughtins up!*"

The sisters giggled. Heads together, they watched Mrs Wilson and her ill-mannered kelpie and, trailing after them, a girl scuffing at pebbles.

"That must be her daughter," said Lottie. "The one she's always talking about. I hope she doesn't eat all the biscuits. Do you think she likes biscuits, Lalla?"

"She has long legs," observed Alicia.

"It's her skirt," explained Lottie. "That's how girls dress now. I wouldn't want *my* child to show so much of her body, would you?"

At the word "child" a weak warm feeling turned over in Alicia's stomach, making her conscious of her breasts, and burning like a slow summer fire along her arms and legs.

"Ask them to come up, Lottie," she said.

Lottie looked concerned. "Are you sure you feel up to it just now? Shouldn't you wait a little? But you always were the impetuous one. I remember . . . Very well, dear," sighed Lottie when Alicia did not answer.

Mrs Wilson was talking at her, taking possession, before she was even in the room. "And how are we today, Miss Wentworth? Your sister tells me you're having one of your dizzy spells. Just as well her migraine cleared up when it did, eh? Have you tried a little bit of red flannel next to the skin? No? Thought you'd know that one. My uncle died wearing red flannel. Next to the skin. Red."

Mrs Wilson's girl, coming softly to the bedside table to glance over Alicia's treasures, smiled to herself.

"That's my little girl," said Alicia, nodding at the Copenhagen, a china girl bent lovingly over her doll. "I'm very fond of my little girl. See how she's holding her baby's hand? I wouldn't part with her for worlds. Do you play with dolls?"

The girl's eyes widened. She shook her head.

Mrs Wilson laughed. "Only wish they'd stay that age, Miss Wentworth! But these days it's whatever the others are doing, and wearing, and saying, and you wear yourself into the ground keeping eyes in the back of your head."

Alicia flicked her fingers at the sharp cold eyes of Mrs Wilson's kelpie. "Good dog. Nice dog."

"He never did take to strangers," said Mrs Wilson. "Marvellous watchdog. Wouldn't be without him."

"And your daughter . . . does she like biscuits?" asked Lottie, nodding at the silent, bored girl rolling and unrolling the end of Alicia's crocheted runner.

"Biscuits? Yes, biscuits and chocolate thickshakes and Mick Jagger and souped-up motor cars and anything else that goes, Miss Wentworth." Mrs Wilson laughed. "Some of us don't know what's best for our own good."

The girl's head swung up. "There's some I know'd give a lot to eat what they like and stay as skinny as me!"

"Now miss!" said her mother. "I didn't bring you here to tell us how cheeky you are."

A sulky mask settled over the girl's face. She picked at the verdigris on Alicia's handmirror. Alicia thrust her jaw forward and sucked at her teeth. There was something about the girl that she seemed to recognize. Brittleness, that was it.

The girl blinked. "Beg yours?"

Alicia held out her hand, blotched and transparent, a boiled-in-its-jacket potato. "Come here, dear."

The girl, shrugging, stepped closer. Her glance rested briefly on the old woman. Her hand fell lightly in Alicia's own, smooth, cool, fragile as her china girl. The old woman's head ducked. "I have a treasure!" she whispered, and drew from under the bedclothes the biscuit with the hundreds and thousands. The girl turned towards her mother. Her fingers were crushing a sprig of rosemary, plucked no doubt from one of Mother's borders. Alicia's breath caught on the morning-sharp fragrance of the herb. "Do you know, dear, I was going to pick a bowl of roses for Mother this morning. I wonder . . . would you . . . "

"Yes, she'll do your flowers, Miss Wentworth. Keep her out of mischief for a bit." Mrs Wilson gave the girl a shove. "Look lively, miss! Take the dog with you."

The girl pulled her hand free and slipped out. Alicia saw her dawdle around the lilypond, setting her feet down carefully, self-absorbed, a princess disguised as a waterbird.

Mrs Wilson leaned out of the window. "Pick them roses for Miss Wentworth like I said! Hurry up now!" The girl hunched her shoulders and dragged at a couple of blooms. Mrs Wilson shook her head. "Will I be glad when school goes back next week! Discipline, that's what kids need. But her father just idolizes her. And then it's *me* that has to come the heavy hand."

Flat irons, thought Alicia, smiling at Mrs Wilson's hands. Rolling pins, butter pats.

Mrs Wilson peered at her. "Beg yours?"

Alicia beckoned Lottie. "Isn't it extraordinary," she confided. "Mrs Wilson's dog has eyes like yellow scissors — and Lottie, *so has Mrs Wilson!*"

Lottie's hands clasped and unclasped. "Lalla! You sound so uncharitable sometimes. I know she means it kindly, Mrs Wilson."

A clever woman, Alicia, will die an old maid.

"Sweet charity didn't wed *us*, Lottie!"

Mrs Wilson laughed. "You might just be lucky at that, Miss Wentworth! Men! Time and again I've begged her father to take her in hand. You know what he says? Let the girl alone, woman, let her have a bit of fun . . . Fun! That's men for you!" Mrs Wilson's contempt cut like glass. Lottie nodded knowingly. Lottie is clever — she really does know! thought Alicia, looking at her sister's chin going nod nod nod. "You haven't a hope these days," Mrs Wilson continued. "Fun! Times have changed since I was a girl. Boys. It's boys boys boys all the time now. And the gear these girls get out in! Just asking for trouble, some of them. Not that *she's* a bad girl, mind you, I wouldn't say a word against my own daughter . . . "

Lottie's voice became dreamy. "We could have married. A young man courted my sister for weeks and weeks . . . " Alicia picked up her handmirror. Me? she asked herself, astonished. "But of course he was quite unsuitable. It would have been a disaster. Mother pointed that out. How could one set to after our kind of upbringing and scrub floors and bake one's own bread and sew and patch for perhaps five or six children? So Lalla sent him away. Didn't you, dear?"

Alicia did not reply. But it wasn't like that at all! protested her silence. Memory swirled like morning mist. His face appeared at the garden gate. He was perhaps eighteen, with fashionable side-burns, and hair that hung almost to his shoulders. He evidently spent much of his time in the sun, since his face and arms were the colour of . . . Alicia groped . . . of Father's tobacco-stained fingers. But it was his shoulders that she looked at again. *He* would not retreat to the garden whenever he wanted to smoke. He leaned over the gate to cast a quick look around the garden. The kelpie's ears pricked. The girl sulking over the roses raised her head. The boy beckoned. Hair rose along the kelpie's neck and along his back. Alicia's blood bolted. She took a step towards him. *No, no, I mustn't. I can't.* And I did turn back! cried Alicia, plucking at a hole in the thin frayed sheet. What else *could* I do, with my hands full of her roses? . . . *Alicia, what you feel is merely . . . physical. We are not animals, child — Give me those roses! — Happiness, you say? My poor child, happiness is for the birds and the bees . . .*

"And of course Mother was absolutely right, although we couldn't see it at the time. We took Lalla away into the country for a long holiday . . . "

Alicia's laughter crackled like trodden sugar. "Oh, I was so excited! All the preparations! And the packing! Can you believe me, I dreamed it all again last night, Lottie! So odd . . . I'd forgotten . . . "

Without so much as a backward glance at the house the girl dumped Mother's cherished roses in the lilypond and ran straight across the beds of iris and rosemary to the waiting boy. The kelpie, given the slip, began to scratch and gnaw at the closed gate. Alicia laughed. Oh, to run, run! *Lovely Alicia, petulant, bored/Plucks a rose and holds it in her teeth* . . . Drops of blood speckled her lips. Prunus blood-red and pink hedged her in. "And when I got out into the street I found I'd forgotten my skirt and I was wearing only my slip — and Lottie, *scarlet* bloomers! And that's really very odd, Mrs Wilson, because we never go on holidays."

"Is that so?" said Mrs Wilson. "You can have too much of a good thing. Holidays! How's that girl of mine getting on with your flowers, Miss Wentworth?"

Smile, dear. Alicia smiled. "Your dog seems upset, Mrs Wilson," she said. She watched Mrs Wilson jump. "Perhaps he hates being shut in, do you think?"

"She's gone! Was it one of them surfies, would you say, Miss Wentworth? Good-for-nothing long-haired layabouts! My God, the little devil, there's no end to it!" Mrs Wilson rushed downstairs.

"I -- I think I'll just go down to the kitchen and tidy up before Mrs Wilson starts cleaning," murmured Lottie. "I wouldn't like her to find everything in a mess. Whatever would she think?"

When Lottie's footsteps had died away, Alicia looked again at the silver handmirror that once had belonged to Mother. Alicia! she whispered to the girl in the glass . . . *You can't keep secrets from me, my girl. Mothers always know* . . . Like the buzz of a wasp caught against glass Mrs Wilson's voice rose from the garden. Stinging with pain, the girl's words rang like a bell. "But what have I done? What have I *done?*"

Hush! crooned Alicia, feeling immeasurably strong as that strange pervading warmth again dragged itself to her fingertips and right down to her toes. Cradling the mirror on one arm, she slipped open the top buttons of her nightdress and gazed upon her breasts that, firm as a girl's, delicate as a winter rose, flowed with milk . . . There, my darling! she murmured, rocking the mirror. The garden grew silent. Alicia! she whispered to the child in the glass. Alicia! Alicia! . . . over and over until the word withered, sucked dry of all meaning. Horrified, she flung down the mirror. A swirl of mist hid the sun. She looked up. The walls moved. Rain fell from the ceiling. She heard the child scream as it shattered in silver fragments.

The Sea

Summer. Heat staggering over bone-bare paddocks, and the scream of cicadas. The evenings were cooler — so cool, in fact, that little Franz Stein curled himself small against the draughts that crawled through knot-holes in the weatherboards and over his face and neck. He flung away so that his back was against the wall . . . pulled his eiderdown right up to his chin. No good — his feet shivered. He wished he still slept with one or other of his sisters in the larger bed. They said he was too big for that now, too big even to stay in the same room with them; they wanted Father to move his bed into a corner of the kitchen. So they could giggle and whisper all the more, he thought, listening to the two of them.

"Tell me, too!" he demanded, sitting up.

"Lie down and go to sleep!" hissed Lieselotte. She had left school the minute she turned fifteen, and because she spent all day helping their mother and sometimes Mrs Reed in the brick house, and owned a bottle of scent that made her smell like Mrs Reed, she thought she was someone. Tears stung his nose. If he pressed his eyes tight shut he could almost remember the time before Brunhilde the baby when he had slept in Mother and Father's room. Through the wall behind his head he heard Brunhilde cough. Then his father's voice, a low murmuring, insistent . . . A little laugh from his mother. His eyes sprang open. A face peered at him through the window, the moon's, huge and white, mocking — like the kids at school. The sheets of iron which Mr Reed had nailed over the shingles creaked and cracked as though the moon itself were walking about on the rooftop. Franz pressed his face into his pillow. Breakfast, he would think about breakfast . . . Mother ladling oatmeal from the black pot on the open fire, hot toast spread thick with blackberry jam (Linda Reed in the brick house had butter, too), water bubbling in the fountain hanging from an iron bar that Mother swung out to fill Father's thermos . . .

But when morning came Father told Lieselotte not to light the fire. No oatmeal. No toast. It was too hot. Mother had to boil the water for the thermos on the primus stove which she pumped carefully, not too much. "Couldn't I try *today*, Mother?" begged Franz. "Just once . . . Mutti?" His father brushed him aside. "Where is my breakfast, Gretchen?" Verena took the billy from the coolgardie safe and poured milk into five chipped enamel bowls. She was whistling, a funny little tune that made Franz want to sing, or throw a cup in the air. "That one's mine, isn't it, Lieselotte?" he cried, noisy as spoons, as Lieselotte cut hunks of bread and dropped them into the milk. "I *think* it's that one . . ." But you couldn't talk to Lieselotte. Her face stayed shut. Into Father's bowl she poured a cupful of red currants that she had picked from the twisted old bush growing beside the copper-house. When I am a man I shall eat red currants, thought Franz, watching the stream of bright berries. If he wanted to be mean he could dob Lieselotte in for pinching handfuls of currants when she thought no one was looking.

"Is my lunch packed?" asked Father in German. He had another new job, outdoors this time, working for the Country Roads Board, and it was time for him to meet the workmate who gave him a lift into the depot every morning.

Mrs Stein nodded towards the table where Lieselotte and Verena were spreading dripping over thick slices of bread.

"Get me some carrots, Lieselotte," Father ordered, again in German. "What sort of a midday meal is bread for a man, Gretchen?" he complained, turning to his wife. "Is this what we were promised? Every day I sat down to soup and meat in our home, remember?"

"But this isn't Germany, is it, Father?" Lieselotte dumped freshly-pulled carrots out of her skirt onto the table. She snapped shut the catch on the canvas strap and flung Father's lunch box along the table towards him. "This isn't — "

Franz flinched as his father's hand struck the girl across the mouth. His heart raced with excitement. Father's hand could split kindling for the open fire. Lieselotte did not scream, or cry, or bleed . . . only hissed "Well, stickystare!", rolling the remaining carrots back and forth along the table until their father had left the cottage. Then she swung in front of her mother.

"I hate it here! Hate it!" she shrilled. "Carmel Murphy has gone to a job in the city. She's working in her cousin's flower shop. I want to work in a flower shop. Why can't I, Mother? What's here for me? Mother!"

"Comb the child's hair," said Mrs Stein, nodding at Franz. She slipped open the top buttons of the loose dress she wore and put the baby's soft greedy mouth to her breast. "You cannot jump over your shadow, Lieselotte."

From the carved cedar mantelpiece, hollow now with borer, Lieselotte seized the old blackened comb which they all used. "Come here!" Franz dragged away. A few more teeth snapped. "Do it yourself, then!" shouted Lieselotte, snatching up the aluminium billy from the table and flying from the room.

"Mad dog!" commented Verena, hacking slices of bread and heaping them with the thick brown juices from the bottom of the dripping tin. Franz felt hungry all over again.

"She has gone for the milk, that is all right," said Mrs Stein, changing Brunhilde to the other breast. The sweet milky smell made Franz draw closer. The greedy head nudged and twisted, the fingers opened and shut on his mother's breast. As soon as Verena had wrapped his lunch in a sheet of newspaper Franz set off. If he waited down near the dam, Lieselotte on her way back from the dairy might let him pinch a mouthful of milk from the billy. Every morning Franz used to fetch the milk until his father caught him drinking it. Then they knew his story that Mr Reed could spare only half a billy was a whopping lie. So going for the milk became Lieselotte's job instead.

He scuffed along the track until his sandshoes were choked with dust. Already the sun had sucked all colour from the sky. It was cooler under the gum tree by the dam. Where the gum leaves had drifted to one end the water was stained black. Rushes grew at the other end. Sometimes Linda and he came with a bit of meat on a string and caught yabbies in a net. Not very often, though. Mrs Reed said a grown-up had to be present when the children were playing near water, though when Linda asked her to go with them she was usually too busy. Fallen fence posts lay half-submerged in the water. He was about to step out onto one when he saw lying along its length a snake with yellow bands around its body. With bitten breath he stared. The snake stared back, then flicked its tongue as it eased into the rushes. Franz seized one of the dried cow-pats lying around the dam and hurled it after the snake. Something to tell the teacher. *A snake nearly bit me* . . . Lieselotte had better be careful. She often paddled around in the dam at dusk when she thought no one was looking. What an age she was taking at the dairy! He was terribly thirsty. He set off to look for her.

The cow, already milked, was munching an armful of

grass hay thrown down to her behind the cowshed. He could hear Lieselotte laughing. There she was, sitting up on the post-and-rail fence along the front of the shed, sitting so straight that the sun lit up her face, her chest pressed tight against her grubby shirt, her skinny brown arms clasped around one knee ... Laughing down at Mr Reed who placed his pipe on top of the gatepost and leaned back as though he had all day to roll the tobacco in the palm of his hand.

"There's plenty of ponies you could practise on," Mr Reed was saying, "If you're really keen on riding. How'd you like to ride the little grey for me in the local show? Or the skewbald?"

"I want to ride your chestnut mare!" shrilled Lieselotte.

Mr Reed laughed. "My wife says I spend too much time with the ponies. I do, I admit. But sheep ... hell, there's no comparison with horses!"

A shred of tobacco fell into the bucket of milk at his feet. As he scooped it out with his free hand and turned to flick it away he caught sight of the little boy. "Well if it isn't young Franz! Good day mate and how's the world treating you?" he cried, so heartily that Franz drew back. He preferred Mr Reed the way he was when *he* fetched the milk.

Lieselotte stopped in the middle of a laugh. "What do you want, Franz? Why aren't you at school?"

"Bit early, isn't it?" said Mr Reed. "I reckon Linda's hardly out of bed yet."

"Did Mother send you?" Lieselotte asked quickly.

Franz shook his head. "Just ... thirsty," he muttered.

"Here, have a drink of milk." Mr Reed took a tin mug from its nail on the wall, wiped it across his shirt, pushed aside the froth at the top of the bucket and filled the mug. Franz drank gratefully. Mr Reed grinned down at him. "That's my mate."

Lieselotte hopped down from the rail then and became very fussy, joggling him so that the last drops of milk splashed over his face. "Just look at your shirt, Franz, buttoned all wrong! And your hair! Stand still while I straighten you."

"Needs a currycomb." Mr Reed winked at him. Franz laughed. Mr Reed had white strong teeth, a faint scar across one cheek, eyes bright as the colourless sky. Lieselotte laughed too, laughed and laughed so that Mr Reed stopped looking at Franz and looked at her instead. Franz hung the mug on its nail. He decided not to tell Lieselotte about the snake after all.

As he walked along the hot road he could see the Murphys still busy in their cowshed; and Billy Boyd running away with an empty bucket from a lumbering calf. No use asking for milk, though — everyone was always too busy. At school he could find no one in the playground. He looked in the shelter shed, the lavatories, behind the pine trees where the girls played houses with walls of pine needles. The school itself, a single-roomed weatherboard building, was still locked. He peeled off a few flakes of pale green paint. Smoke curled out of the chimney of the teacher's residence, but you weren't allowed past the hedge that stood between it and the playground. Franz peeped . . . a closed front door, a lawn neat as a blackboard, and — his heart jumped — two dandelion clocks that the lawn-mower had missed. One for himself and one for Linda. He darted behind the hedge, grabbed the clocks and raced back into the playground. He wished Linda would hurry. He was sick of waiting for people.

At last children began to straggle into the playground. Billy Boyd had brought a length of rope so Verena made Franz and Billy each take an end under the cool of the pine trees.

"Come on, Franz, turn it properly!" bossed Verena

who could skip pepper and wanted Maria Murphy to see.

"Linda! Linda! There you are!" he shouted, dropping his end of the rope over which all the Murphys were jumping, and rushing to meet her as she entered the playground. "I thought you weren't coming to school today. What happened? Were you sick?"

"No. Blow your nose, Franz." He never remembered.

"Look — I found you a clock. What time is it?"

He thrust it at her with such a gulp of laughter that all the school children turned to stare — the Murphys even stopped skipping. Linda grew crimson.

"Shh! Everyone's going into line."

The teacher said a short prayer. Franz didn't listen to the words. The voice roared over him comfortably. Suddenly Linda nudged him. " . . . and *one of us* arrived at school far too early this morning. And what is more, *came into my garden!*" All eyes turned upon Franz. His face and neck burned, even his arms felt hot. He grinned proudly. Not even Linda had been singled out at assembly. He liked school. He especially liked sitting beside Linda who smiled and smelt nice and was his friend. Sometimes he just lolled in his desk and looked around the room. If you stared hard enough at people they went into your head and then you could like them.

"Finished already, Franz?" called the teacher.

Franz shuffled. "Haven't started . . . sir."

"Haven't started?" The teacher stood with arms flung out, his mouth round. "Haven't . . . *started?*" The room tittered.

Franz grinned, since that seemed expected. As he puzzled over the sums set for his grade that morning, he heard the teacher say *Come, dear children, let us away*. He looked up — but it wasn't playtime. The teacher was reading something to the sixth-graders.

Now the salt tides seawards flow;
Now the wild white horses play . . .

Horses! He could hardly wait until he was big enough to gallop over the hills with Mr Reed, rounding up sheep for shearing and dipping —

Margaret! Margaret! . . . That was his mother's name, though Father always said Gretchen . . .

Sand-strewn caverns, cool and deep,
Where the winds are all asleep;
Where the spent lights quiver and gleam;
Where the salt weed sways in the stream;
Where the sea-beasts . . . This was a sleepy story, and sad, too — he could tell from the teacher's voice. But whatever were seasnakes, and whales that *Sail and sail with unshut eye, Round the world for ever and aye . . .* ? Maybe they were looking for something. Yes, that was it — something was lost, a horse, one of Mr Reed's horses for mustering sheep, and they were calling his mother to help in the search. He knew he was right when he heard *The hoarse wind blows colder . . . gusts shake the door.* He shook Linda's arm: just like home!

Linda stared at him. "Go on with your work, Franz. The teacher will get mad!"

He glanced down at the desk. Nothing at all in his book! He looked across at Linda's but her arm was curled around it like a seasnake so that was no help. Hastily he scrawled a few numbers, the first that came into his head. When the teacher came to his desk he scored a thick red line across the page. "That's what comes of inattention, Franz."

At playtime he asked, "Linda, what's the sea?"

"The sea!" cried Maria Murphy, one of the sixth-graders. "Franz! Haven't you ever been there?"

"No. Have you?"

"Of course we have," Pauline Murphy, who was in his own grade, replied disdainfully. "We go every year at Christmas, and stay with our grandma."

"Well what is it then?"

"When you come to the edge of the land," said Linda, "There's all water. That's the sea."

"Oh. Like a dam." He remembered the snake in the reeds.

"*Much* bigger. It goes right over the edge of the world. And it's full of fishes — "

"And ships — "

"And seaweed — "

"And whales and horses!" shouted Franz.

"Not horses, silly!" laughed Maria.

"There are! There are!" cried Franz, remembering the story.

"How do you know if you've never been there?"

Just as he was thinking of flinging a pine cone at someone, Billy Boyd came to his rescue. "Sometimes people swim racehorses in the sea for exercise."

"So there, Maria!"

"And then they gallop them over the sand."

"What does sand look like?"

"Oh . . . it's a sort of dust, only it's yellow. And it's full of shells."

This wonderful new world so intrigued Franz that he said nothing as he and Linda walked home after school. *Down, down, down. Down to the depths of the sea* called someone inside his head. The sea! That was what he was looking for! Where Father would sit down to soup and meat every day and Lieselotte would work in her flower shop and Verena would skip pepper faster than Maria Murphy and everyone would call him *one of us* . . . A rasping northerly pushed at the two children. Dust whirled in their faces.

"Let's go under the bridge, it'll be cooler," puffed Linda.

They hopped from stone to stone, skirting the muddy pools where frantic tadpoles dashed in an inch of water.

Franz leaned against a stone pillar. It was nice under the bridge, it was a *sand-strewn cavern, cool and deep* . . . he might stay here forever. After a while he saw Linda watching him, puzzled. Catching his eye, she smiled.

"I know what you're thinking about," she teased. "The sea, isn't it? My Auntie Bonnie and Uncle Nev have just come back from Surfers Paradise. They've got lots of coloured slides. When I grow up I'm going to Surfers Paradise." *Down to the depths of the sea* sang the voice. "You know what, your hair's a bit like that spiky yellow grass that grows on the top of sandhills," Linda chattered, since Franz did not reply, her head on one side, smiling at him, until he smiled too. She patted his arm. "Franz, your mother can't help it if — "

But Franz jumped into a puddle and squelched amongst the stones and sticks and ooze, liking the cold trickles that seeped through the worn soles and uppers and over the tops of his sandshoes. "I'm a whale, Linda. Here's a wave." He kicked the surface of the puddle and shouted as it showered them both.

"You'd better help me clean my dress, Franz," said Linda, dipping her handkerchief in a pool and scrubbing at the greenish-brown splatters. "Else I won't let you come to my house."

Franz went with Linda into the brick house after school because Mrs Reed always had good things to eat. Today it was a hot buttery sultana scone for each of them, and a fruit drink with blocks of ice bobbing about in it. Linda picked the sultanas out of her scone and passed them to Franz who chewed and swallowed hungrily. Just as Linda was showing her mother her gold star for being good all day, Mrs Stein arrived pushing her battered pram that contained as well as Brunhilde a huge bunch of carrots and a cabbage. She tumbled the vegetables onto the table.

"Danke schön!" said Mrs Reed. Mrs Stein laughed.

Mrs Reed poured her a cool drink. Now my mother has a friend, thought Franz happily. He gave an ice cube to Brunhilde who held it on her tongue for awhile, then spat it out, crying and clutching her fist to her mouth. Franz shouted and threw himself about with laughter. "There now," crooned Mrs Stein, reaching for the little girl. *And the youngest sate on her knee* — that was how the story went, thought Franz, wishing Brunhilde had stayed at home. He saw Linda look quickly away as his mother unbuttoned her dress. Her breast spilled out, heavy and sagging. "Now we go home," said Mrs Stein cheerfully, pulling her dress together and dumping Brunhilde back into the pram.

"I'll see that Franz goes home," Mrs Reed called. She always said that. Franz couldn't help laughing . . . as though he might forget, or lose his way. Sometimes he liked Linda's mother, and sometimes he didn't. He took his stool over to the sink and knelt up on it, very close to her face.

"Mrs Reed — " he began, edging closer.

Mrs Reed tightened her shoulders. "What is it?"

"Those cherries are red to me," he said. "Are they red to you, Mrs Reed?"

Mrs Reed sighed. "Yes Franz. Red cherries."

"They're red to me, too," said Linda.

"But you might really see them green."

"I do not, silly. They're red, aren't they, Mum?"

"But you might see them green and call that red, Linda."

"Oh I do not! I don't call green red, do I, Mum?"

Mrs Reed picked Franz up, stool and all, and dumped him back at the table. "The cherries are red."

Mr Reed came into the kitchen then. "Tea going?" He brought with him all the exciting smells of work, smells that caught at the nostrils: dust, and saddle-leather, and wool, and the sheep manure that Father dug into the ground to make the vegetables grow.

"Mr Reed — "

"G'day, mate. Tea going, Lo?"

Mrs Reed looked at the clock. "You're early. It isn't five yet."

"Hot work in the yards. Pull the kettle over, will you?"

"I can't just now. You'll have to wait. I've got to keep the vacola at a hundred and seventy for another twenty minutes yet."

"I'll have a beer, then. Get me a glass and the bottle opener, Linda."

"I wish you wouldn't drink in the middle of the day."

"Fair crack of the whip! What are you bottling cherries for now, anyway, if you're off to town tomorrow?"

"And who likes cherry pie in the winter and cherries and ice cream in the summer, might I ask?"

"Did you have to leave it till the last minute? Those cherries have been sitting around for a week."

Franz's heart raced. He loved these conversations. His head turned from one to the other. It was like watching the big kids at a game of hand tennis.

Linda began to dance around the kitchen. "Town? Are we going to town tomorrow, Mum?"

"You and I are, dear, for a few days. To stay with Auntie Bonnie and Uncle Nev."

"Goodie good! But isn't Dad?"

Mrs Reed looked hard at Mr Reed while her hands went on packing cherries and pouring syrup into the jars.

"Christ, Lois! You know I can't get away at this time of year. I've got those wethers to move onto the hill, and that bit of fence to do up before I can put them there."

Mrs Reed studied a bottle of cherries against the window. "You could have done that last week."

"Last week I was busy with the ponies."

"Oh yes! The ponies . . ."

"And if I wasn't here we'd be burnt out for sure. Hell!"

"The Steins could look after things for you. Little enough in return for living in the cottage, surely. And all the hay you used to keep in the cottage just rotting out in the open. I thought he was going to help you build a proper hayshed."

"He will, when I get around to it."

Mrs Reed laughed. "We're weak reeds, Ron, that's our trouble. Weak reeds . . ."

He went over to her then, letting his arm fall around her waist and dropping his head onto her shoulder. "You know I want to come with you . . . Any other time of the year . . ."

She pulled out of his clasp. "That's what you said last August. And May. It's all right for you, off with the ponies to shows and gymkhanas at the drop of a hat while I stay home watching the hay rot and the fences fall down. I need a holiday, Ron. Sit on the beach somewhere. Take Linda to a pantomime. Swimming lessons. Shopping. Somewhere nice. Away from this everlasting north wind, and the dust. At least give your daughter a chance, Ron."

He poured himself another beer. "What time are you leaving?"

"Bonnie and Nev are driving up in the morning."

"Staying for dinner, I suppose. I'll have to put on a clean shirt and say grace and listen to your brother-in-law planning his next trip to the Gold Coast."

"You know they'll never eat a meal with us. Bonnie doesn't like the country."

"God, your sister! You could eat off the floor in this house. I bet she's never bottled a cherry in her life, either." He looped a pair of cherries over each of her ears. "You ought to be packing instead of hanging over that stove in this heat. Scones, too!" He took another, saw the little boy's eyes following it, and passed it to him. Franz grinned. He liked Linda's dad.

Suddenly the hot wind dropped, died, and in its place sprang a breeze that carried with it a strange, cool, salty smell that caught in Franz's nose and made his eyes blink. He stopped chewing. "What's that funny smell?"

Mrs Reed leaned her arms on the sink and, letting her gaze rest on the distance, breathed deeply. When her answer came, he felt he'd known it all the time. "That? That's the sea." She laughed lazily. "Haven't you smelt it before, when the wind changes from north to south?"

"Jeez . . . the sea . . . Tell me again about the sea, Linda."

"Wait a minute." Linda ran into her bedroom, returning in a moment with a large shell which she held against his ear. "I found this on the beach last summer. Listen . . . *that's* the sea."

"Jeez . . . " he breathed, his eyes shining as he listened to the faint roar of distant waves. *Down to the depths of the sea* sang the voice in his head. "I wish *I* had a shell," he said wistfully. He pressed the shell to his ear. "Mr Reed — I can hear the *sea* . . . Do you think I'll ever see the sea, Mr Reed?"

Mrs Reed laughed. "Of course you will, Franz. Everyone goes to the beach sooner or later."

He grew as still as the shell itself as he saw Mr Reed raise his eyebrows in his direction, speaking a silent question to Mrs Reed.

Mrs Reed stared at her husband. "*What?*"

"Why not? You'll be there only a few days . . . won't you? . . . and Bonnie's house'd hold a dozen kids . . . "

"It wouldn't do at all! Heavens above, Ron! I wouldn't dream . . . And the child's sister is light-fingered. I watch her all the time she's here now. Who else could have taken that bottle of perfume off my dressing-table?"

"Well if a bit of scent is all she pinches from you, I wouldn't lose any sleep." He laughed to himself, reaching for his hat as he rose to go. "Like to bring up the cow, kids?"

"But aren't you going to wait for your cup of tea? Just when the kettle's on the boil? Oh . . . men!"

Linda trotted along beside her father, while Franz, pretending to be a dog, circled around them, barking and leaping. The chestnut mare, tethered in the shade, laid back her ears and danced at their approach. Under her brilliant coat the muscles swelled and rippled. "Steady, girl," said Mr Reed, approaching her slowly. "Cut it out, Franz!" He held the mare on a short rein until she stopped snorting and trembling and dropped her head to his arm. He patted her neck, grinning down at the two children. Franz gazed up at Linda's dad. He was the only person who could ride that crazy horse.

Franz, riding an imaginary horse, galloped the cow towards the shed.

"Don't race her, Franz, she loses all her milk!" shouted Linda.

Franz kicked at the milk-streaked dust. Always something!

Back at the shed, he climbed up beside Linda on the railing where Lieselotte had perched that morning. Mr Reed sat on a wooden block with his head pressed against the cow's warm flank. Milk drummed in the bucket.

"When it gets dark," Linda said dreamily, "You can see the lights of the city glowing in the sky." A faraway look came into her face. "When I grow up, I'm going to live in the city. In a house with two toilets like Auntie Bonnie's. Franz can visit me."

"When I grow up," said Franz, "I'm going to visit the sea."

"Cow's ready to take down to the dam, Linda." Mr

Reed put his arm around Linda's shoulder. "She'll miss you while you're away."

"I'll look after her for you, Mr Reed! I'll bring her up in the mornings and take her back every evening. I'll do it!"

Mr Reed grinned down at the eager boy. "Thanks, mate!"

As they trailed along behind the cow, Franz told Linda about the snake. "And Lieselotte swims in the dam every afternoon. Bet she's there now . . . Shh! Let's give her a fright!"

They crept along the little gully across which the dam was built, clutching each other and giggling when pebbles dislodged and rattled away, and climbed into a patch of bracken from where they could look across to the dam. Sure enough, Lieselotte was splashing about in the water. She turned on her back and swam lazily, as though supper time and the washing up were hours away.

"My sister can swim," Franz boasted. "You can't, Linda."

But Linda was staring at Lieselotte. "She — she's taken all her clothes off!"

Franz shrugged. "Who swims in their clothes?"

"I mean . . . bathers."

"Doesn't have any."

Lieselotte stood up, leaning forward to press the water from her body. She smiled to herself as her hands brushed her stomach, her breasts, the thin bones of her face. She had pinned up her long hair so that her head looked smaller and sharper and her neck longer — like someone I don't know, really, thought Franz uneasily.

"She's rude, and it's rude to stare!" Linda whispered. "Come away, Franz."

Lieselotte was staring at herself in the dam. Franz picked up a stone and flung it. The reflections shattered, ripples broke over Lieselotte's feet. She started backwards, shouting in anger as she saw the two children. Laughing loudly, they ran away, crashing through the bracken and flinging open the gate of the cow paddock. "Boy, was she mad!" That was the sister he knew.

The next morning Franz was out early to watch for the car from the city. At the brick house there was no one in sight, though when he put his ear to the door he could hear footsteps and voices, and drawers being opened and shut. He knocked.

Mrs Reed, wearing one of her best dresses, flung open the door and talked past his shoulder. "No, not this morning, Franz. We're very busy today. People getting ready for a holiday are always busy, you know."

"Goodbye Franz!" Linda called. "We're going soon. You'll be at school next week and I won't. Goodbye!"

As the afternoon burned away, everyone at the cottage grew hotter and crosser. Even his mother slapped him just because he had a suck of Brunhilde's dummy. Lieselotte began to nag at him to split some wood so that she could light the copper and have a bath.

"Make him, Mother! It's his job."

"What does she want a bath for? She swims in the dam every day."

Lieselotte sprang at him. "Telltale!"

He kicked her as hard as he could and ducked. Lieselotte screamed and flew after him. She could run very fast. At the cowshed she caught him. They fell in a heap, her bony knees digging in to his chest and her fists pounding him. "That will teach you! Telltale! Spy!"

He heard the clank of the milk bucket. Lieselotte was pulled off him. "Steady on, Lieselotte," said Mr Reed, holding her arms. The girl glared up at him for a moment, then stepped backwards, her neck very red and her hands clasping her arms where he had held her. "Come on, Lieselotte," said Mr Reed gently.

Lieselotte smiled stupidly. "We were going for a walk," she muttered. "To get some kindling," she added. "To light the copper — " She turned suddenly and walked away, her head very straight. They watched her for a moment, then Mr Reed turned to Franz with a shrug . . . That was girls for you, the look said.

Franz scrubbed the dust from his face. "I'll get the cow, Mr Reed!"

"Thanks, mate." Mr Reed leaned against the gatepost and took his pipe from his pocket.

Franz was so pleased to be helping again that he galloped the cow all the way from her paddock. He hopped up onto the railing. "Wonder if Linda likes the lights," he chattered. "Wonder if she's found me a seashell . . . Mr Reed! . . . There's a snake down at the dam."

Milk streamed into the bucket. "Snake, eh."

"Yes, and Lieselotte swims there every evening. Bet she's down there right now. She might get bit."

The jet of milk wavered. "Snake, did you say? Down at the dam? When?"

Mr Reed listened like a schoolkid waiting to get his gold star. He finished milking, hung the bucket on a hook, unbailed the cow and turned her out of the shed. Franz clattered down from the gatepost. "I'll take her down to the dam, Mr Reed. Mr Reed! You said — Mr Reed!"

But gee, he *said* — protested Franz, dragging one foot along the ground. A dandelion clock like a goggling moon stared at him from a hundred eyes. He swiped at it, muttering fiercely . . . *I* want to see the sea!

shocked. She's only a schoolgirl. Who put it into her head to see a film like that, anyway? Bill, would it be Bill?" Or Harry? Or Stephen? Nice open kids you liked your daughter to mix with, kids who combed their hair and looked you in the eye . . . "*Fred!*"

"Maybe she just reads the papers."

"But why should a nice young girl concern herself with filth and vice? Prostitution — homosexuality — cruelty — you name it, we saw it."

"Yes, that beggar driving the spurs into his horse wasn't very pretty. Prostitution . . . Were they prostitutes, Edna? I thought they were just two sisters looking for a bloke."

Looking for a bloke . . . She heard the telephone ring, Susan's bedroom door fly open, the girl's eager voice . . . Young people couldn't wait five minutes these days. Wherever was the loving girl who had always rushed to her mother with the first jonquil, a new bruise, a hug if she thought she'd been naughty? Edna Green had to lean against the sink, her stomach heaved so. You thought you were a fortress, and all the time the enemy prowled within.

"When we were young, we weren't lusted after by every young fellow who said good day. We just had fun together. Bicycling after church. Picnics. Tennis parties. And dance! Remember how we'd dance all night, Fred? Real dancing, mind you, not all this jigging and gyrating."

"Yes, they were good times."

They had met at a dance. Fred Green's got his eye on you, her girl friends had giggled, staring back at the tall shy young man sloped against the wall by the door. Their eyes could afford to be bold. They were all engaged, or had an understanding, or were married with little children asleep outside in the car. Edna's saving herself, they had teased her. Saving herself? She hadn't liked that, and had swept around the floor more eagerly, more dashingly, so that when at last he had pushed his way between the couples and stammered out his request for the next dance — the last but one on the program — a terrible faintness had crept right through her and almost choked her reply. His hands — she could see nothing but his hands knotting and unknotting inches from her face . . . such strong clean hands . . . The child of one of her girl friends had staggered into the hall just then, blinking against the lights and the noise, and Edna had hugged the warm, sleepy body with a blind, fierce pity for this diffident man with the restless hands who mistook her terror for coldness . . .

"Young people can so easily get the wrong impression," said Edna Green to her husband. "I think you should speak to Susan, Fred. She might listen to you. Whatever I say is just water off a duck's back. Life isn't like that film. No wonder young people don't listen to their parents any more when they're brainwashed by rubbish like that. Films should tell people the truth about life."

Fred Green laughed to himself. "Maybe if you told them the truth about life, no one would ever get married. I dunno, Edna, I reckon that film was a pretty good send-up of women in love."

"Love! Is that what you call it? Lust, more like it! No wonder she tried to lock the brute out of her room."

At the memory of it she felt a peculiar blush spread from her stomach right up over her neck and face, down her arms, down even into her rubber gloves so that she had to turn on the cold tap before she could plunge her hands back into the water. What if some brute had tried that on with *her!* . . . Who — *Fred?* She drew back, but the idea pressed against her, sly, inviting. Startled, she glanced at him. He sat lost in thought — in that film, was he? Her blood bolted. The brutality of it! The arrogance! That poor girl struggling to lock her door, the wretch forcing his way, that male body poised above hers — *love,* was it? Anyway, what could a young girl like Susan possibly know about love? The blushing, stammering boy from the Y who called for her every Thursday and rang her up at weekends hardly held her hand . . . *did he?* Edna Green felt a moment of terror. Sick to the stomach. Like that time when the pains began. She had thought she was being torn in two. Afterwards, lying limp and empty with the baby in the crook of her arm, she had held her breath in amazement at the tiny, perfect fingers that clutched hers. When the blind, eager mouth drew at her breast, she had felt a gush of love as painful as the violent spasms of her womb. She would sit holding Susan for hours. Fred would say she was silly, a baby's place was in its pram, did Edna expect him to wait all night? While he waited anyway, cross and helpless in the face of her silence as she looked up at him over the child in her arms . . .

She squeezed the dishmop between her fingers. "Would you break down a door, Fred?"

Fred Green looked startled. "You know I wouldn't, Edna."

Little pulses beat in her neck. "Or force yourself on an unwilling woman?"

The kitchen door flung open and Susan Green rushed in. A crocheted knee-rug hung around her shoulders, and pulled over her head was her mother's old black felt hat with the upturned brim that the silly girl had unearthed somewhere. Edna Green stared. It might have been herself she was looking at . . . yes, that girl stood as close as yesterday. All that dancing! The plans! The veiled seeking! Girls were taught to be modest then. And look at her now . . . A threadbare garment of a woman, tattered and patched and about as sought-after as a duster.

"Going out, Susie?" asked Fred Green in surprise. Edna Green looked hard at her husband. "Yes . . . well. Time I got going myself. We've been talking about that film, Susan." His cup jumped about in its saucer as he carried them over to the sink. "What will you women think of us men?"

Susan Green pulled a funny face at her mother. "What's eating him?" She spun on tiptoe, swept a tin from the pantry and cut herself a hunk of chocolate cake.

"*Susan!*"

Swallowing as she talked, Susan Green said, "Stephen just rang. His dad's lent him the car for an hour. We're going for a drive before lunch. Okay?"

Edna Green looked sharply at her daughter. She saw a warm pink flower on the verge of blooming. "Stephen? But I thought it was Bill."

"Listening, were you?" said Susan Green archly, dashing crumbs from her mouth with the back of her hand. She never had been a dainty eater, thought Edna Green sadly, she always liked her food too much. But this going without breakfast, and eating chocolate cake first thing in the morning — it wasn't right, that wasn't how they had brought her up. And then that film!

"Susan . . . "

"Yes?" The girl swung around, holding open the outside door so that a fly drifted in. "Yes Mum, what?"

A car horn blared. "Drive carefully," begged Edna Green.

"Sure." The girl laughed, and waved as she ran past the window.

Together

The day the doctor tells Laverne she is well enough to take over things again, Midge announces she is moving out into a flat of her own. For weeks she has been planning what she will say to Laverne. She draws a string bag through her fingers as she speaks, concentrating on a frayed thread so that her wits won't snag against Laverne's attention.

"It's not very far. Just around the corner, really. On the top storey, looking right out over the city." She pauses, held aloft on a promise that stretches to the horizon. The other woman says nothing, just lets her eyes follow as Midge twitters about the kitchen. "There's a continental grocer right on the corner. And guess what, he sells baklava. I know, because I went in and walked right around, just looking and breathing. Such lovely smells!" She closes her eyes and sees again the grocer's busy hands slicing bacon, draining olives, wrapping the delicious little biscuits that ooze honey at each bite. It is his strength that she breathes in, the self-contained world of masculinity that Laverne ignores and Midge puzzles over. She goes on breathlessly, "We can see each other often, Laverne — every day. There's a heater in the bathroom, and a tiny bench in the kitchen just big enough for my typewriter, and the telephone — here's my number, look — and a divan for a visitor. You'll love the view, Laverne."

She begins to collect her things from the kitchen, her own mug, cutlery that once belonged to her mother, a lidless saucepan. Her fingers are shaking, and a spoon clatters into the sink.

Laverne is silent for so long that Midge slips into her old place, on the arm of Laverne's chair, and resists the impulse to lay her head beside hers on the plump cushion. Laverne apparently does not notice. She has turned up her sleeve and with the tip of her finger is rubbing a vein in her marshmallow skin. At last she says "Please tell me one thing. You're very fond of baklava. Have you any idea how much a packet of baklava costs?"

Now, Laverne never bothers Midge about money, or shopping lists, or bills to add up — all that sort of thing. So what is she driving at? The years fall away and Midge is a child again, blurting out her opinions in front of everyone and Laverne is ordering silence so that Midge can try again. "We'll make a thinker of you yet, Marguerite." Her wits are delicate balloons that she juggles while Laverne and all the others wait with eyes like barbs. But she is conscious only of Laverne. That bitch!

"You think I can't do it, Laverne? I won't be able to manage? I'm helpless on my own, is that it?" She jumps to her feet. "I tell you this, I can't work here any more."

"It's because I've been sick. You've had all the cooking and cleaning to do. But I'm better now. And you can get back to your work. As before. All day to yourself in this flat."

Midge looks around the room. "Do you know, I sit here during the day and I watch the silverfish come out when the flat is all quiet and you know what they're up to, creeping around the walls and falling into basins and scuttling into my notebooks when I throw things at them? They're chewing the place away. See that photograph that my mother had taken just before I left home? *Look* at it, Laverne. The face is almost completely gone. And I *can't work*."

Laverne says politely, in that way she has, "And

when you take all your things from here to escape the silverfish, how do you know you won't carry a few with you and it will begin all over again?"

Midge stares at her, narrowing her eyes. With her invalid's pallor and her silver-gilt hair, Laverne herself is a silverfish — and that really is a joke, because Laverne is a big woman, fat, and she never scuttles. She turns now, slowly, as fat people do, and says "What's funny? We've been together a long time, Midge."

"You make it sound like a marriage. Well, you know what I think about marriage. Didn't my mother finally pluck up courage to leave that disgusting drunkard my father after years of — "

"Yes yes yes." Laverne twists as though in pain and Midge, terrified that she is about to have a relapse, stuffs clothes from the ironing basket into the string bag without caring whether they are hers or Laverne's. Laverne, grunting, stoops to straighten the crocheted rug that has slipped from her knee. "For heaven's sake. A working partnership, I would have said . . . I'm still some use to you, I think," she goes on, plucking at a pulled stitch in the rug. "Who suggested the plot for that story of yours about the burglars who phoned in first and left their phone off the hook so the old lady couldn't phone out? Neat, eh? Original? You hadn't known that, had you? Not many people do."

Midge breathes deeply. Is there no way to reach her? "So what about your work, Laverne?" she pleads. "Do you think I don't notice at night? You stare into space, you doze off in front of the radiator, you even read the newspaper you're using to wrap up the rubbish. Where's the future in that?"

"Well I read about the burglars, didn't I?"

Midge stands very still. "I mean," she says, "You don't spend any time on preparation these days. *Your* work. Oh yes, I hear things! You just rehash the old stuff from years ago. The things you gave *me*, I shouldn't wonder. And they're *bored*, Laverne! You used to be so good — so good."

Thinking about it is so awful that now after years of shielding, by one person or another, it is she who should protect Laverne, and she longs to throw her arms around the kind, soft woman who is saying plaintively "I worry about you, sweeting."

"And all those pills you take. Pills to make you sleep. Pills to wake you up again. You've a drawer full of poison, Laverne. Where's the future in *that*?"

"Now that I'm well again I'll work properly, Midge. You'll see. We both will."

"I am going, Laverne." This sounds so ruthless that she reseats herself for a moment on the arm of Laverne's chair, saying things like "I'll be all right. Don't worry about me. I'll manage."

"How?"

"As I do now. From my work."

"Oh Marguerite." Laverne's head rolls against the back of her chair, and her breasts shake with laughter. The arm of the chair vibrates. Midge jumps up angrily and prowls around the little sitting room, fingering Laverne's Persian wall hangings, kicking the fat velvet sofa. It is Laverne's flat all right. And the rent? the food? her new suede jacket that her last cheque was supposed to cover? A terrible suspicion rises to choke her . . . but she cannot bring herself to find out . . . she thinks she would kill Laverne.

She has a vision of her mother, weary, irritable, ironing far into the night because she is now the breadwinner and Midge must have food and clothes and books. She pats the string bag. "I'll take in ironing."

Laverne catches her breath. "Do you know how much a woman gets paid for an hour's ironing? And the back ache? The varicose veins? What a waste of your time. Leave all that to me. Haven't I always taken care of that side of things? I can do it with my eyes closed. I have to look after you, Midge. It's a promise I made to your mother."

"Laverne! You never even met my mother."

"It was a silent pledge."

What can one say in reply to an impossible person? Clever with fear, Midge tries again. "You know what I dreamed, Laverne? That I was in a coffin and you were shutting the lid and *I was still alive!*" She shudders. Laverne's mouth opens. Shuts. Her hands twitch. Midge can't bear to look, it is a silverfish struggling in the chair.

Her heart knocks triumphantly. "Goodbye, Laverne."

Downstairs she realizes she still has Laverne's key to the flat, but she will not go back, no, she will ask Laverne to come and collect it, or post it back, throw it down a grating, even — anything rather than walk back up those stairs.

One goodbye is enough.

As she runs along the street, her case bumping against her knees and the string bag bulging, the wind pushes at her back and seems to lift her so that she flies over the pavements. She is smiling, and strangers hurrying home smile back involuntarily at this thin, flying girl who looks so extraordinarily happy. She pictures her typewriter all ready on the bench in her own kitchen. Ideas rush into her head. The continental grocer, closing his shop for the day, bows "Madame . . . " as she flies past, and she smiles at him, too, glorying in the power of her own joy.

Reaching her block of flats, she lingers a moment, conscious of the solitude that waits upstairs. Downstairs, a party is beginning. Someone is handing around cans of beer, a boy is strumming a guitar, two people, arms clasped around each other's waists, heads buried together, are swaying in the centre of the room. The girl's hands slowly rub her partner's back, and Midge frowns, such a lassitude in her limbs after the fight with Laverne and all the running that watching the couple she thinks she will fall to the ground. So she looks at the guitarist who is alone, like herself, and she pretends he too is waiting and when he looks up he will see her breathing there and will run to the door to greet her — But he does not look up.

When she enters her flat the phone is ringing. She is sure it is he. Tip-toeing, she lifts the receiver, speaks.

It is Laverne.

She is ringing, she says, to say goodbye. It takes Midge a moment to understand her, because her voice sounds funny, blurred. "Laverne? What — "

"Goodbye," says Laverne again, faintly.

"What *is* this?" shouts Midge, as though raising her own voice will make Laverne more distinct. "Aren't I seeing you again on Sunday when I collect the rest of my things? You know I am. Laverne — I can't hear you — you've *what?*"

Laverne says, since she is no further use to Midge and therefore no use to herself, she has decided to take all the tablets in her drawer, they are taking effect already and she is so glad Midge has gone straight to the flat because she really wanted to say a proper goodbye.

Midge looks at the little holes in the handpiece and says "Oh you monster."

"Goodbye," says the handpiece, and then there is a crash, and Midge can just picture Laverne sprawling out of her chair and the handpiece dangling and bumping on its cord. "Bitch!" she shrieks. There is no answer.

Because she has had to telephone so often lately, she knows by heart the number of Laverne's doctor. She dials. There is no response. This time she listens carefully for dial tone — there is none. Only a faint crackling in the distance. And she realizes with suffocating horror that she is still connected to Laverne, that until Laverne puts her handpiece back on the set Midge will stay connected to her, like a child tied by an umbilicus to a dead mother.

The thought crosses her mind as she runs down the stairs, *let her die.*

Oh help me, someone, help me, she moans. The door of the downstairs flat flies open as she passes and the guitarist staggers out. "Oh help me!" cries Midge, clutching his arm. He lurches against her, saying "Sorry, mate," as beer from his can sloshes over her arm. Disgusted, she pushes him and runs. Runs. In the pocket of her suede jacket is the key to Laverne's flat. Thank heaven, thank heaven, she thinks, grasping it until her fingers ache. The wind whips her cheekbones as she runs.

Adult Education

Outside the newsagency Chattie Cookson fusses with her watch. If she dashes in now and settles the paper account without stopping to bandy more words with Mr Jolley the newsagent about the Cooksons' big move to Canberra, she will still be in time to catch the butcher on her way back to the car. Paper bill, T-bones. Chattie nods. If there's one thing she is clever at, it's organization. Chattie, where's a new tube of toothpaste? Mum, I can't find a pencil. Chattie, was it this morning I changed my singlet? . . . Yes, organization. Direction. She seizes Jim's cheque book and hurries into the newsagency.

Of course she does squander a precious minute or two at the counter. Mr Jolley runs true to form — Chattie has only to nod obligingly. Mrs Jolley nods too. In a high mirror behind the counter Chattie is startled by the sight of their heads going nod nod nod like a pair of muppets while Mr Jolley hunches forward and conspiratorially taps on the counter. Yes it's a step-up for Jim sure enough. A real challenge, too, since he'll be a kind of pioneer up there in Canberra. But hasn't Mr Jolley always said . . . Eh Mrs Cookson? (Chattie smiles.) Eh Mother? (Mrs Jolley smiles.) Mr Jolley is delighted with himself. He picks up Chattie's cheque and out of long habit makes a show of studying the signature. "Too right, I could see it a mile off, Jim's a moral for a job like that."

Jim, Jim, Jim! "I'll find it a change, too, Mr Jolley," she replies, more tartly than she intends.

Mrs Jolley fiddles with a jar of chocolate freckles. "You'll miss all your friends down here, Mrs Cookson," she offers.

Chattie smiles. Because she and Jim started so young, most of the children of her present friends are still toddlers; at tennis, at coffees, at the monthly meetings of the craft club, their mothers mull over teething and playschool and shoe brands till Chattie could scream. "I'm looking forward to a change of view, Mrs Jolley."

"No doubt about it, they've picked the right man in Jim Cookson," Mr Jolley repeats, putting the receipt at last into her waiting hand. "Next thing we'll be opening the papers and seeing Mr and Mrs James Cookson jetting off first-class all over the world. Eh, Mrs Cookson?"

Chattie laughs. "That's politicians." The closest she is likely to get to the political life is the visitors' gallery in Parliament House. Nevertheless she is flattered, and turns to leave in a dazzle of excitement. Perhaps that is why she is careless and lets her eyes wander; immediately they are captured by the brilliant dustjackets of a tableful of books by the door. She stops. Great sweeps of sand, yellow as butter, and in the foreground a tiny figure — male? female? — setting forth towards red and yellow rockpiles. So little and so far to go! Chattie picks up one of the books.

The title doesn't mean anything to her, nor does the name of the author. She flips the cover open and skims. "Harrington Vane: explorer, poet, mystic . . ." says the dustjacket. She opens at random and reads, not poetry as she is expecting, but everyday prose — no, that's not right, not everyday by any means. The author has a curious way of describing a journey to the inland as though really he is looking at something else. This is no ordinary travel book, no ordinary traveller. Intrigued, Chattie reads the dustjacket more carefully. The word "Canberra" jumps out at her. Harrington Vane, explorer, poet and mystic, has recently been appointed Visiting Fellow at the university in Canberra! Now, if that isn't an omen . . . Dear goodness, Canberra must be full of wonderful people. Not that Chattie expects ever to come in close contact with any of them. Academics and writers are a touch above the Cookson ambit. Still, just to know they are about . . . She glances down at the dauntless manikin striking out for the unknown. Oh yes, an omen indeed! She dashes back to the counter, takes out the T-bone money, and with a gulp of breath as though she has breasted a high and windswept hill, purchases Harrington Vane . . . She bites her lip. Too late now. Shepherd's pie for dinner.

The move to Canberra is at last complete. Their furniture is unpacked; new drapes and carpets are paid for. They have borrowed just that little bit more than they really intended for the lovely house that looks into the valley of the Murrumbidgee. They have debated the pros and cons of the different sorts of education for Jamie and Cheryl, public, private, experimental. Contacts of Jim's have invited them to dinner; Chattie has reciprocated. Jim throws himself into his job, working late at night and bringing home papers at the weekend. Nearly every day any time between twelve and two he rushes home for a hot lunch, as he eats pouring out his successes of the morning, his plans for the afternoon.

Chattie hasn't much to offer Jim in return. Each morning by half past nine the kitchen floor is rubbed over so well it seems a shame to walk on it. Shopping — that's much the same as anywhere. So she tells herself — just in case Jim should ask. The truth is, search as she will in the big tinselly Christmas stocking that is the new shopping complex, nowhere does she come across even the skin-creeping interest of a Mr Jolley. Fancy missing Mr Jolley! Chattie flees home, double-checks her docket, slips her fingers into her comfortable old gardening gloves. These are tracks that she knows. The garden is flourishing. She reads all she can lay hands on about gardening in Canberra, and spends a lot of time at the front of the house, digging, planting, watering. No one passes by, or drops in. Most of the women in the street seem to work. Chattie wonders whether she should look for a job. But what could she *do?* She hardly fancies polishing another woman's kitchen floor. Oh she had ideas once, all right, years ago — air hostess, nurse, indispensable secretary. She sits back on her heels and lifts her eyes to the mountains caught in brilliant autumn sunshine. Across the years comes the voice of one of her teachers. "Chattie, you're a joy to have in the class." A joy to have in the class . . . At first the schoolgirl just stared at Miss Fielding, growing hot all over while everyone else sniggered, positive old Fielding was being sarcastic. "Oh no, I really mean it!" Miss Fielding said quickly. "Always asking questions . . . finding out . . . much better than just sitting there like a row of lamp posts." . . . Pansy seedlings lie forgotten in Chattie's hands as she remembers. Old Crabapple Fielding. Nice old thing. Didn't approve of Jim, though. Used to chase the two of them out of the assembly hall whenever she caught them there during private studies. She needn't have worried. School was sacrosanct. Chattie smiles, recalling that pearly morning by the waterhole, the first time she saw Jim naked; how fiercely she had stripped for him then! Funny how all that fades, no, drops into place alongside other priorities like work, schools, keeping up a neat house. They've been Chattie and Jim for so long now, Chattie and Jim, Chattie and Jim, Chattie and Jim — She jumps to her feet, scattering seedlings as she runs out to the footpath.

It is five past four, time the children were home from school. The children! The children! But the thoughtless creatures have begun to dawdle home later and later. Jamie once or twice hasn't turned up till his dinner is actually out on his plate! His father just laughs. She doubts whether Jim has even heard her complaint. These days he eats his dinner with a report propped in front of him.

One morning while rearranging her shoes at the bottom of a wardrobe she comes across the book with the red and yellow dustjacket. She looks hard at the foreground figure and for a moment sits back, daydreaming; makes to toss the book back amongst the shoes, changes her mind and goes out to the kitchen to reread in the daily paper a notice which has caught her attention.

Over dinner while she is wondering how to begin, Jim suddenly tells her that he has decided to do a short course in accountancy to help him with his work. Jamie and Cheryl look at each other. "*School*," they groan.

In her lap her fingers pick at her serviette. "I'm going to a class, too," she announces. "For fun." She glances around the table and wishes that Jim would look as though he were really listening, that the children wouldn't stare so. "It was in the paper today. Adult education. Yes, I know I've done classes before, Jim, bread-making and slimming and dried flowers, but something different this time. Reading books. Every Tuesday morning" — she breathes deeply — "on the university campus . . . No it wouldn't be the same just going to the library. I look at all those books along the shelves and my mind goes blank . . . Your hot lunch? Well, I'll just have to prepare it after breakfast, won't I, and leave it in the oven . . . You *will*, Jim, you will get used to it."

She enrols in a class called "Leave the Dishes in the Sink" because that is just how she feels. She looks around at the other women in her discussion group and hopes they aren't too clever for her. There are no men in this class which is a relief really. By the end of the course perhaps she'll have confidence enough to take part in a real conversation with a man, not just one of those bantering games men feel they owe to women. The tutor introduces herself as Clair. It is all first names here. Chattie likes this idea. Cookson, after all, is Jim's name. She isn't so sure about Chattie, either, the name that has stuck for more than thirty years. She would rather like a change . . . Carlotta, perhaps . . . Odile . . . Isadora.

The tutor asks each one to give a short autobiographical account "just to get to know one another, girls. You first, Lise," she prompts Chattie's neighbour, a solid, blonde young woman with eyes as green as parsley. Her husband's research takes him out of Canberra for weeks at a time, Lise tells the class, leaving her in a little flat with three children under four. "That's fine for him, isn't it? What am I? Some sort of peapod?"

Everyone laughs. Chattie relaxes. She finds herself telling the class about Harrington Vane's remaindered book in its eye-catching dustjacket that has become for her a symbol of quest.

Lise nudges her. "Don't for heaven's sake tell Hal that." And as Chattie looks startled — "Harrington Vane. Vane by name and vain by nature, that one."

Chattie is surprised, even a little hurt, at such a spiteful remark, and would like to ask Lise whether she has ever read the book, but the tutor is talking again, and at the conclusion of the class Lise hurries out ahead of everyone. Chattie catches sight of her greeting a lounging, sullen young fellow whose whitish-blonde hair straggles across his shiny leather jacket. Lise talks animatedly for a moment, then he puts on a helmet and hands her another. Chattie claps her hands to her ears as they roar off on his motor-cycle. Funny the sort of men women marry, she muses. But lovely all the same to have him meet you and go off together and talk over your doings.

At the dinner table that evening she says "In my class there's a woman of seventy-eight who says she wants to go on learning till the day she dies. Isn't that wonderful?" She comes to the crux of the comment. "*I* want to be like her!"

Jim looks at her patiently. "But what *for*, dear?"

She sits next to Lise the following week, and each week thereafter. Funny, she thinks, how we like our own places, we stick to them, we're not adventurous really. Lise makes sharp, amusing remarks that Chattie enjoys. She decides to forget the Harrington Vane comment. One morning during the coffee break Lise says to Chattie, "Hal is back again from the Centre. With enough material for three more volumes at least. I suppose he'll want me to type it all up, as usual. Oh by the way — I passed on your adulation about his last book, the one you found in the newsagent's."

So Lise is married to Harrington Vane . . . Harrington Vane . . . the mooching youth whose hair needs a trim. Chattie becomes quite breathless. Even more so when Lise continues, "We're having a bit of a nosh-up on Saturday evening. Folks dropping in any old time after nine — ten — you know. Like to come?"

Like to come? Chattie can't remember an invitation in years that hasn't come about through Jim's work, or from friends who were friends of both of them. She rushes home and all that afternoon rereads Harrington Vane. Again she is struck by an obsessive quality about the writing. What is it besides sand and spinifex that the author is really looking at? She will ask him. That young man whose hair Jamie would admire can't really be too frightening.

She takes extra care with her appearance on Saturday evening. Lovingly she takes out her black velvet slacks and her cream silk shirt. Horrors, there's that button still missing from the front of the shirt! Lately she has been using the day set aside for sewing to dash off to the National Library. No time now to search out a matching button — tosses aside that shirt, riffles through the rack for another — the red one? heavens no! — sees the missing button in of all places her make-up tray, calls Cheryl to bring needle and thread quickly, quickly; and is after all ready on time.

"You'll do," says Jim. He is wearing his new safari suit. Jim is getting on very well at work these days, and is quite jaunty about Chattie's new friends. "What time did she say? Sounds more like bedtime to me."

Dead on nine they arrive at the Vanes' university flat. Jim takes her elbow to steer her up the front steps. His knock is evidently not heard above the noise from inside, so tentatively he opens the door. The tiny flat seems full of people already. Lise in thin cheesecloth waves wildly from the steps to the mezzanine level where someone is filling glasses. Chattie's darting eyes take in bowls of hakea and golden everlastings; shields and bark paintings instead of prints on the walls; and suspended from the top storey stairs, one of those ducky cane basket chairs. No sign of Harrington Vane. She feels Jim's clutch relax as he spots a familiar face. "Jim's wife, are you?" says the acquaintance. He introduces his wife. "Cookson?" she repeats. Her face lights up. "Not Jamie's mother? Such a nice boy, he was round at our place yesterday after school to see Nancy, we'd have asked him to stay to a meal but we thought you might be expecting him. Such nice manners, it's a real change these days . . . " Dear goodness, thinks Chattie, is it going to be one of those evenings after all? She is really annoyed with Jamie now — how dare he follow her here! She smiles politely at the woman and lets herself be swept aside by someone who is impatiently pushing. With a gulp of excitement she sees it is Harrington Vane. Now or never! She blocks his passage and says "Hello. I'm Chattie Cookson."

The young man grins. "That's your bad luck."

She is so amazed that all she can do is rush on. "I wanted to tell you, I enjoyed your book."

He sways towards her. "What's that?" His complexion is like pastry mix.

"Your book — I enjoyed it."

"Book? Book?" Wine jiggles from his glass as he makes a puzzled gesture. There is a button missing from one cuff of his jean jacket.

"You are Harrington Vane, aren't you?"

"Vane? Good God no. That's Hal over there, by the stairs, earbashing some elderly Young Liberal by the look of him."

She looks, and sees talking to Jim a squarely built man of about fifty; he has black curling hair touched with grey, and a short black beard. He is using his hands to emphasize some point, and Jim is laughing.

Lise comes up then and leans against the young man. "So glad you came, Chattie. Sorry I wasn't there to introduce you to people but you're managing all right, aren't you? More drinks, anyone?" She moves on, and the young man follows.

"Sorry lady," he flings over his shoulder. "Wrong number."

"I am so relieved," Chattie retorts. However could she have mistaken him for Harrington Vane! She looks across to the corner under the top storey stairs where people come and go like moths around Vane. Jim is still there. He seems to be enjoying himself hugely.

Letting herself drift in that direction, she sips like an insect at her wine as she joins in with more skill than she has ever suspected the sprightly, shallow talk of people who brush wings and part. Unemployment — conservation — she smiles, nods, raises an eyebrow. It is so *easy!* At length she is close enough to Vane to catch occasional phrases, hear his laughter. Jim has moved away. When at last Vane is talking to only one person, Nancy's mother, the wife of Jim's acquaintance whom she spoke to earlier, she turns so that she is now part of his circle. Nancy's mother smiles her recognition; Vane looks her up and down rapidly, nods, and goes on talking.

"You agree?" he is saying. "Of course you do — It must be like a beautiful woman, always with that element of surprise."

"You mean," Nancy's mother ponders, "away with mathematical precision. Follow nature?"

"Exactly. Every woman since Eve knows all about the art that conceals art."

It transpires that they are talking about gardening. Now this is a subject close to Chattie's heart, after all those spare hours spent in her front garden. She breaks in. "I love oldie worldie gardens, all planned out for colours and scents — you know? Violets and pinks, lavender, hearts-ease. I saw a hearts and diamonds garden once — "

Vane, interrupted in his flow, says "Yes? Yes?" and returns to Nancy's mother who is hanging on every word. Chattie, taking tiny sips from her glass, bides her time. Cool and golden as her wine, Vane's voice flows around her like nectar. " 'A garden is a lovesome thing, God wot!' And the first prison, too, till luckily man sinned himself out of it." The two women flutter with laughter. "What was it Pope said? — he lived in an age that was crazy about gardening, you know — 'Men, some to business, some to pleasure take; But every woman is at heart a rake.' " He pauses while Nancy's mother relishes his pun. Chattie, busy recollecting, catches her breath.

"I know one about men! 'A man of words and not of deeds Is like a garden full of weeds.'"

There is a small silence. "Mother Goose," she adds.

"Oh yes, Mother Goose!" Nancy's mother giggles. "'Girls and boys come out to play, The moon doth shine as bright as day.'"

"Women and gardens are governed by the moon." Vane's musings bob before Chattie like moons, like motes, like manikins. "'There is a tide in the affairs of women, Which, taken at the flood, leads — God knows where.'"

Chattie grows pink. "That's Shakespeare . . . isn't it?"

"Byron. *Don Juan.*" He holds her gaze until she looks down, confused, and excited too.

"You're absolutely right about the moon, Hal!" cries Nancy's mother. "I always sow by the moon."

Chattie says lightly, "Don't you get around to it during the day?"

She is as surprised as Vane and Nancy's mother at this witticism. Smiling to herself, she finishes off her wine. Vane, still talking, refills her glass from a bottle on the bookshelf nearby.

Nancy's mother hurries on, "I've been meaning to ask you, Hal, what trees do you recommend we plant at the front of our house?"

"But my dear girl, you already have a forest of trees at the front of your house."

"Yes, but not enough. I want a thick screen. I want to block out the neighbours."

Vane tops up their glasses while he considers. "How tall are the trees now?"

"About twelve feet."

Chattie catches Vane's eye. She says, "How tall are the neighbours?"

Nancy's mother smiles uncertainly. Vane laughs. Chattie, savouring triumph, looks into her wine glass.

When she raises her eyes, Vane is studying her, and Nancy's mother has turned in response to someone else.

Vane makes an observation that she puts aside to think about later. "You are a more interesting woman than I at first thought." Then, briskly, "I'm Harrington Vane. And you?"

"Chattie Cookson. Chattie."

He says, so softly that she has to lean towards him, "But you aren't, are you?"

She stares at him, reddening, for one terrible moment believing that he is making fun of her. But of course she is wrong. He says smoothly, "I shall call you Charlotte. It is Charlotte, isn't it?"

"Charlotte is so old-fashioned."

He laughs. "Is it? Tell me about yourself."

Where to begin? "Your book — I've read it three times — I never dreamed I'd have the chance to tell you — ask you — "

Now she has his full attention. "It really meant so much to you?" At his suggestion she sits in the basket chair, shrugging herself comfortably into its plump cushion, and swinging gently as he talks. "I am fascinated by the Centre, Charlotte. I return again and again. Lawrence once wrote to Katharine Susannah Prichard about 'its Sleeping Beauty terror'. I know exactly what he meant."

This is heady stuff. Chattie begins to float. "Your family doesn't see much of you, then?" she asks, wondering how she would feel if Jim's work constantly took him away from Canberra.

"Lise and I understand each other. We are independent people. Why should married people ever be otherwise?"

"Oh I quite agree!" she exclaims, remembering Chattie and Jim, Chattie and Jim.

"You do? Remarkable. Most women are unable to

see human relationships in that way. My first wife, for instance, a lovely girl, but limited. Fortunately Lise and I see eye to eye over most things — essential things. Though she's making a mistake this time, and I have told her so. This present friend of hers is so — so *crass*. She is making a fool of herself."

Chattie can't help but agree. Aloud she comments, "You'll be in Canberra for awhile now to write your new book, I suppose. That must be hard work."

"Writing a book is like making love, Charlotte. Have you ever considered that?" Without waiting for a reply he continues. "Writer — lover — each is an artist. He searches, he selects, he discards. He glimpses perfection. Feels ecstasy. And the world marvels, and acclaims him for the artist that he is. Isn't that so? . . . Hmm?"

Chattie frowns. "But the woman? What happens to the woman? You — he — isn't she just — "

"The woman?" He turns to refill her glass. "The woman? My dear Charlotte, have you ever read a book or seen a painting or a piece of sculpture that could exist without its creator?"

After a moment she decides to laugh. He must be right of course. All the same . . .

He sees her frown and says quickly, "What's the matter? Something's bothering you? Let me rearrange that silly cushion." She can feel his breath, warm as sunlight on her neck as he fusses behind her. His hand reaching down tugs at the cushion, then, so lightly that she can't really be sure, takes hold of her velvet-clad backside, moves, takes hold again. She jolts upright. "There, that should stay in place now. You can sit back," he says, straightening, and she huddles away, ashamed of her suspicions, doubly ashamed of conveying them to him like a silly schoolgirl.

"There's one thing about your writing that puzzles me," she babbles. "I can't quite put it into words.

That's why it's so good listening to you explain things."
She assures herself that she is perfectly collected again.

"You and I have a lot of interests in common, Charlotte," he remarks casually. "I like talking to you. Let me take you to lunch one day at the university — Your husband too, of course, if you wish," he is quick to add. Chattie stares up at him. She is remembering that manikin on the dustjacket of his book — driven on to strange places by some compulsion. " . . . not really Jim's cup of tea," she hears herself declaring. Vane continues smoothly, "Monday, then? If it's fine we can eat outdoors, by the lake."

Just as casually she agrees, telling herself what could be more natural than a man and a woman lunching together to discuss his work? She sees the table for two under the gum trees, the carafe of wine, sunlight freckling through the leaves as she leans forward with eager questions . . .

"No, please, no more wine," she protests but he fills her glass anyway.

"Can you find your own way about the campus, Charlotte?"

She replies with some pride. "Oh yes. I go to the university each week for my adult education class."

"Ah yes. Adult education."

"Clair, our tutor, says ask yourself two questions. What is the author trying to do? Is he successful?"

"Wonderful perspicacity, your tutor. Is she here tonight?"

"Food, everyone!" Lise calls from above. "Up here on the table. Moussaka! Moussaka!"

Vane nods at Chattie. "That's settled, then!" and indicates that they move upstairs to supper. But Chattie's questions are still unasked. "Isn't there one thing you've overlooked, Hal?" she cries, catching his arm. "You journey into the Centre. You return and write a clever book — "

83

He smooths her hand. "So? Something so urgent that it won't wait till Monday?"

What is it that she is trying to say? The persistent, niggling thoughts jump out. "For you, the Centre is a challenge — "

His fingers are creeping under the silk of her cuff. "Every encounter is a challenge . . . hmm?"

It is as though she can hear two conversations at once: her own perplexed words, and the gabbling pulses in her wrist. "But the Centre stays the same — doesn't it? I mean, it is always there — regardless — whether you contemplate it or not — Is it clear what I am trying to tell you?"

"Perfectly clear." She stares at the brownish-yellow pits in his teeth as he begins to laugh. His face bobs closer. "What an attractive woman you are, Charlotte."

Is that all a man can say to a woman? She jumps to her feet. Oh the wolf! The fox! The pig! He hasn't listened to a word she has said!

As she stands up Jim catches sight of her. "There you are, Chattie!" he booms. "I've been wondering where you'd got to. Supper's ready. Some Greek dish, very nice too. Your wife is a good cook, Hal — Chattie is a good cook, too," he adds.

Vane nods. "I believe you, Jim. Your wife has been telling me so much about herself."

Chattie gives a conversational laugh, but her fingertips ache with anger. Smirking fools! Ignorant! Arrogant! And a woman like herself so *helpless* . . . Oh pull your socks up, Chattie, where's that superfine sense of direction? Inspiration strikes her. She opens her eyes very wide. "Jim! You'll never guess. Hal wants the two of us to have lunch with him at the university on Monday!"

"Is that so? Well, that's very nice. We can go on with our talk, Hal — We've been discussing the pros and cons of a planned city like Canberra, Chattie."

Chattie says softly, "Is it like a woman, Jim? Canberra?"

She flashes a dazzling smile at Harrington Vane, then turns in triumph to Jim. But as Jim tucks her arm under his and turns her around saying "This way, old girl", she asks herself where on earth she is going.

Nuclear

His workmates at the paper mill came back at him with things like "Take a holiday, Ray. You're letting it bug you." And laughed.

As he stepped off the bus that brought the night shift back to the town, Ray Skerritt couldn't bring himself to turn with his usual wave. He hunched his head into his upturned coat collar. Letting it bug him, was he? Their chiaking bit into him with the insistence of the morning's chill wind. As though getting away from it all on a holiday could in any way lessen the danger! He could hardly credit that ordinary, decent blokes — his mates — could be so short-sighted. Young Ted Parker from next door was just behind him but Ray Skerritt strode on. Be damned to the lot of them! They said things like "There's men hungry for jobs, Ray. You know that." And "You some sort of greenie, Ray? Or a red?" Even Ted Parker disbelieved him. "Reckon I'll be off up there like a shot once they start mining, Ray. Danger money and all that. If you ask me, there's more danger out here at the mill clearing a machine, like we done this morning." . . . "If we *don't* sell the stuff — " An older chap had chipped in then with that craven argument about invasion from the north that the politicians were fond of touting. "Look here, Ray, I fought them fellers when youse was all kids. You young blokes today, you don't know you're alive. You're a family man, Ray. You want some future for your kids, don't you?"

"But that's just it!" he muttered, tearing the first tentative blooms from a wattle tree overhanging the footpath. "Some future for the kids!" As he crunched along the gravel drive at the side of his house, he could hear those kids of his through the weatherboard walls, Alvie thumping around in her bedroom — last minute packing, he supposed — and the little ones Trish and Billy in the bathroom having one of their interminable, pointless rows that nearly drove him mad. Of course he should go straight in and break it up, reason with them gently, set an example, but God he'd had it this morning. Bone weary. What with not coming home at midnight as he'd expected but working right through till the day shift came on; and the frantic rush to clear the machine after the break in the great sheet of paper; and then that argument on the way home in the bus.

His old dog Brownie whined a greeting but he ignored that, too. Sleep, that was what he needed. Oblivion. He didn't even bother to hang up his mill workers' "Work Safely" overall, just dropped it in the back porch and stepped into the laundry to slosh cold water on hands and face. In the kitchen there was no sign of his family yet, but the woman Raelene had already arrived. She looked up from the hunks of bread she was piling with raspberry jam for the school lunches.

"Cuppa tea? You look buggered," she greeted him in her cheerful, raspy way. "It's a killer all right, that night shift. Blue could never get used of it. Take a pew — kettle's just on the boil. You just done a double? Oh jeez." She shook her head in sympathy.

"Thanks, Raelene. I'm fair done in." He couldn't be bothered sitting down straightaway; just stayed propped where he was, by the kitchen table where she was working.

"This marge is certainly a cinch to spread," she commented, glancing up. "Though I do like butter meself, mind you."

"Bad for your arteries, Raelene," he teased, relaxing

in the warmth of the kitchen, and the warm, yeasty smell of the woman.

"Ah, get out with you. I haven't croaked yet."

"They make that jam from pumpkins and the pips from little bits of wood, did you know that?" he went on. He liked the way she slapped jam and margarine right to the crusts of each slice.

"Go on? Marvellous what they can do these days, isn't it? There's that kettle." As she turned towards the stove she collided with him, breast and thigh pressing him against the table as she shoved past. "Woops," she said blithely. "Clumsy old me. Porridge is ready. Them kids should be here any tic. I'll give them a hoy . . . Mrs Skerritt's told me what she wants done this morning," she continued, busy with the porridge plates. "The washing, and a good tidy-up, and the lunches for the rest of the week in the freezer. Real good idea, I reckon, her having a bit of a break before the baby comes. My sister Shirlene, that's the one with all the kids, she's got a real nice house and a good husband, mind you, but she never gets a minute to put her feet up. And young Alvie going with your wife too, now isn't that a good idea? She's a real card, that Alvie. Like my sister Darlene. Real smart."

With a sigh of relief Ray Skerritt took his steaming cup of tea and sat down amongst the sandwich crumbs.

"Here's the paper. Picked it up on me way in. Tea okay?"

Ray Skerritt nodded briefly. His attention was rivetted by a feature article on the second page. Bearing out exactly what he'd been trying to get across to the others on the bus! Now what would they have to say? Conscious that Raelene was asking him something he looked up frowning, but she said without repeating the question "Oh I c'n see you're busy with the paper, I won't keep botherin' you." He nodded again, ideas aroused by the article jostling for attention while his eyes followed Raelene as she turned back to the stove: a big, mousey-coloured woman with her hair straggling out of plastic curlers and an ugly sleeveless green dress stretched across rolls of flesh and rolling buttocks. "Rough as bags", people said of Raelene, and in the same breath, "heart of gold". There were stories by the dozen about Raelene, half of which Ray Skerritt dismissed as spite — or envy — and the other half, well, what did they expect her to do? Life certainly dealt a rough hand to some people. Father of her first kid wouldn't marry her; that fellow Blue in and out of gaol; both sons in homes now. One of life's battlers, was Raelene. When it came to survival she would run rings around those women she regularly cleaned and ironed for, wives of the bosses out at the mill, engineers and the like, with their big houses and big cars and big heads full of dollar signs. He reckoned he knew to a T what *they* would all say about this article in the paper. He fell to wondering what Raelene would make of it.

— Or his own family, come to that? He regarded them sombrely as they straggled to the breakfast table, his three kids and then his wife Joan. "Just a cuppa for me, love," Raelene said to Alvie, sitting back with a sigh and cradling her cup in both hands as she sipped. "Jeez, this is good-oh, isn't it, a nice big family all sitting down together. Puts me in mind of when we was all kids, me and Darlene and Shirlene."

No one said anything for a moment, because of Blue, and those awful boys who got sent away.

Then Trish piped up. "Shouldn't read at the table, Dad!" Getting too cheeky for words, that one. He saw Alvie's eyes gleam as she sensed a battle. Or was it all the muck she'd painted on? Lord knows what her aunt and uncle would make of her.

"Go and wash your face, Alvie," he grumbled.

"Oh Ray! She looks very nice," his wife interceded. She'd had her hair done the day before, and she was wearing one of the new maternity smocks she had run up especially for her stay with her sister and brother-in-law. Silly idea, this going away. He looked away from her to his eldest child.

"You'd be better spending the week at school, Alvie," he complained. "You kids today . . . I don't know."

"Mum needs me!" Alvie cast an appealing glance at her mother, who smiled complacently. The girl smirked at her father. "Dad, I'm so dumb at school, missing a few days won't make any difference. I might as well leave anyway."

Ray Skerritt sighed. Short-sighted little beggar. "You've got to stick at things, girl. You don't know what you're good at yet. You don't give yourself a chance, that's your trouble. Everyone's good at something!" he concluded pompously.

"Yeah?" Raelene laughed, swaying against Alvie to give her a nudge. "Even me, eh? Well, that's good news. I been waiting around for years and years and I still don't know what it is, but!"

His wife yawned. Joanie was good to look at, even yawning, Ray Skerritt decided. "Pardon me!" she cried, turning it into a laugh as he caught her yawning again. Her words twined around him like a cat. "What's news this morning, Ray?"

"This article, Joanie — " he began eagerly, then caught his breath as she turned to Alvie to remind her to be sure to pack a skirt because Uncle Rupert was a bit old-fashioned. "Sorry — what was that, dear?"

"This article — " He grew more excited as he talked. "It says here — listen, no listen, Joan — it says here what I've been trying to get across to you all for months, only no one wants to listen, no one thinks it concerns him personally — all right, or *her,* Alvie — you don't see that it's us, housewives, workers, family, whatever we are, my mates at work, me, you Joanie, Alvie, Billy, Trish, Raelene — it's only Ray Skerritt talking off the top of his head again, must be some kind of nut, we're all right, Jack! But just you look here! Here it is in black and white, it isn't just me spouting, it's facts and figures — "

"But *what* is?" interrupted Alvie. "What are you on about? What facts and figures?"

"Uranium. That's what I'm on about."

Everyone sighed. *That* again.

Ray Skerritt thumped the table with his folded newspaper. "We own twenty-five per cent of the world's high grade ore. You know what that means? Wealth, Trish. Power. The chance to be a big frog in the pond instead of just a little tadpole — for awhile, that is, until the frog blows itself up. Power! Greed! And that's as far as our fine politicians and big shots and mineral magnates can see, every damned one of them. Hooked on the *now* society, the quick quid."

He saw a slow, purring smile cross Joan's face. She breathed in slowly. "Well, we could all do with a bit of that, everyone of us, that's for sure. Couldn't we, Raelene?"

"Too right."

"I'd like a bit of spending money now and then instead of having to run to Mum every time!" Alvie muttered.

Ray Skerritt threw down his newspaper. What was the use? "Any tea left in the pot, someone?"

Alvie jumped to her feet. "Come on, Mum, we'll miss the train. Get the car warmed up, Dad! 'Bye, you lot!"

Raelene, filling Ray Skerritt's cup, laughed. "You have fun now, Alvie. An' take care of your ma. We'll be jake here."

All the way to the station Ray Skerritt talked, speedometer needle just past the limit, hands drumming on the steering wheel. "You know what the answer is?" He jerked his head at the windscreen.

"Watch it, Dad!" Alvie exclaimed. "You're all over the road like a dog's breakfast."

"The sun. The sun, Alvie. Solar energy. Here we are living on this huge mass of land, the lucky country, clear skies, hours and hours of sunlight, yet we'd rather face the prospect of a nuclear inferno from man-made fusion than try to make use of old sol up there. You know what we do instead? We give aid to the poor countries so that they can afford to buy our weapons to shoot up whoever hasn't starved to death in the meantime. The whole world's gone crazy!"

"Ray! Ray! You take it too much to heart."

"Of course I do! Someone has to care about these things — " Out of the corner of his eye he saw Joan ease her round belly as he swerved into the station yard. He put his hand over hers. "Look, don't you let Chrissie rush you around all over town every day, will you? She's a pampered woman, your sister, compared with you — that big house, no kids, Rupert's money to splash about how she likes. You take things easy."

"I will, I will. I wasn't planning on much shopping, Ray, just a few clothes for the kids, and one or two special things for the baby. Heavens, if it's coming into a world as horrible as you say — "

As he lifted their cases onto the luggage rack he said "You won't stay any longer, will you, Joan? Just the week."

Alvie danced up and down in impatience to be gone. "You think she's old Brownie at home on the chain, Dad?"

"Old Brownie?" Ray Skerritt laughed, looking across at Joan. "Your mother?"

Joan Skerritt took some coins from her purse. "Run out and buy us a couple of magazines, Alv."

"Alvie — " Ray Skerritt followed the girl into the corridor. "Here's something to buy yourself something special in town."

The sulky, irritable expression that Alvie usually wore when he tried to talk to her vanished as she stared at the notes he had given her. "Gee Dad! Are you sure — "

"Course I'm sure! You run along now. It's not every day you go off for a posh holiday in the city with your aunt and uncle, is it?"

It occurred to him that he had just sold out to someone, Alvie, or Chrissie and Rupert was it? All the same he returned more cheerily to his wife. "Everything apples? Looks like you've got the carriage to yourselves."

Joan Skerritt put her hands on his shoulders and looked at him fondly. "Cheer up, you old battler. You'll be all right. There's casseroles in the fridge, and lunches in the freezer. Get Raelene to come back if you're stuck. And Parkers are right next door."

He held the big-bellied woman close, rubbing himself against her. "Hell it's going to be good when all this is over, isn't it? Joanie?"

Home again, he garaged the car, then stopped for a moment by the kennel near the patch of dock where the old brown heeler lay snoozing. He looked like a bit of old mill felt, left over from the paper machine. Wind rattled the dock leaves, and old Brownie shivered as Ray Skerritt stooped to pat him. "Poor old boy," he muttered. "Poor old Brownie."

As he turned towards the back porch, Raelene battling with the wind at the clothes-line caught his eye. Good God, she'd gone and washed all three pairs of his "Work Safely" overalls! "Hell Raelene, what am I going to wear on shift tonight?" he grumbled.

"Jeez I'm sorry, they was all there in a heap on the floor, I just thought — " Half-laughing, she continued to apologize as he went inside, following him through the kitchen and along the passage. "Told you I wasn't no good at things, didn't I?"

"It's all right, Raelene. Forget it, will you?" He was relieved to escape into the mess of his bedroom. How deserted it seemed without Joan. He couldn't find his pyjamas, tossed somewhere under the rolled-back bedclothes; started to straighten the bottom sheet, couldn't be bothered, pulled his dressing-gown from the hook at the back of the door instead. A shower was what he craved right now, then sleep. He hoped Raelene would be off soon. He couldn't take the crashing of brooms this morning. When he returned from the bathroom, the grime and stink of the mill washed away, hair rinsed and combed, teeth cleaned, Raelene was in the room tidying up for him. He watched her smoothing the sheet, thumping the pillows.

Raelene looked up. "Soon be finished. Reckon you feel dead-beat, eh? Blue always said the night shift was the worst."

"You miss Blue?"

She straightened, one hand massaging the small of her back. After a moment she laughed. "Well, that's how it goes. Eh?" She stood by the window, staring out into the garden. "I reckon them overalls'll be dry by tonight. Look at that wind. Real good drying day. Keep up like this and Mrs Skerritt'll have no trouble getting the nappies dry next month."

How safe she made it all seem, talking about next month as though the future were something you just took for granted. "Come away from the window, Raelene." He hated that pale flying sky. All he wanted was a safe world, a kindly, sharing world where there was no wind, no harsh argument, no ugliness. "That dress — it's ugly. Take off that ugly dress." She turned to him with her slow, kind smile.

He stared in fascination at the goldy-red hair under her arms as she raised her hands to the zip at the back of her neck. "My sister Shirlene, she's the one with six or seven kids, she never wanted to do anything but get married, and I reckon that's what she's good at."

The ugly dress fell around her feet.

"Go on, go on." He felt sick with terror sometimes, thinking about things.

She unhasped her sagging bra, then the safety pin at the waist of her bloomers. "And Darlene — remember Darlene? She come back here last year with her boyfriend and that snazzy little sports car. She's bought a cafe business for herself along the Hume Highway some place, and I reckon that's what *she's* good at, business."

He studied her without really listening: the escaped curls like tendrils on her neck; the big dark nipples; the rolls of flesh and then the triangle of hair reddish-gold like the hair in her armpits.

"Funny, isn't it?" she chuckled. "You and me — Ray and Raelene — "

"No!" he said harshly. He didn't want words. He'd had his share of words today. Peace, he wanted peace, that was all a man wanted. He had to hold her, taste her, bury himself in the comfortable, consoling, irresistible butter of her flesh. They fell together across the half-made bed. "Hey steady Mr Skerritt," she murmured. "We got all morning." Her hands smoothing and brushing might have been spreading the kids' lunches. "I know how it is," the husky voice breathed in his ear. "All them months, it's hard on a feller. I know how Blue was when my second kid was on the way. All them months and me like a mountain. Poor Blue, I reckon he's not gettin' much fun where he is right now." She squeezed his face into the warm dough of her breasts. "Better? Feels good for me, too . . . You know what?" She began to giggle. "We never closed the venetians.

Them overalls I put on the line before, I pegged them all at the shoulders and in this wind they look just like three men having a race, only they never get nowheres."

Godammit, he thought, straining against her, does she never stop talking? Involuntarily he groaned. Raelene began to gabble. "Oh jeez the sky — the clouds — the clothes-line — oh jeez Mr Skerritt! Everything's flying away! *Hold me.*"

"Stop it!" he shouted. He stared down at her in horror. What in God's name was he doing? And the back door, it wasn't even shut, was it? What if Mrs Parker next door dropped in to ask after Joan? He rolled away, too weary right now to bother about anything.

From beside him came a small voice. "I wasn't no good then?"

He didn't reply. He fixed his gaze on the three pairs of overalls on the clothes-line, dancing and straining full-bellied at the end of their pegs, their muscling backs saying "Work Safely", "Work Safely", "Work Safely".

Chanson d'Automne

People do ring at the oddest times. This time it's just as she's preparing the vegetables — and her husband isn't even home yet to help with dinner. Her hands flutter. An accident? Snatching up the receiver, now she can't reach the television set to turn down the volume; she has to dash with the phone cord extended into the second bedroom which they use as a study. "Hello?" As she recognizes the caller her voice resumes its usual assurance. "Of course — do go on. What's the problem?" It is one of her students, a hopelessly disorganized, lonely, anxious girl, quite out of her depth, living alone on a diet of chips and soft drink, the young wife guesses. She likes to help this girl but dreads being cornered by her. Somehow it's easier over the phone, when she can't see the poor bewildered too-fat face, all blotched and snuffling with tears.

"Call around for a few minutes later this evening if it doesn't work out," she finds herself saying in a surge of generosity, waving to her husband as he drops his briefcase by the divan and goes with two glasses to the refrigerator. "Five minutes is all we'll need," she emphasizes. "So I can check that your plan is sufficient for the essay. You're just going to have something to eat? Well, so are we. *After* dinner." And she smiles her special telephone smile.

When she returns to the kitchenette a half-peeled potato is growing brown on the bench and her husband, oblivious, is stretched out on the divan. "I've poured you a drink," he says, waving his own glass. "In the fridge." He doesn't even notice her offended stalking back to the chopping board, so intent is he on the nature program that they usually watch together. This week it's a documentary on the Bighorn, rare sheep of the Canadian Rockies. They are graceful, handsome animals, she sees, looking up, each one intent on survival as autumn heralds the approach of winter. The biggest male seems to divide his time between warding off lesser rams and, with outstretched neck and flaring nostrils, pursuing his patient females. At the stupid, enduring expression on the ewe's face as the ram briefly mounts, she slams across to the set and switches it off.

"Hey! What did you do that for? That's an interesting program," protests her husband, rising. "What's the matter?"

"When we both work . . . " she replies pointedly, gesturing with the vegetable knife at the tomatoes and lettuce unwashed, the chops in their soggy butcher's paper.

"Oh, is that all? Sorry. I was going to do something, but you were busy on the phone. Who was it, anyway?"

She sighs. "Just one of my students — that girl, actually, the one I've been telling you about. Helpless Harriet."

"Oh God! Your Good Samaritan act again. What did she want this time?"

"Oh just the usual. An essay she's bogged down in. References she can't follow. I've asked her to drop by for a few minutes later tonight, as a matter of fact."

He groans. "Oh God. Was that wise? Why do you do these things!"

She says angrily, "How can I tell what's *wise*? She's a bore, she's a half-wit, she's sure to fail at the end of the year, but why shouldn't I spend five minutes or even half an hour with the poor thing occasionally, if it's going to make her feel less desperate? Sometimes talking to Harriet I get the feeling I'm the only person who *cares!*"

He shrugs. "You're the wrong shape, honey chile. What she needs is a man."

It's his standard joke, and she laughs exasperatedly.

"Well, isn't it?" One by one he drops the tomatoes back into the sink, then, turning slowly, fastens his arms around her. They kiss, pressing their thighs together.

She pulls away laughing, reaching to turn off the griller even as she protests, "Not now."

"Why not now?" Already with one hand around her hip he is guiding her out of the kitchen. "Lock the door!" "Pull the blind!" Laughing, they collapse on the divan. "Why not now?" he repeats as she reaches to kiss him. It occurs to her that she can hear their blood beating in time.

They are startled by the doorbell, a timid jangle that seems so loud they freeze like children in a game of statues.

"Good heavens!" she whispers. "It's her! It must be. That student. Oh what will we do?" Giggling, she catches her breath.

She feels a throb in the pit of her stomach as he squeezes her breast. "Shall I ask her to join us?"

She scrabbles at his hands. "Don't be absurd. I'm going to answer the door. Quick, take your things into the bedroom."

She slides off the divan and fumbles for her skirt and blouse, trying to pull herself upright as he comes after her. He chuckles over her shoulder, "You know something? Of all the animals it's only man who does this face to face. That's a thought, isn't it?" She protests at his insistence. "But it's not obligatory," he adds, urging her over the divan so that it supports her arms and her head turns sideways in the bloom of the cushions. She thinks *it's no use* and she begins to laugh, short gasping sobs as he enters her from behind, his arms crossed on her belly and his hands squeezing her breasts, kneading, moulding their bodies together. Straightening her arms she thrusts against him. A muscle inside her that she is still discovering contracts and he cries out with pleasure. His mouth nuzzles her and she feels his teeth, holding her. She wants to bite him, too, she twists her head and nips his hand, hard, so that he hisses in surprise. His body arches. In the anguish of flesh made one she cries out unaware. Neither hears the second tweak of the doorbell; nor, after a moment, the sad, receding footsteps. The arms of her husband clamp. He groans. His head falls against her neck, his body grows heavy and slack. Little pulses subside. The young wife shivers. It is her blood, only hers, that she hears.

Cream Sponge on Sunday

Everyone took it for granted that one day Douggie Wilson and I would get married. We had been going around together for so long, since we first shared an ice-cream lick for lick as our dear parents were fond of reminding us, that we hardly questioned the future that stretched ahead hazy but certain as the distant ranges. We were too busy with studies or having a good time. I kept telling myself we were lucky — some people looking for the right partner get into terrible hassles.

Vern Bonnor for instance. Everyone knew the story of Bonnors, Vern and Lilith Kelly and Vern's first wife Grace, a fretful invalid in a wheelchair who persuaded Sister Kelly to leave the hospital to nurse just her, out there at Bonnors' farm. How people talked! Lilith Kelly was a vivid girl who as a trainee nurse had arrived in our town fired to do something noble, church mission work it was said, and who nursed Grace Bonnor and bore Vern Bonnor two love children instead. Isn't that a romantic story?

Of course it was all past history by the time we were growing up, Vern and Lilith were long since married, but occasionally people remembered. Those eyes, they recalled, teacups brimming with delicious indignation at the indiscretions of Sister Kelly. Looking right into you every time she came around with the thermometer as though she meant to convert you. Well she converted Vern Bonnor all right, laughed some wag. Good luck to him, too. Hush! cried the teacups. Sin is no laughing matter. And Vern Bonnor at that nurse's insistence cutting down all the old cypress and pine trees so you could actually see the house. Oh scandal! Oh shame!

I couldn't help feeling there was something grand about Vern Bonnor and Lilith Kelly, something bold and extreme. I was always on the lookout for the heroic.

"Like Anna Karenina!" I declared. Our class was doing Tolstoy that year.

"Old man Karenin, that's the one I feel sorry for," Douggie commented. "Brooding about Anna and cracking his knuckles."

Douggie's reasoning was way off sometimes. The trouble was, he couldn't see the glory in situations the way I could. I was loud in my support of the lovers, although all I could remember clearly of our local *histoire d'amour* was Lilith falling off her bicycle in the middle of the main street and a bus load of high school children jeering. She had been shopping and I suppose was on her way back to Bonnors'. From her carrier an onion rolled right to my feet like a gift, but I dared not pick it up. I took my cue from the big kids then.

But I always regretted that onion. "I would do it, Douggie!" I declared. "Sacrifice everything for something I believed in. Stride naked into the storm regardless of the wails of the rest of you huddling under umbrellas!" I suppose Douggie just laughed. He was used to my histrionics.

During our last term of high school he grudgingly agreed to my suggestion that we sacrifice pleasure for work, i.e. see a lot less of each other for awhile. We were both studying frantically to get over that terrible hurdle of end-of-year exams, Douggie to go into partnership with his father after several more years of hard work, and I — well, I just enjoyed learning things. In fact, every now and then I felt a blankness at the prospect of leaving school. Our families treated me with indulgence. There was no real need for me to work so hard. I was already well-qualified for the job that my father had offered me in his office while I waited for Douggie.

Sometimes, as I gazed through the classroom window at mist swirling down from the ranges to blot out the farms, the town, the other side of the playground, it was the future I saw closing in.

"You have to remember, Douggie," I said, dishing out one of my epigrams, "the wages of virtue is infinite boredom."

"That's for sure. Let's duck out for a couple of milk-shakes at the Blue Bell." As we shared each milkshake with two straws, Douggie told me he was working into the early hours of every morning. He was certainly edgy. "There are limits as to how far any sensible person should go overboard about things," he growled, squeezing my knee under the table.

He was probably right. One morning during exam week I awoke to the devastating certainty that not seeing Douggie didn't matter very much. In fact, I enjoyed the novelty of being alone. I wanted nothing better that morning than to walk right out of the town, past the farms, past Bonnors' place, right to the top of one of those distant hills from which I would survey the world.

When I ran outside in my walking shoes, Douggie was waiting for me in his father's car that was a sort of perk to get through the exams. The previous evening he had pleaded with me over the phone to spend the morning with him in the school library because he had his most important exam that afternoon.

I hesitated by the car door. "I've changed my mind about the library, Douggie."

"So have I. Get in." He put his foot on the accelerator and we shot right out of the town, pulling up in a

103

quiet little dirt lane with one of those old-fashioned hawthorn hedges on one side and calves in a paddock on the other and a couple of beady-eyed magpies watching us from a gum tree.

We kissed for a bit, then I sat up, pushing away Douggie's anxious hands and straightening my skirt. "Let's go back now."

"It's no good," Douggie said, clutching me. "I can't study. All I can think about is you. You've got to let me, Julie. We're as good as engaged. It's the only way I'll get calm enough to face that exam today."

I stared at him in dismay. Yesterday, I wouldn't have hesitated. Today — I was scared of any commitment.

"It's the exam, Douggie," I began. "Let's talk about this later, when it's over."

"Of course it's the exam, haven't I just said so?" I began to feel frightened, not of Douggie but of the overwhelming logic of emotion. "Don't you see, it's the only way — it'll be all right, truly it will," he begged.

"I can't think straight." I fumbled with the door catch. "Let me go, Douggie."

"Hell, we're going to be married, aren't we, what's come over you all of a sudden? ... Oh, you're very fine, aren't you?" he went on bitterly. "You've got to have the names in the book and the three-tiered cake and the bits of confetti first, is that it? You're as narrowminded and respectable as the rest of the town."

"It isn't that, Douggie," I pleaded.

"No? All your talk about novels and heroines and freedom to love — !"

He flung me away so that I half-fell out of the car, reversed in a spatter of red mud and roared off towards town. I felt bad about his exam. But when the last sound of the engine had died away, and only the wind was roaring in the treetops, I remembered the walk I had planned. I climbed through the fence and set out across the paddocks, cows ankledeep in clover looking at me with eyes like pansies. In the distance I could see the green roof of Bonnors' place nestling in the foothills. Vern Bonnor had a way with animals, my father said. He never raised his voice, never rushed. On sale days you could always pick his stock; they were the quietest in the yards. I admired a man like that. I hoped Douggie wasn't going to flunk that exam. I began to walk faster.

It was only with the first Mrs Bonnor that Vern was at a loss. They said in the town she was a fair terror. Once when I was very small, long before Lilith Kelly had come to the town, my parents were invited out to Bonnors' for dinner. I think my father had just concluded some business for Vern. I went too, sitting up to eat with the grown-ups, though I don't believe Mrs Bonnor thought much of that. She had to set an extra place in a hurry, her wheelchair jibbing like a bad-tempered horse. The knife and fork were very heavy, I remember, and the peas had such a nasty, metallic taste that I pushed them aside with the bits of gristle. I looked up to find Mrs Bonnor staring at me. She had such hard round eyes and a little pinched-up mouth like a pea-shooter that I burst into tears. "She's overtired," apologized my mother, and before I had touched my pudding I was packed off to sleep in a spare room, where for hours I was kept awake by a branch of one of those huge pine trees scraping across the iron roof. I thought it was Mrs Bonnor screeching at Vern.

I liked Vern Bonnor, though, a tall, rangy farmer with faraway eyes and a kind smile if he happened to notice you. You'd see him around the town sometimes, sale days mostly, resting his eyes on the distance the way countrymen do when they're wondering about rain or wool prices, or just easing their backs. They said Grace Bonnor would never come into town. Vern did all the shopping. The cooking and cleaning and washing too, by all accounts. The house at that time was so dark the kitchen light was never switched off. Creepy! No wonder Mrs Bonnor was so cranky. Poor Vern, he was a bit odd himself, they said. Put you in mind of a clock with a busted spring. It was a real shame, you should have known him when he was single, he turned the girls' heads then! And dance! Dance the legs off a supper table, Vern could, that was in the good times, before all the troubles with his missus, poor woman. Hard on a bloke like that. When Lilith came along the years dropped off him like oak leaves at budburst . . .

Lilith, I mused, plodding on over the tussocks. The very name portended well. Adam's other wife, his dark spirit, his daemon lover . . .

Bonnors' house was the rambling kind, with a verandah all round and windows set deep like a countryman's eyes. Wisteria blooms looked as though they had been dipped into the sky and hung to drip blue globules from the spouting and verandah posts. The garden was full of old-fashioned flowers like picotee and heartsease and hollyhock and sweet alice. I sensed something very still and peaceful, soporific almost. From a mound of leaf mould a thrush regarded me as I followed a stone path around the side of the house to the back garden, where a woman was staking tomatoes. The warm, rich smell of damp soil mingled with the scents of mint and flowering currant and crushed tomato vine. Lilith Bonnor caught sight of me. She was a tall, well-built woman who moved and spoke gently. Her eyes were like the thrush's, bright and quizzical.

"Julie? Yes, I do know you. Though I don't go into town much these days. There's so much to do out here, what with the children and the garden and helping Vern when he needs me. Oh, it's a busy life, I can tell you! . . . A drink of water? Of course. Aren't you sensible, taking a break between exams?" She smiled at me, brushing with sap-stained fingers at a straggle of hair that had escaped from the old shoelace tying it back. "What will you do when they're over?"

"I don't know." I stubbed at the earth with my toe. "Stay at home — go away."

"I see." She thought for a moment. "Nursing is a good career for a girl."

"I suppose so." Endlessly I saw her bicycle pass, swerve, spill . . . How I wished I had retrieved that onion. But I wasn't that sort of kid. Could I ever be? Maybe Douggie was right, I was really a coward at heart —

"Let's have a cup of tea," Lilith was saying, "and you can tell me all about yourself . . . See that huge stump? You wouldn't believe the bulbs that shot up that first spring after Vern took out the pines, Julie. Things he said his grandmother had planted years before. Smothered in pine needles. Smell the soil now." She scooped up a handful of fine brown earth and held it to her face, breathing deeply. "Lovely!" She offered it to me, and I sniffed too, and nodded. She didn't expect me to talk.

The kettle on the woodfire stove was boiling, so she made the tea in a fat brown teapot and carried it across to the kitchen table. "How nice it is talking to you!" she was saying, rearranging some marigolds in a mustard jar. "You must come out again — for the whole day if you can. I'd like that. What about Sunday? Bring your young man. We'll just be pottering in the garden or down at the yards. You'd like to see the others, wouldn't you? If you can't manage the whole day, come for afternoon tea. I'll make a cream sponge."

Startled, I glanced back from the dreaming garden to the calm domesticity of the kitchen. My adolescent soul rebelled. Could this be the woman whose reputation had sweetened all those teacups years ago? Meeting her eyes I remembered with a taste of panic how people said she made you feel she wanted to convert you . . . "I — I'm not sure — Douggie — study — " I muttered, coming up with a social phrase of my mother's, "You really mustn't put yourself out, Mrs Bonnor."

"Oh I always make a sponge on Sundays." Lilith laughed, leaning towards me, inviting me to share in some joke she had against herself. "Vern and the children expect it now. Sundays would seem funny without a sponge."

As I stirred my tea Lilith's words swished round and round in my mind. I took another sugar cube on my spoon and watched it drown in the creeping liquid. Was this the apotheosis of love? Was the wages of grandeur . . . cream sponge on Sunday?

That evening I took a sheet of stiff, plain notepaper and began to write: Dear Douggie, After due consideration I've decided I'm not cut out to be a Wicked Woman, as you say. Or even a Wife . . .

Nature

Lola began to peel an orange with her teeth. The dentist had told her not to but so what? What a fuss about one little rabbit, she thought scornfully, leaning on the broom handle while her mother on hands and knees by the clump of tea-tree wheedled "Here, Pumpkin. Nice Pumpkin. Give it to me, puss — Hurry up with that broom, Lola!" she shouted, then swore as a branch snagged her hair-do that she and Lola had spent ages over because it was Saturday and Frank was coming. "Help me, can't you? Don't stand there asleep!"

Lola spat pieces of orange peel onto the path where she knew Frank would see them. "What's the use? It's the cat's nature, isn't it?"

"And him such a lazy thing at home!" her mother repeated. She couldn't get over it. While she had been hopping about in a flurry of tidying, pushing towels and bathers into the laundry and chewing cachous because Frank disliked smoke on her breath, the big orange cat had come miaowing around the back door of the beach house, terribly proud of his catch, lashing his tail and raising his head to miaow again when Lola's mother opened the flyscreen. "Will you just look at this!" she had exclaimed. "The poor little thing's still alive," she had added in what Lola called her soppy voice. As she bent down to rescue the rabbit, the cat exploded like a cracker in her hand — snatched up the rabbit by the back of the neck and fled wide-legged into the tea-tree.

"Come on out of there, Mum, you'll pick up a tick," Lola urged. "And Frank'll be here soon."

Her mother stood up and brushed sand and leaves from her jeans and that blouse they'd had a row over in the shop because Lola had commented it made a woman of her mother's age look as though she was trying to be trendy. "Wherever could he have got it, do you think?"

Lola sucked at the wire braces on her teeth in that ugly way she had. "There's a warren over there in the scrub. I found it last weekend. When you and Frank went off fishing."

Her mother pushed a straggle of hair into place. "Fair dos — you could have come too. Don't act up, Lola. We're having a pretty good time here, you and me."

"There's *him*, too," Lola muttered.

"Who — Frank? Well do you mind! Frank's here half of Saturday and all day Sunday. I don't call that very much . . . Not much at all," she repeated wistfully, looking around her. Lola followed her gaze. The house, built by Frank on land he had bought, stood by itself on the edge of the cliff. A sandy track ran inland towards a line of trees which marked the highway joining one coastal town to the next. Behind the house was tea-tree scrub where Frank said they could see kangaroos if only they would get up at daybreak. Below was the glittering, swelling sea.

"It's a bit lonely here for you all week, I can see that," her mother continued. "No one your own age for miles around, though you did say you met a girl on the beach yesterday, maybe she's from the farmhouse by the turn-off — didn't you find out? I suppose it was her father sold Frank all this land. There'd be more people around if Frank'd sell off a few blocks . . . Funny creatures, men. But how'd we ever get to have a holiday in a posh house at the coast if it wasn't for someone like Frank, answer me that now!" She nodded towards the carport where Frank's second car was left for her use. "I reckon I can put up with a bit of sand and sky for a bit." Her next words caught Lola's attention. "And Wilkinsons are down this weekend, I ran into missus in the laundrette, her boy's going to look out for you at that cabaret thing that Frank's taking us to at the pub tonight — now what's wrong with that, Lola? I thought you were bored out of your brain doing nothing . . . I dunno, when I was your age . . . Every Saturday night off to a dance — That's where I met your father, did I ever tell you that? A real ladykiller, your father. You don't want to dip out on a bit of fun when it's offering, Lola. I can't understand you lately. You don't see me hanging back, that's for sure — nor your father either," she added. "Him and that dollybird!" Her eyes narrowed. "And that's another thing, Lola," she continued cunningly. "By rights you should be spending these holidays with your father. If you'd rather go back to the city to stay with him . . . "

Lola thought about the Saturdays that she was obliged to spend with her father. Sitting stiffly in a posh restaurant not knowing what to say to one another. All three of them. The woman like someone cut out of a magazine. Her father's fingers drumming on the table edge. Afterwards back to his unit to listen politely to records or finger the pages of books. Maybe a cup of coffee and a dry little cake that stuck to her tongue like paper. And him and the woman and Lola all trying to hide their relief when it was time for Lola to leave. And then her mother's greedy questions as soon as she got in the door — who was with him this time, what was she wearing, what had they said . . .

"No thanks."

"There you are then! You're a heap better off down here. What is it you've got against Frank, anyway? He's real good to you. You're lucky, he likes kids. Just wear a bit more than that bikini when you come to the table, will you? He's a bit of an old maid, I'll admit that. So might you be if you'd had to live his life up till now. But he'll get over it. He's learning." She laughed her throaty chuckle that ended in a harsh little cough. "Now here's something a woman has to remember, Lola. It's easy for a man to pick up a dollybird, maybe half his age." She brooded for a moment. "But it doesn't often work the other way. So I reckon we owe Frank something, you and me both. So put a smile on your face, miss, because here's the car now."

They glared at each other. Lola thought furiously, creep, he makes my skin creep and he doesn't even know and *you* don't know — The big car spattered gravel as it screamed level.

"I must have done it in record time today!" Frank leaped out of the car, tie loose, suit coat off, then hesitated, his eyes swallowing Lola's mother. Reassuringly she moved close. As he bent to kiss her his pink scalp shone like the icing on a bun. He looked around for Lola. "Hey! Give us a bit of a welcome, kid!"

A hammer began to beat in Lola's ears and throat as she pushed forward and raised her face — trying at the same time to hang back because of her mother's comment about her bikini. So that for a frozen moment they just stood there, Frank leaning down with a ripening kiss and Lola nearly beaten to pieces by the knocking in her head. As soon as Frank's mouth touched her cheek she scrubbed the spot furiously. Frank was full of questions. "What's new, eh? Been fishing? What's the surf like today?" But he really didn't want any answers. Like two people dancing, Lola thought, tears pricking her eyelids as she watched her mother urging Frank towards the house so that he stepped right over the orange peel, and chuckling and brushing against him as he opened the door.

In the doorway her mother turned. "Coming in for something to eat, Lola?"

Lola shook her head. "I'm not hungry. I'm going down to the beach."

Frank leaned over her mother's shoulder. "Better not swim till we come down, Lola. Want to try out my new fishing rod? It's in the back of the car."

His big fingers with the ginger hairs at the knuckles lay outspread like gasping fish across her mother's thigh.

"No thanks."

Frank shrugged. "Suit yourself." And the door closed between them.

As Lola took her big black-fringed towel from the clothes-line, a movement near the tea-tree caught her attention. Pumpkin the cat was lying a few feet away, his eyes half-shut, the end of his tail flicking lazily from side to side. The rabbit huddled between his paws, so still that Lola thought it must be dead. Pumpkin nudged it with his paw, then sprang up and tossed it over his shoulder. The rabbit landed on its feet and began to run while the cat ran lightly along behind. Suddenly the rabbit dodged. The cat pounced. The rabbit screamed then, a high-pitched protest of terror that started up the hammers again in Lola's head.

Throwing the towel over her shoulder, she hurried along the cliff top, well away from the house and their usual beach, and climbed through a fence, scattering dust-coloured sheep huddled in the shade of the scrub on the other side. Her destination was a tiny, crescent-shaped beach that she had discovered the previous day, accessible only from the cliff top. It was on this beach that she had talked briefly to the girl her mother had asked about. Lola stopped at the cliff edge and looked over. Below her the sea rolled endlessly on to the white sand. Rolled, and retreated, and rolled back again to grasp the shining flesh of the shore. Lola clambered down carefully, following what she supposed was the girl's track amongst the rocks and shrubs. The girl herself, in tattered denim shorts and a man's shirt tied in a knot across her stomach, was squatting by the water's edge. She was a funny kid, Lola thought, shooing a small brown bird that ran in front of her instead of taking flight . . . a bit dumb maybe; she had never been to the city, wasn't even sure where the city was. But she had a lively, couldn't-care expression that both attracted and irritated Lola, and a truly all-over suntan because she had her own beach to herself, whereas Lola without her bikini looked like a zebra. Also she was easier to be with than young Wilkinson, say, whose hands were always sneaking around girls' ribs like two little ferrets. Lola came up to the girl and stood so that her shadow fell across her.

"Hello, Lola Laceface," said the girl, without looking up. "I thought you weren't coming today."

Lola cringed. In a rush of confidence the previous day she had told the girl how the rockapes at school made fun of her braces. Now the girl glanced up, waiting, so Lola put a smile on her face. "What are you doing?"

The girl held out her hands. Lola saw a collection of shells, smooth and ridged, pink, black, iridescent.

Lola nodded knowledgeably. "I did a project on shells. I got it all out of a book. Maybe I could help you. Are they for a school project?"

The girl laughed, and let the shells slide into an advancing wave. "I just enjoy finding things. I might keep them for awhile or throw them away and do something else. This beach is full of secrets." She stood up. "It's hot, isn't it? I'm going in for a swim." She stripped off her shirt and shorts and ran naked into the water. Diving, she reappeared and let a wave carry her back to Lola's feet. "Hurry up! Why don't you try skinny-dipping?"

"Coming." Lola threw her bikini onto her towel and waded out slowly, shivering as the water nudged her, and receded, and returned like something alive to nibble and tug.

When they were tired of swimming they went for a walk. Lola kept thinking how Frank would admire the girl's straight back — no need to chivvy *her* about lunking along. Then she got to thinking about how her mother changed as the weekends approached: she was friendlier, more fun to be with — yet more distant, too, because the source of her warmth was Frank. A shadow slid across her mind; when the girl asked her not to tell anyone about the beach, she simply sucked her wire braces and said nothing.

"Promise, Lola?" the girl repeated.

"All right," Lola said at last. "If you tell me one of your secrets."

The girl looked at her sharply. "The whole beach is a secret."

"You said there were others."

"All right, I'll tell you — well, show you, actually. But you mightn't like it . . . This way."

They went around the rocks at the promontory and clambered onto a ledge that grew narrow and slippery as they moved around the cliff face. Crabs scuttled out of their way — Lola saw their eyes looking out from crevices. A gull screamed past. "There!" cried the girl. Below them was a rock pool, its glittering blue-green surface alive and dark with kelp. The girl gripped Lola's wrist. "Here comes a big one!" The sea swelled, the pool began to heave and rise and a tongue of water climbed up . . . up and foamed over their feet. Lola pushed back hard against the cliff face. The girl said dreamily, "I often come here. If you fell into that kelp you would disappear and no one would ever know. Will you jump in with me, Lola Laceface?"

"Stop it!" cried Lola, shutting her eyes. "You're making me feel giddy. I'm going back to the beach." She hesitated. "You'll have to go first."

"All right." The girl edged past, then stepped nonchalantly along the ledge and jumped onto the beach. Lola inched after her, catching her breath as she slithered the last few feet.

The girl put out a hand to steady her. "Okay?"

Chilled and shaken, Lola flung away. "That was a crazy place to go . . . dangerous . . . Are all your secrets so mad?"

The girl laughed. "Mostly. Now what are you going to share with me in return?"

Lola hesitated. The girl was crazy, that was for sure, and wasn't it about time she returned to the house in case the others were worrying? And then she remembered the way Frank had closed the front door . . . She looked around. "I don't know. There's this, I suppose." She shook out her beach towel.

"Golly, just look at the size of it! More like a bedspread. Where did you get such a splendiferous thing?"

Lola felt very pleased. She patted the towel fussily. "Come on then, sit down, there's room for you, too. Frank gave it to me for Christmas."

"Who's Frank? Your boyfriend?"

"No. Mum's."

The girl looked at her sideways. "Do you like him?"

Lola glanced around nervously, and moved to pull up her corner of the towel.

The girl caught her hand. "No don't. People cover themselves up far too much. Golly you're cold, Lola Laceface! Why are you cold on such a beautiful day?"

Lola shrugged, and pulled her hand away. "I don't know. Maybe I should run around on the beach for a bit. That's what Frank's always telling me, anyway."

The girl smiled. "I know a much better way to get

warm . . . Don't you want to know?" She leaned closer. Her eyes swam like green rock pools. "Do you like dancing?"

"Oh yes!" And Lola gabbled a string of fibs about every Saturday night off to a dance, and the cabarets, and all the boys looking out for her. It sounded good. Lola herself was impressed.

The girl stood up. "I come down here when I want to dance. That's another of my secrets. Watch."

Light sprang to her face and arms and breasts as she stretched towards the sun. Swaying like a flower in a rock pool, she began to chant in a soppy poetry-class voice that made Lola giggle, "Lord of earth, lord and father of water! I am your handmaid, your lover, your daughter!"

"Stop it!" Lola giggled. "You're crazy! Aren't you? Aren't you? I'm going home!"

Then the girl leaned down and, putting her fingertips under Lola's arms, drew her to her feet. "Not yet, I haven't told you the best secret of all." Raising her head as though listening, she began to move, slowly dancing, not looking at Lola or touching her except with her fingers. Like strands of kelp those hands held her while the girl wreathed and swayed and the tide licked almost to their feet. Lola could not take her eyes from the girl's pink-tipped breasts, the arched throat, the dreaming eyelids. Had she gone to sleep or something? Closed a door like the others between herself and Lola? I'm not a shell just to be tossed away, Lola thought angrily. She recalled how Pumpkin the cat had prodded the inert rabbit. Tentatively she drew her fingertips across the girl's throat. At once the girl's hands came to life. They slid upwards in long stroking curves, they took hold and pressed, they explored the shape of her nipples. Lola gasped. From her taut breasts to the pit of her stomach curled the greedy warmth that possessed her these days when anyone, even old Frank, so much as touched her. Oh help me, she breathed. The girl pressed again. Lola staggered. As the girl caught her Lola listened urgently for her own scream of protest, but no sound came.

Flight

Today, Michael says, maybe today he will see about booking that gallery. "Alison? It's as close as that!" And afterwards? She can walk out of whatever classroom she happens to be teaching in and they'll hop on the first flight out and then — New York! Paris! London! "Well? What do you say?" Alison smiles, then frowns. Isn't he going to do a bit more on the big nude first, the focus of the exhibition, before approaching the gallery? Last week, didn't he say . . . Now Michael is frowning.

At this point the phone rings. One of the high schools wants Alison to teach today in place of a teacher who is ill. "Don't go. Stay with me," Michael tempts her, running his toes up her leg under the breakfast table. "Oh Michael!" she protests, laughing, her hand over the mouthpiece, a pulse beginning to throb as his sly toes knead. "I thought you had to *work!*" She makes herself say into the telephone yes, she is free today, she will be there by first bell, and, banging down the handpiece, to Michael that sometimes she wonders if he'll ever be ready for that exhibition and that's the truth!

Then she has to scrape back her chair so that it crashes over backwards and rush away before she relents and says to hell with canvas and deadlines and teacherless kids, that isn't what they came interstate to find together, is it? Because she knows that if they aren't firm with themselves now they'll be caught, trapped, the way Michael was when she first met him, talented and ambitious and without a thing finished because of all those distractions, all those people wanting to sit around and gab, interesting people, full of ideas, but for someone like Michael distractions nevertheless, his resolution threadbare she told him, until at last he recognized the wisdom in her constant urging. This scene is bad news for me too, she would say, let's get right away, let's make a start where we don't know a soul, just the two of us . . .

She holds herself together today only by using what she calls her standover tactics. And the kids rebel openly, or sit sullen and stupid. The moment the last bell rings they snatch up books and haversacks and bolt towards the door. Alison flings herself into their midst. "Stop! Where are your manners! I haven't said — " She grabs a boy's arm, yes, *that* boy, the tall fidgety one who has driven her crazy all day with his whispering and nudging and dropping things so that in retrieving them he can sprawl across the silly giggling moonflower sitting next to him. "You! Come here!"

For one horrible moment she thinks he will shrug her off, or pull her along with him as he keeps walking. Why should he obey her? She is only a relief teacher. But the boys freezes, hunching forward so that as his head slowly turns he is looking up at her, wide-eyed, a parody of obedience.

"Yes, Miss?"

"Stand up properly, can't you — like a decent human being — " The cliche flies out like chalk dust. What on earth is happening to her? Now all she wants is the incident finished, the boy out the door, herself on her way home to Michael and safety. But the boy won't cooperate. He is playing another game. At once he straightens, peering down into her face, standing too close now so that she has to step backwards.

"Yes, Miss."

Alison glances towards the door. His girlfriend, pink

with silent laughter, skips out of sight. Alison panics. "Take that bin in the corner and the one from the next room and before you go home fill both of them with papers from the grounds — just down there — where I can see you from this window."

"I'll miss my bus, Miss."

"And I'll miss mine!" she snaps, easing herself towards him because she is jammed up against the blackboard ledge.

He shrugs, watching her. Well then, says his look, let's be decent human beings and forget about this silly business of the rubbish bins, shall we? I've got a little chick waiting out there, Miss, and no doubt there's someone hanging around after you . . . He smiles, a daring, young-old, exploratory smile. She feels her breasts tighten shamelessly. His teeth are like appleflesh. He is so delicious, this brat, and she is tired of games, of playing Miss the school teacher and breadwinner and homemaker and social exile to help Michael and suppressor of spontaneous hungers. "Don't you understand?" she urges, but of course he does not, he scrambles to pick up the bin and she shouts "Hurry up! Where I can see you! Full, mind!"

Trapped at the window, waiting for the boy to appear outside, she follows the flight of a flock of white birds dipping and whirling high overhead. White cockatoos? Pigeons? No — some species she can't identify. Beautiful things, how lucky they are, she muses as the wind rises and the white birds circle higher. They must be right over her home now — she hopes Michael has seen them from the light, leafy bedroom they have turned into his studio, screened from prying eyes by a wisteria vine twining and twisting along the front verandah. Has he missed her today? Is he wondering what has kept her? She pictures him out by the letter box, looking impatiently towards the bus stop. She leans her forehead against the cold glass of the window and hangs on hard to that picture. Michael hasn't much idea how difficult her job really is. The permanent staff ignore her; students plot against her — the boy with the bins, for instance, has probably dumped them and run. She hopes that he has. He has frightened her. Divested her of her dignity, no, more than that. She never wants to see him again. At that moment he comes into sight, mooching after scraps that the wind is rattling across the footpath and poking them with his toe into one of the bins. When he comes to the big metal bin by the corner of the building he kicks off its lid and from it cheerfully fills his two small bins. On his way back to the classroom he looks up to Alison's window and waves.

Before he can get there Alison flees, down the back stairs, across the oval and into the storm water drain that borders the school grounds. When all out of breath she reaches the traffic lights at the crossroads she clambers up the bank and saunters along the footpath like any ordinary Miss. The precocious spring sunshine beats on her head and neck as she trudges uphill. High above, the white birds swing lazily on eddies of air far removed from the torments of the flesh. Michael waves a book at her from the hammock she has slung under the old acacia in the front garden.

"Hello. Back already?"

"How was it today?" She drops to her knees beside him and buries her hot face in the coolness of his shoulder. "Have you been watching those marvellous birds?" She feels Michael shift his arm so that he can hold both her and the book so she tries again. "What are you reading?"

"This? Oh — something Woodie lent me. I can't put it down."

She stands up then, brushing leaves and golden fluff from her knees. "This wattle blossom is suffocating me. I'm going inside."

"Can you put the kettle on? I'll be with you in a minute."

On the kitchen table a fly crawls amongst the breakfast crumbs. He never thinks to tidy up. Frowning, she threads half a dozen dirty mugs onto her fingers and carries them towards the sink. As Michael comes in she waves them at him. "Have you been entertaining, Michael?"

"I told you — Woodie lent me this book. He and a couple of the others dropped by this morning. They wanted to see the studio. Gemma thinks my ideas for the nude are spot on. She really knows what she's talking about, that one. Then we all went into town for a quick lunch at a vegetarian place that she knows about. You really must come with us next time — you'd like all that crowd."

"How can I, when I'm in the classroom all day?" She hears her mother's martyred tones when her father is late home after bowls.

But Michael is oblivious. " — hommos, and hunza pie. Oh, and some drink called a banana smoothie. Doesn't that sound erotic?"

"Oh!" says Alison. She imagines Gemma, whom she sees in her mind's eye as a tall, serpentine woman with sleepy eyes and ivory skin and a long dark cloak, murmuring Try it, Michael. Isn't it *erotic?* . . . She walks quickly from the kitchen and throws open the studio door, as though the ghost of Gemma might still be lurking. The big empty canvas that Michael had turned to the wall in despair now faces her, alive and vibrant with colour.

"Yes," he is saying proudly. "I thought you'd be surprised. After lunch I was so bursting with ideas I tore home and simply worked like a madman — you should have seen me! I had no idea I had it in me. And then I just collapsed in the hammock with Woodie's book. And then you came home."

"Yes," she says slowly. "I came home."

Michael begins to squeeze a tube of blue paint. "I'm just going to touch something up," he says. "I might work on till dinner's ready." He stoops to scrape up a squidge of paint from the old canvas they have spread to protect the floor. "How was your day, anyway?"

She sinks into his old leather armchair that she picked up at a garage sale. "There was a boy in my class — Are you listening, Michael?"

"Yes — a boy. Look, if I add a bit here . . . so that your eye goes from there . . . What do you say?"

"There was this boy, I tell you! — " She unbuttons her shirt and reaching up draws his hands to her breasts. "This boy — " Michael's hands feel heavy and cold. She jumps to her feet. Clever with fear she begins to woo him, running her tongue over his lips, urging herself against him, drawing her hands over his back and thighs in long stroking movements, until at last she feels his preoccupation dissolve, her own panic subside.

"So there was a boy," he scoffs. "You make too much of everything." His hands are alive now, inspired, creating, slipping off clothes and fears, spreading, moulding, lifting her to him until through that crazy plunging body cleaving to his she reaffirms her need of him and at the same time with a shuddering bound is released, is nothing, is everyman's, sheds place, time, soars, circles, shivers a little. Something is digging into her back — a paintbrush. She sits up.

"Yes, you're good for me, girl," Michael murmurs. "Throw a rug over me, will you?"

Alison runs her hands over her body, rejoicing in her nakedness, trying to feel through her fingers what Michael has just felt as he held her. Through thick blue globules of wisteria bloom she looks out with lazy contempt onto the hustle and burl outside.

A man is approaching slowly along the street. She

watches him indolently. He is dressed in a white overall, and he carries a metal rod. Every now and then he prods it into a piece of rubbish, lifts it, and pokes it into a sack. In the wind his trousers flap around his legs like flags. Then the wind ceases altogether, and Alison's magnificent white birds swoop to settle on the road and nature strip. And they are not birds at all, but scraps of paper, meat wrappings, lunch bags. Along comes the street cleaner, catching each one with the rod and dropping it into the sack before it can rise again wildly, and Alison is afraid.

Interior

. . . your mother, for instance. It's funny, isn't it, how when you go back to see your folks all the years drop away and for a couple of hours you're a kid again? As you turn into the old street and there it is, the peeling weatherboard cottage behind the straggly hedge where you grew up into whatever sort of creature you are now, you're not driving yourself and your own blossoming kids in Roddy's new stationwagon — no, you're cycling home late from school with your pals and your father is hanging about by the letterbox to see what's keeping you this time. The old worrywort. You mutter something to your pals, making them laugh, but all the same you pedal a bit harder, the stationwagon shoots forward, and the old boy gestures frantically at you to stop. Stop! The gateposts — too narrow! — better let him bring the car into the drive, and you get along in to see her, she's been up since daylight, she's a ruddy marvel; he keeps saying Sit down, sit down dear, it's a grand occasion today, just tell him something to do — but d'you think she will listen? Shoo! shoo! she says, let her get on in her own way in her own kitchen — especially today, it's a grand occasion, remember?

A ruddy marvel . . . He runs his hand tenderly over the gleaming bonnet. He loves cars. He has never owned a new one, only second- or third-hand jalopies that he spends hours tinkering with and tuning and polishing. So you give the kids a wink and you all pile out in the street, you, and the kids, and the soccer ball, and the eski containing the smoked chicken and pate and mousse and two kinds of slaw that will save her the trouble of having to think about lunch, and you hand over the keys, and then you run, all of you run (only you run harder than anyone), around the side of the house where the honeysuckle still catches your hair — up the sagging back steps into the warm embrace of indoors.

She is in the kitchen, of course. She wipes her hands on the tea-towel and holds out her arms. Imperceptibly you hesitate; the others rush past. As she stands hugging your children and turning eagerly from one to another, her wispy hair flying and her round face like a fresh floury scone, you say with a touch of impatience, "There, that's enough, go easy with Grandma, why don't you run outside for a bit?" Shortly you hear them kicking the soccer ball in the back yard, and the plunk of the ball and their shouts become part of your breathing, the rhythm of your pulses.

You have your mother to yourself.

As you unpack your eski with a flourish you hear her demur, "I was thinking just a bite of salad out of the garden . . . Dad's grown some lovely tomatoes this year, he's real proud of them."

For the briefest of moments your hands pause over your carefully selected pates and coleslaws. Then your ears decide not to hear. "And how is the old boy these days?" you ask hurriedly. "You're still surviving, I take it?"

Your deflection succeeds . . . She laughs faintly. A look passes between you, an understanding look, born of the conspiracy of women. Her blue eyes shine like a patch of watery sky.

She never laughs outright, your mother.

Just then those children of yours cause a diversion as they troop back into the kitchen. "I thought I told you — " you begin, upon which they toss you a look and cluster around their grandma. "Grandpa's fixing Mum's car out there and he wants us to help him hold things and pass things but as soon as we do he says we're getting in his way!"

Your mother's reply is indistinct because she has turned away into the dining room, but you hear the younger boy exclaim "But he says just kicking the soccer ball to each other is getting in his way!"

You close your eyes. Nothing has changed . . .

You hear the rattle and chink of cutlery as your mother artfully talks the children into setting and decorating the dining room table instead. "Scones next!" she says gaily, returning to the kitchen and testing the oven with her hand. She begins to put together flour and butter and milk and an egg in her own inimitable way that you never tire of watching.

. . . Suddenly you are the little girl who even on tiptoe can barely see over the benchtop.

"Let me help!" you hear yourself plead.

Your cry rolls like a raw egg off the sloping benchtop.

"When I got married I could hardly boil an egg," you grumble.

" — so Roddy likes to tell people," you add hastily.

"And how is Roddy?" your mother asks, rubbing butter and flour together.

You talk about Roddy for a bit. Then — looking about you — "Isn't there *anything* . . . ?"

She shakes her head. "You just rest up a bit. All that long drive. It's not as though it's every day — "

So you go on leaning against the sink while she stirs, and adds, and stirs again. You go on leaning and you say "And how are you, Mum? How are you, *really?*"

To which she replies "Oh — fit as a flea, fit as a flea! Don't you worry about us!"

Is there just the faintest rebuke in the way she says "us"? Your *mother?* . . . Before you can pursue this thought there is another interruption; your father this time, clumping up the back steps and into the kitchen. Stripped to his singlet now, he is a thin, muscular man, balding, with tufts of hair over his ears. He is carrying an old-fashioned metal bucket in one hand, and with a rag in the other he is mopping his forehead. He throws himself onto a chair and stretches out his legs, mopping and sighing.

"Oh, it's hot work. Hot work."

"Leave it, Dad," you urge. "Really, it's not necessary. And on a day like this — "

His reply is directed towards your mother who is now cutting the dough into circles with that cutter your father made years ago out of an old tobacco tin. He says "What I need is some warm water in this bucket — "

"Have a beer instead," you persist. "Roddy sent you up a dozen, shall I get one out of the fridge?"

" -- warm water, and a few drops of detergent."

You say drily "Try the laundry, Dad. Hot water, cold water. Detergent in a bottle at eye level, directly above the taps. Where it has always been."

"Well all right, all *right!*" he returns. "All I want is a bit of help, a bit of warm *water!*"

Your mother murmurs "Give me the bucket, I'll get it," and has gone and is back again as quietly as breathing. "Here, Dad, I found you a bit of clean rag."

He looks up then. He clasps her wrist. "Now that is what I call devotion! No, don't move. Stand still. I want to look at you. I swear I am married to a marvel." He heaves himself up from his chair and pulls her towards it. "Now you sit yourself right there, Mother. You sit down, dear, and don't move. You have your family all around you to help today. You stay there and just tell us what to do." Still holding her wrist he guides her onto the chair. When he lets go there are greasy fingermarks on her flour-dusted skin.

As soon as he goes she hops up again.

You think you are going to explode. That man! That woman! Ever since you can remember, hasn't it always been the same? "Oh Mum!" you expostulate as the back door slams.

Your mother laughs again, that half-laugh that when you lived at home used to drive you mad. "Now don't you start in on me!" She tumbles hot scones from the oven tray onto the cake rack. "Tell me, what else can I do?"

"But a bucket of *water* — !"

She shrugs, and changes the subject — and hasn't that always been the same, too? "Let's see how the little ones have got on with that table."

It's a grand occasion, that's for sure: she is using her linen tablecloth that she was given almost new when she was married, the one with the tiny darns and the tea-stain that she covers with the salt and pepper. The children have set out the special heavy cutlery in a very individual way; beer glasses out of the cabinet; serviettes starched so stiff that they slide off your lap; and they have thrust a bright bunch of marigolds into that hideous green vase someone ought to drop when your mother's not looking.

You begin to feel like a visitor.

When you look up from rearranging the knives and forks, you are startled to see that your mother has climbed up onto a chair and is scrabbling around in the dresser.

"Mum, what on earth are you doing?" you cry, giving her such a jump that the chair actually wobbles. You steady it, and taking her arm help her down onto the floor. She is clutching a plate. She is just getting out the dinner service, she says — you remember? the old willow pattern. "I thought . . . since it's not every day, dear . . . But they're pretty dusty, they'll all need a good wash," she adds apologetically. "I got up early especially and then I clean forgot."

"Oh Mum!" you exlcaim. "Your very best plates! It's only us — let's use what's out there in the kitchen."

"But that's only the breakfast set," she says, frowning, and looking from the plate with its timeless pattern of love and recalcitrance and pursuit to the table and back again at the plate. "I wouldn't want to use the breakfast set today — "

"But *we* don't mind!" you assure her. "Mum, do you think the children would even notice?" She stares. You rush on. "And what's in the kitchen is clean already, so why make more work with all that extra washing, eh?" You take the plate from her and stretching on tip-toe replace it out of her reach. "It's only us!" you repeat, dashing back into the kitchen and flinging open her tidy cupboards. "Look, here's my old rabbit plate, you can just see the pattern — oh I do remember . . . Oh yes! And here's — "

"But it's chipped!" she objects. "They don't match! We use those old things every day, Dad and me!"

"Now Mum!" you say firmly.

She sits down then, and you refuse to see those old fingers knotting and unknotting. "We want today to be something we'll all remember!" you cry gaily. "What's the sense in our coming all this way to see you if — if — "

She looks down at her hands.

She sighs.

"All right, dear, whatever seems easiest," she murmurs.

What else can she say . . . your mother?

The Ringbarker's Daughter

Now that Richard was back home for the summer vacation his mother had begun to urge him to get about more, join the local tennis club, ask some young people around to play records. Last time she was in town, she said, young Mary and Sarah were asking after him. They hadn't set eyes on him since their New Year's Eve party. He liked them. Didn't he? Richard? He mustn't lose touch completely with the people in the district. But Richard preferred to mooch around the farm on his own. He took to riding all over the property, and, when he had renewed acquaintance with each paddock, to daydreaming along the wide, overgrown stretches of back road over which drovers once used to move stock.

His father was delighted to see the lad taking so much interest in country things; he had been secretly afraid that boarding school might somehow have changed him. "Let the boy be," he said to his wife. "Give him time. He'll want to get off into town soon enough." And with renewed enthusiasm now that Richard was home again, he began to plan the repairs to the sheepyards that he had been putting off for months.

One morning, riding along the boundary of his father's property very early in an effort to shake off a nightmare, one of those hideous, creeping things he thought he had left behind him at boarding school, Richard came across two rabbit trappers. A man and a woman, they were going around the traps they had set the previous evening in gaps under the netting fence. Richard frowned; wasn't there anywhere he could go off alone without being reminded that he was alone? Riding closer, he saw that they were strangers; the man was about his father's age, the woman nearer his own, just a girl, a little older, maybe. The man looked up briefly as he released the jaws of a trap, nodded at Richard, wrung the rabbit's neck, gutted it and handed it to the girl. As a blowfly darted over the steaming guts flung so heedlessly into the clean morning, all the aura of Richard's nightmare washed back over him. He felt sick. Who were these people? He urged his mare forward.

"Excuse me," he began. "Excuse me — "

The man sat back on his heels, waiting. He was a big, strong-looking fellow with a broken nose like a boxer and sand-coloured expressionless eyes. The girl sidled closer to him, staring up through a tangle of dark hair as Richard began speaking.

"Those things can catch dogs and possums as well as rabbits, you know. Do you have permission to set traps here? This is my father's property — "

"It is?"

"Yes."

"Your father's, you say?"

"Yes."

"Not yours, squire?"

"No. Look here — "

The girl gave a snuffle of laughter, her eyes darting from one speaker to the other. Her big toes poking through holes in her tennis shoes wriggled.

"Cut that out, Evie — Now tell me, do I look the sort of bloke that'd take what wasn't his?"

Richard shot the girl a furious look. "Then you do have — ? My father knows — ?" he stammered in an effort to recover some dignity.

The man winked at him. "What do you reckon, squire?"

He turned back to his traps, and the girl followed. Richard heard her laugh again; as she slapped the man across the back with a dead rabbit he threw his arm around her in a brief hug.

"Come on, damn you!" Richard muttered to the mare, hitting her hard across the neck with the leafy switch he had brought to brush away bush flies. He burned with rage and shame. These last few months had been nothing but a series of humiliations. He was, it seemed, the only boy in his wing of the boarding house who hadn't knocked off a girl; not only hadn't, but hadn't even *tried*. The butt of jokes of kids who boasted of sweaty grapplings in the backs of cars, in parks, in picture theatres, he found himself plagued day and night by their graphic detailings . . . "Daydreaming again, Richard?" He would snigger at that, picturing whoever had burst in upon him coming face to face with the prowling monsters of his imagination. His body gave him away. Safe, so he thought, amongst old friends at Mary and Sarah's joint New Year's Eve party, he had been stunned to feel his right hand sneaking across Mary's back and under her arm. She had turned to him, her eyes mocking, her lips plump as the strawberries on her mother's pavlovas. "Yes I am wearing one, Richard. I'm a big girl now." To Richard her clear voice rang around the entire room. Shortly afterwards, queuing with Sarah for more fruit cup, he had begun squeezing against her, rubbing himself against the friendly solid flesh of her thigh. "Got an itch, Rich?" she had asked, quirking her eyebrow in that way she had. He had wanted to plunge into the fruit cup there and then and drown amongst the floating passionfruit seeds. Now, cantering through the pearled morning towards the safety of cornflakes and boiled eggs, he burned again at the memory of that New Year's Eve. He had disgraced himself. How, then, was he ever going to achieve anything worth boasting about when all his encounters ended up in disaster?

After breakfast, craving the solace of his everready fantasies, he saddled the mare again and set her to amble along what was known as Mollison's back road. This was a potholed track that wound its way amongst scrub and spindly gums, past the huge persistent rabbit warren in Mollison's old gravel pit, past the settler's two-roomed weatherboard cottage abandoned years ago to possums and spiders, across the ford in the creek and eventually if you had all the time in the world into the township itself. Richard's destination was Mollison's scrub, a patch of stony, neglected bush around the cottage where in spring you could find indigo and egg-and-bacon and bushman's bootlace in minature bloom beneath the wattles and dogwoods, and in summer you could stretch out on a sunbaked, lichen-encrusted rock and give yourself up to the small secret life around you. As the grazing land grew poorer and he left the cleared paddocks behind him, he saw with momentary disbelief that someone very recently had set about ringbarking Mollison's scrub. Right around each sizeable tree was a creamy gash from which an axeman had lifted the life-sustaining bark. Like people unaware of some horrible terminal illness, he thought, wattles and messmates and manna gums continued to move their leaves and cast rapid shadows as they had always done. He rode on miserably. How could the Miss Mollisons, those nice old ladies who could recall the days when there were still koalas in the district, and who listened each spring for the pallid cuckoo's first cunning notes — how could they let anyone do this to their last little bit of real bush?

Just ahead of him dogs began to bark. Looking up, he saw smoke issuing from the chimney of the cottage, and on the track a battered truck pointing towards the township. Close to the cottage two small boys were throwing stones at a stack of bottles. He reined in abruptly behind a patch of native cherry as a girl came out of the cottage. It was the girl he had encountered before breakfast, Evie, the man had called her. She shouted at the dogs, and they stopped barking. Then the man came out, carrying a drum which he hoisted onto the tray of the truck. He seemed to be having an argument with the girl. Richard could hear his voice, cajoling, then angry, and the girl's shrill in reply. A couple of times he gestured towards the truck. Once he turned abruptly to the boys who scuttled out of sight into the bush. Head down defiantly, the girl began to walk along the track in Richard's direction. What happened next Richard decided later he must have exaggerated — the result of too much fantasy-making. As the girl continued walking doggedly away, the man ran to the truck, roared the engine and shot backwards. She had to jump for her life — so it seemed to Richard, peering through his screen of native cherry. The truck jerked to a stop, the girl climbed into the cabin, and they drove off in the direction of the township. After a few seconds Richard heard the engine cut out. They were probably at the creek, he thought — maybe she hadn't wanted to go with him to get water, and he had reversed the truck in a rage. All the same . . . to almost run someone down . . .

Over midday dinner, keeping his voice very matter-of-fact, he remarked to his father, "There's someone in Mollison's old cottage, I see."

"That's right. The Miss Mollisons put a bloke on awhile back to do something about their bush paddock. I reckon he must have done a bit of sweet talking to get that job. And a good thing, too — that patch of scrub's useless, rabbits everywhere."

"There seems to be a whole family," Richard continued. He could not bring himself to say more; the morning's humiliation over the rabbit traps rose in his throat.

"What? Oh yes. Wife and two or three kids. Bit out of the way for them, I reckon. Beats me why anyone would choose to live in that old cottage. By the way, I've ordered that timber for the yards, Richard. Should be here by the end of the week. Eh?"

But Richard was no longer listening. It had suddenly struck him that when he heard the truck stop, he should have galloped after it: maybe he'd taken her away to beat her? Bury her in the creek bed? He saw himself arriving just in time, the mare in a lather, the girl cringing, the man's fist upraised. *Hoy! Let her go, you brute! Quickly, hop up behind the saddle and put your arms around me — tight — and away!* And as they rode like the wind along the creek to his secret cave above the waterfall, she was no longer the girl from the cottage, she was Mary, Sarah, Evie, every naked girl he had ever imagined —

That afternoon he returned to Mollison's back road. He couldn't keep away. His fears and fantasies were crazy; they were ridiculous. All the same, suppose . . . And then the world swung back to normal as he caught sight of the girl herself, a ferret box slung over her shoulder and her dogs racing in circles. She was making towards the rabbit warren in Mollison's old gravel pit. As sheep resting in the shade moved away in alarm, he decided he really would say something severe about taking dogs into a sheep-grazing paddock. The poor old Miss Mollisons might want their bush cleared but dogs on the loose was quite another matter. Oh yes! Tying the mare to a shady sapling, he climbed through the fence and set off up the hill in pursuit.

She stood sulky and silent, a rabbit net trailing through her fingers as he crunched across the gravel and confronted her. Her torn, faded dress was too big, he noticed, and her tennis shoes too small. Her protruding toes, quite still now, waited humbly for his outburst.

"Want a hand?" he asked.

She grinned, tossing her hair out of her eyes. "Reckon I'm just about out of nets. This one's bigger than I reckoned."

"We could block up the rest of the holes with a stone or something."

When all the entrances to the burrows were secured, she opened the box in which two ferrets were scratching impatiently. As she grasped one, the other ran sniffing and squirming over the gravel, so Richard, to show her that he too knew how, seized it by the back of the neck and pushed it into a burrow. Then he sat down with her under a big old gum tree to wait. Her dogs, hot and panting, flopped down beside them and licked at grass seeds between their toes.

"You go rabbiting every day?"

"Most."

"What do you do with the rabbits?"

"Eat them. Feed them to the dogs. You can take some home if you want. Sell the skins someplace, least-ways *he* does, he drives the truck, he won't let me — Shh! I heard a bolt!"

She jumped to her feet as a rabbit leapt out into an entangling net. Standing with her foot over the hole she wrung its neck, renetted the burrow and poked the ferret back inside. Another rabbit flung itself into a net. He attended to this one.

"This isn't your farm, is it?" she asked presently. "Why aren't you workin' on your own farm today?"

He felt twinges of guilt, remembering how after dinner his father had said to him hopefully, "I'm off to look at a ram I might buy. Want to come?"

"I'm on holidays. From boarding school."

"School!" She turned to him, and he watched ideas rapid as wind-shadows passing across her face. "Is it one of them places for bad boys?"

He began to laugh. "Come off it! Do I look like a bad boy? Evie?" He leaned over and shook her bare toe.

She jerked her foot out of reach and he went red, remembering those superior girls at the New Year's Eve party.

"I got a brother in one of them places," she said, shrugging, so that he went red again at having laughed. "For nicking things — big things." She moved closer. Her eyes were the colour of massy summer storm clouds. "You ever get caught nicking things?"

He shook his head, not adding that he couldn't recall ever nicking things.

"Me neither. That's 'cause I only nicked little things — lollies, and a pineapple, and a couple of shirts for me and Cissie from Woolies. Not much chance now, but, stuck out here in the bush." She looked at him, her expression curious, warm, quite unlike the colourless stare of the man that morning. "So then, why — ?"

"Because I'm getting educated. Because my dad wants me to. I'd rather be living at home instead of miles away in that prison, though," he muttered.

Evie shivered. "I'd be shit scared if I had to go to prison. He reckoned Cissie'd end up in prison, that's what he kept telling her anyway. And you know what? That was all a big load of bull. Cissie never went to prison. She got married instead. She's got her own bedroom now, and a mirror, and a new hairbrush, and oh — all her own things."

"I've got my own things at home, and my own room," he went on.

"Have you? Wish I did." She looked puzzled again. "Then why do you do it? Go away to school?"

"As I said, Dad's keen on the idea. Mum too. I don't

know." She nodded, and he leaned towards her. "I don't want to make a fuss — you know — upset them by refusing to co-operate. I mean they're my parents, they think it's for the best and maybe they're right, maybe I don't really hate it as much as all that . . . I don't know."

"You an' me both!" Evie exclaimed. "We gotta be where we don't want to be, you want to be with your folks, and I want to get away from mine. You know the one thing I've made up my mind to do? I'm gonna get to hear a rock concert. I've got all their pictures pinned up round the walls back there, all the different bands. Helps to keep the draughts out of that dump." She laughed, looking to him to laugh too. "I'm gonna get right up close and I'll be wearing a new dress, right? and new shoes, and a little gold chain and I'm gonna cheer and yell and clap till my hands drop off. And all of them spunky guys up there on the stage, him on the drums" (she beat imaginary drums) "and him with the guitar" (she strummed) "and him singing" (she held her fist to her wide-open mouth and screwed up her face) "they'll look down and they'll say, Who's that girl in the new dress and the little gold chain cheering and yelling and clapping till her hands drop off?" She laughed again. Her whole body was alive with the momentum of her dream, her dark hair tumbling around her face, her eyes shining as though all the lights from the stage were reflected there.

Richard smiled. "Well. That shouldn't be too difficult. Going to a rock concert sometime."

"For you, maybe."

"Since you've made up your mind, though," he persisted, half-teasing, unwilling to let go of her exhilaration in which everything seemed possible.

"Sure. That's all it needs. Making up your mind." She fiddled with a safety pin that held the front of her dress together. "Do you like your ol' man?" she asked abruptly.

He thought about all those jobs around the place that in homesick letters he had promised to throw himself into. "He's a good bloke. What about you?"

"I hate him." She pulled her dress in tightly around her knees. "I'm gonna kill him one of these days — that's if he don't kill me first."

Richard grinned. "You seemed friendly enough first thing this morning," he fished, unwilling to bring up the truck reversing episode himself, but hoping that she would.

"You reckon?" She placed her hand palm down on the gravel beside his. "You keep your nails nice, don't you? Look at mine — all bit down to the quick — He's working down the bush someplace today," she went on. "Two ol' ladies give him a job the other week, ringbarking an' that. He's real handy with an axe, he wins all the woodchops at shows. He was fencing before we come here. Where? I dunno. Where we left Cissie. Someplace where it's flat and dusty and the bush is all little. Fencing's okay. Ever been fencing? Ringbarking's not a bad job, neither, better'n fruit picking — your back givin' you hell all day and the boss givin' you hell 'cause you've broke next year's new shoots. Anyway fruit picking's finished now. He don't go much for fruit picking, he don't like being around lots of people, he reckons."

"Not much fun for you, always on your own," Richard commented, unconsciously echoing his mother's concern for himself.

A rabbit bolted into a net; he let Evie jump up although it was his turn so that he could lean back against the tree and watch the swell and spread of her haunches as she squatted and her swift, capable hands as they killed and cleaned and renetted. "I'm real glad you come along today," she was saying. "I left my transistor back home."

He took a deep breath. "I'll come back again tomorrow, if you like."

"And will you learn me to ride your horse? Jeez, I've always wanted to ride a horse! You know what? My ol' man used to ride buckjumpers at shows, he was the best buckjump rider for a hundred mile. I wish you would let him make that horse of yours buck — will you? We better keep out of his way, but," she added, coming down to earth. "He don't go for other folks around, he reckons there's enough of us on our own."

"How many?" Richard asked indolently, watching her breasts moving under the faded dress like small shy animals that think themselves unobserved.

"There's five of us now, that's me, and him, and her, and me two little brothers, and there used to be me sister only she's ran away, that's why he won't learn me to drive the truck — "

"How come? I don't follow."

"Taking it to the garage, that's how she met her boyfriend, see, he's a mechanic, she used to do the shopping and take the old truck to get petrol and then she run off with him." She glanced down at him. "Cissie had got herself in trouble, see."

Richard nodded. It wasn't a particularly uncommon story, so he was surprised when, eyes widening, Evie leaned right up close and lowered her voice. "Big, big trouble. One night she just screamed it out at him, *him,* I mean, and then they had a terrible row, I thought he was going to kill her. She reckoned she'd lose it for sure if he hit her again. I reckon that's what he wanted. Anyway she run away then and the mechanic said he'd marry her, he was real decent about it, and when *he* found out she wasn't coming back no more he tried to kill him too. It took five men to hold him — " Richard detected a note of pride, as though she were talking about some buckjumping contest. "Can you believe that? *Five!* — and then the pleece moved us on and we come here."

"Well," he murmured, smiling at her, a bit bored by now with all this fuss about the runaway Cissie. "That's okay, isn't it? I mean your sister getting married to the mechanic and everything. She's all right now, isn't she?"

She said slowly, "You reckon her going off with the mechanic like that makes it all okay?"

"Well of course." He was puzzled by her doubts. "It's always happening around here," he added to reassure her.

"Yeah, she's okay. Cissie's lucky, I reckon." She started to chew her thumbnail and he caught at her hand, saying don't, it made them look ugly. She looked at him moodily. "Real lucky. He said she was a bad girl and she'd have to go to prison but she didn't care, she was fed up with him anyway, always pesterin' her, Cissie do this, Cissie do that, Cissie come with me in the truck while I get a bit of kindling, come on quick now or I'll knock the livin' daylights out of you. So she run off anyway and the mechanic was real decent about it. Like, it wasn't his fault, was it? They went to live with his ol' lady, she was real good to them . . . " Her face lighted up; she was thinking about Cissie's new things, he guessed. "What would your ol' lady do if you got some girl in trouble?" she asked abruptly.

"What? Oh — I dunno." He sniggered a bit, and shifted from one buttock to the other. Then there came powerfully to mind the milky smell of chilled newborn lambs wrapped in grain bags by the kitchen stove and milk-filled sauce bottles heating up in a saucepan of water. "She'd look after it, I guess — both of them, I mean. Crikey!" He began to laugh. "I reckon my father'd have something to say to me, though."

"Chuck you off the farm, maybe?"

"No. Not as bad as that. He likes having me around, helping, and that."

"An' it'll all be yours one day, the farm?"

"I suppose so."

She looked at him sideways. "An' before too long maybe you'll find some nice girl and her and you and your kids'll all live in that nice big farmhouse."

He sniggered again, seeing himself in his parents' double bed and one of his naked girls beside him. "Maybe."

"Better'n always on the move, eh? Or going back to that stupid old school."

He groaned. "Let's not talk about that."

But Evie persisted. "What if something happened and you couldn't go back?"

"Like breaking my leg or something? Fat chance!"

"No. Not accidents. Something you had to do."

"Such as?"

But she wouldn't say, just smiled one of those smiles into the distance that Mary and Sarah were so good at, and he thought Boy! if only those kids at school could see me now, alone in a gravel pit with a bird two feet away, they'd reckon I was a mug not to do her on the spot. Hastily he tucked these fantasies away for resurrection later. "My parents think I'm going off on my own, and they don't like it, and your father thinks you're going off on your own — " He lay back with his hands behind his head and followed a dot that was a wedgetail spiralling. "Do you ever feel bad about deceiving people, Evie?"

"No. Jeez!" She wrinkled her nose. "You're funny. I never knew anyone like you before."

"I've known you," he replied, "ever since I started thinking about girls." From a tussock a grasshopper spread golden wings and whirred away into silence; he thought he had never been as happy as he was at this moment. "So you want a riding lesson, do you?" he murmured, to watch her face light up. "All right, then, but only if you promise to do something for me."

She looked at him sideways. "What's that?"

"Go on talking."

She wrinkled her nose again. "What for?"

"I like listening."

She laughed. "Get away with you!" After a moment she asked slyly "What else do you like doing?"

He might have walked right into one of his own fantasies. His hand closed over hers. "Just being here," he said. "With you. Rabbiting. Talking. I get sick of hanging around by myself all day."

She nodded. "A transistor's okay but it isn't the same." She looked at him anxiously. "And you'll come every day?"

"Every day." All days melted into one day as the long summer afternoon opened out. "Your folks don't seem to like the idea of you getting too friendly with a boy, though," he commented.

Evie laughed resentfully. "*She* wouldn't even notice. Ol' cow, she never sees nothin', all she does all day is sit around starin'. Half the time you wouldn't even know she was there. You know what, the silly bitch can't even keep the fire going without I have to rouse on her, and she can't make a decent cuppa tea, the bloody stuff tastes like camel's water." Again her look invited him to laugh. "She wants a good kick up the bum, I reckon."

"Oh!" said Richard. If he had spoken about his mother like that his conscience would have clobbered him. "Your father, then," he said weakly.

"Him?" Her shoulders sagged. "You can say that again."

"What's the matter?"

"Oh . . . nothin'."

"There is." He slid his fingers between hers and squeezed. "Tell me."

"You really want to know?" She leaned over him, turned his head as though to whisper, then ran her tongue around his ear. He pulled her down on top of him then, and they lay there while his blood bolted like a rabbit in a burrow.

"Your hair smells nice," she murmured. "I reckon you must wash it with something real nice at your place. Under a shower with hot water like at caravan parks." Her lips brushed his. "I bet you sleep in a big comfy bed all to yourself, too, eh?" Light as a leaf she breathed against his ear, "Have you ever been with a girl?"

He hedged. "Have you ever been with a boy?"

She took a long time answering. "No. Not a real boy." Overhead the sun roared; the leaves dazzled. His dreamgirl whispered *Don't you want to?*

"Of course I do."

"With me?"

"Who else?"

"I reckon we should."

"So do I."

"Now."

"No not now," he protested dreamily. "I have to use something, you know — some protection."

She shook her head. "It doesn't matter."

"Be sensible, we must use something." First thing tomorrow he would go to the chemist's. He pictured his mother's surprise when he announced that he was coming with her into town . . . the looks she would exchange with his father . . .

"I tell you it doesn't matter."

"Of course it matters."

Evie's body that a moment before had been friendly and pliant now stiffened against him. "Maybe your ol' man has give you some, has he? Seeing as you're such good pals."

"Dad?" Richard was startled, and for the moment ignored her sarcasm. "It's funny thinking about your parents, isn't it? I mean, like us — wanting to do this."

"Is it? I don't care about them."

Her voice was so dismissive, so small and cold, that Richard returned irritably "Well what about *your* father? Maybe *he's* got some?"

"He don't use nothing."

He was shocked at her easy knowledge . . . but then, all scrambled together in the cottage like that . . .

She clung to him suddenly. "You *will*, won't you?"

"Use something? Haven't I just said — ?"

"No not that. I mean — " As he took in what she was whispering his mind reeled at the scope of her imagination; it left his well and truly for dead.

"Put your hand there . . . and there . . . That feels good, doesn't it? I get that *crazy* sometimes," she muttered, her head rocking from side to side. He tasted tears on her face. If this was what his friends at school smirked and whinnied about after lights out or down behind the dunnies, then they were just a bunch of hoons. The realization came to him then — not without a few regrets — that he would never bring himself to talk to them or to anyone about Evie. "I reckon if we do it right now, while we want to — " she was saying.

A rabbit flung itself into one of the nets. He recalled how when you strangled a rabbit you did it quickly, one twist of the neck so that it felt no pain. "It's no good, Evie," he mumbled. "I don't carry them around with me — you know, like the boy scouts — be prepared — "

She began to laugh breathlessly. "You don't — Oh bugger the rabbits!" Jumping to her feet, she released the rabbit, caught the two ferrets which had followed it out and slammed them into their box. "There!" she exclaimed, falling onto her knees beside him and trying to catch hold of his hands. "So you don't have nothing with you — so what?"

He sat up desperately. "So it's no good, that's what. It's no good getting ourselves in a sweat like this, Evie — "

She stared at him. "Because . . . you're not going to do it?"

He had to look away or he would have drowned on the spot in her rain-coloured urgent eyes. "That's right. Not now. Not till I've been into town." He glanced at her; *help me*, his look said. "Tomorrow, Evie. Just one more day." But even as he spoke he foresaw the scene at the pharmacy, every detail of which would be relayed to his mother the next time she came into town: Old Mr Gates, his eyes as shiny as his counter-tops, exlaiming "Well if it isn't young Richard! And what can we do for you, young Richard?" And himself, blushing furiously: "I want a packet of . . . a packet . . . " "Yes, Richard? A packet of . . . ?" "Razor blades!" And Mr Gates, all tact and circumspection as he busily wrapped the little package: "Of course, Richard. Certainly, Richard. We all come to it sooner or later, young Richard." . . . He dragged himself to his feet, wondering how he would ever get from here to the road and onto the mare and home.

She also stood up, her hands gripped together, her mouth thin. "Maybe you've just been havin' me on?"

"You must be joking. Listen," he said. "Once we started it wouldn't be just once, it would be every day we could get together — right? Because that's what we both want — right? And you know what will happen if we don't use anything — " She wasn't helping him at all, she just stared at him with that same frozen expression. "For God's sake, Evie, of course you know! Do you think you're any different from Cissie?" He felt like crying. He was being honourable — responsible — restrained; everything, in fact, that his headmaster had commended in his speech night address — and all Evie could do was look at him as though he were some sort of murderer. "We have to act responsibly," he pleaded. "An unwanted pregnancy's no joke."

"Ah," she said. "You've got words by the mouthful, haven't you? And here's me conned into thinking you was crazy for me."

"*Evie!*" he protested, stricken by the injustice of everything.

Like an echo came a shout from the road — "*Evie!*" The girl started fearfully. "He's looking for me," she muttered. "Maybe he knows you're here." She began to pack up her nets. "Fat lot you care, but."

Richard put out his hand. He couldn't bear to see her look so bleak, so defeated. "What's the matter? Has he been beating you? Don't go back right now if he's mad at you."

She shrugged. "I gotta go back sooner or later, don't I?" She smiled wearily. "Where else can I go?"

"Yes, but just till he cools off — there's a cave I can take you to — " He broke off, recollecting fantasies that had centred around that cave.

"You want to carry something?" She threw the rabbits over her shoulder and began to walk down the hill.

The man was waiting by the fence. His truck was parked on the track, and the two boys were leaning against it, watching. "And how are we this afternoon, squire?" he asked, using his thumb to test the sharpness of his axe. "Out riding again?"

Richard nodded, his eyes held by the man's broad thumb feeling up and down the axe blade. "I gave Evie a bit of a hand with the rabbits."

"I see. Very decent of you. I like young fellers to do the right thing by women." Richard felt his hostility towards Evie's father beginning to dissolve. "By the bye," he went on. "You recollect you give me the nod this mornin' about trappin' along your old man's fence?"

"Yes?" Richard grew wary.

"Well then. I reckon it works both ways when it comes to property. What do you say?"

"Well, yes," agreed Richard, still guarded, remembering his father's description of the man as a sweet talker. "But these paddocks belong to the Miss Mollisons."

"That's right, they do. But it's not paddocks I'm talkin' about." Before Richard could reply he continued "That's the style. No trespassin', eh? No poachin' on another man's terry-tory." He jerked his head. "Come on, Evie. We're goin' someplace in the truck."

She flung the rabbits down. "What for?"

"Get in, I said." He turned back to Richard. "All right, youngster, scram. There's things I got to say to the girl." He picked up a stick and made a feint at her across the fence. "She's a bad girl — aren't you, Evie?"

She flashed a quick look from the man to the boy, a warning, Richard realized, not to him but to her father. He would have stepped away, but seeing in her glance something trapped, frantic, he said angrily to the man "She's scared of you!"

The man's face was mocking. "*Scared* of me? Scared of her ol' man? Is that true, Evie? Are you scared of me?"

Sweat gleamed on her forehead. She twitched her head; it could have been a nod or a shake.

The man chuckled. "Don't you believe everything she tells you. She's a great one for stories — aren't you, Evie? A great one for a bit of bull."

"So *you* reckon," she sulked. "All I ever told him was how good you are at the woodchops — didn't I? Isn't that what I told you? See! And how you win all the woodchops at shows, every one, don't you, Dad?" She looked at her father. The sullen blank look began to fade; her voice grew cajoling. "Why don't you show him how, Dad? I bet he's never even been to a woodchop. Look, there's a good-sized log, you show him how good you are, how your axe is all sharpened up and you stand on the log like it wants to get away from you and when the bell rings you lam into that log and the chips fly and the muscles in your back are like the trunk of a tree and then you jump around so you're facing the other way and your back is all wet and you make the chips fly all creamy and wet and when the log's nearly in two you give it a kick and it rolls away and they cheer, everyone cheers — "

The man watched this performance with amusement, Richard with astonishment. When it was over and Evie's hands were twitching at her side and her breath coming in gulps, the man turned to Richard with a wink. "Like I said, a lot of crap." And then, gently, "Come on, girl. I'll give you a hand over the fence. Leave the bloody rabbits, the boys'll bring them."

As she stepped past Richard she paused. "You, you mutton-head, you wool-brain, you're about as much use as tits on a bull."

Richard threw the ferret box on top of the nets and pulled himself up onto the mare in a fury. I hope he beats her good and proper, he thought. The mare danced under his anger, swinging around so that he was facing the truck and the two people walking towards it. Evie's head lolled against her father's shoulder; his great splayed fingers supported her against his thigh. When they reached the truck he took hold of her hips and jumped her up into the cabin. The two boys walked over to pick up the nets and box and dead rabbits; without looking up at Richard they slunk off in the direction of the cottage.

The next morning the timber for the sheepyards arrived; Richard threw himself into the repairs with such a furious energy that his father was astonished. That evening he phoned Mary and arranged a weekend of tennis with Mary and Sarah and Sarah's brother. He saw his parents exchange a glance . . . all's well, the glance said.

Following the summer vacation it was Easter before Richard came home again. After church on Good Friday he went for a long ride, relishing the bite of the wind on his ears and in his eyes and throat. Autumn rains had fallen, and the paddocks were springing with green. His father had recently joined the rams to the ewes; the cycle of gestation and birth and growth was renewing itself. Only Mollison's scrub waved dry and bleached. The cottage itself was empty, deserted. To make sure he pushed the door open, and found as the only mark of recent habitation a few popstars pinned to the walls.

Over dinner that evening he remarked "I took the mare along Mollison's back road. That fellow doing the ringbarking has left, has he?"

His father nodded. "Month or so back."

His mother drew in her breath. "There was the most terrible accident. There was a girl, poor thing — killed."

He grew very still. "What happened?"

"Her father's truck rolled back over her into the creek while they were getting water. The hand brake didn't hold — you know how it is with these old trucks, always something going wrong. Evidently the father was further along the creek. He looked up and saw it moving and he shouted — oh dear! can you imagine . . . ! Then he had to run all the way to Mollison's to the nearest phone. They said they'd never seen anyone in such a state! But there was nothing anyone could do to save the girl."

He scooped up the last of his dessert, careful not to go on scraping the plate. "It was an accident, was it?"

"Of course it was an accident! A terrible, terrible accident. Oh, there were police out and inquiries and everything but it was an accident, she hadn't tried to do away with herself or anything — "

He remembered Evie bursting with life as she pictured herself at the rock concert. "Why should she want to do that?"

"Well you see, she was pregnant, about four months, poor little thing."

He asked, even more carefully, "How could she be, stuck out there miles from anywhere?"

His mother began to collect their dessert plates. "Dear Richard, that sort of girl always finds a way."

When she had disappeared into the kitchen his father caught his eye. "You never came across her on those solitary rides of yours?"

He shook his head. "It wasn't me, Dad."

"Sure, sure — don't get me wrong, son. Anyway the timing lets you out, doesn't it? Some johnny had got hold of the poor kid before you came home."

"It's horrible." He stood up and walked out onto the verandah. Across a moon-bleached gully three shrill yaps of a fox started the farm dogs clamouring. The white eye of the moon stared at him impassively . . . *Had* it been an accident? Her words glittered in front of him: "I'm gonna kill him one of these days — that's if he don't kill me first." Well, if she had really hated him, it was a funny way she had showed it at the fence, going on about his woodchopping like some woman spruiking at a sideshow . . . A bad girl, her father had called her. A story-teller. What was it she really had wanted? The answer nudged him, then skipped back out of reach. He wished that he had paid more attention to the light, singsong voice pouring things out to him over the nets at

Mollison's warren. Instead he could remember as though his guts were being torn from him only how she had stirred him with her body, her frantic kisses, the taste and smell and jingle of her. He recalled those last minutes with her, her excitement and her fear of the man and then as he had called her to him her acquiescence and her parting shot at Richard.

He smelt again her musky, tormenting smell, saw her dress riding up and down on her backside under the man's greedy fingers and then her ready leap into the cabin, heard the slam of the door, the receding scuff of the sulky boys' footsteps, and then his own blood bolting in horror during the unbearable, unnatural silence before her old man at last revved the engine.

Antique

Because it is old Mr Huggins's birthday there is a tinselly brightness about each face as Maud and Manton and Posy hurry to join him at breakfast.

Manton, dressed in his creams for Saturday bowls, has even foregone reading the morning's paper at the table today. He leans towards his father-in-law who is hunched like Father Bear over his bowl of porridge. "Many Happy Returns has a double significance today, Pop," Manton begins. "One, it's your birthday and two, you're leaving us again, eh? Another stint in the country with Jim and Jean and their lads, eh?" He pauses, glances around automatically for the paper, clears his throat. "Yes, well . . . All packed then, are you?"

Mr Huggins nods. "All packed. All but the clock."

"Why not the clock?" demands young Posy, joggling the table as she reaches across to plonk a parcel the size of a shoe box on top of the shallow rectangular parcel at Mr Huggins's left elbow.

Mr Huggins grunts. He visualizes his clock, not shoved out of sight in his bedroom but as it was for years and years on the farm, ticking away next to the tea caddy on the kitchen mantelpiece. And still going as good as the day he paid for it, he tells himself proudly, so long as it's wound every day. His wife Lottie used to see to that, straight after breakfast. "Always the same number of turns of the key and not one more or the clock gets indigestion — hear that, Joe?" And when Lottie died he took over. Funny thing that, how winding that clock every morning brings him right back to them, mantelpiece, tea caddy, Lottie —

"Why not the clock, Gramps?" Posy repeats.

"How would you fancy being stashed away amongst a lot of socks and shirts and medi-synal apricots?" Mr Huggins retorts.

From the kitchen comes his daughter Maud. As she slides onto her chair she places a small square parcel on top of the others and in front of Mr Huggins two lightly poached eggs on toast, prettily garnished with a sprig of chervil.

"Doesn't he look marvellous!" beams Maud. "You'd have to search hard to find another old boy as well-preserved."

"Not a day over fifty!" says Manton. "Puts us youngsters to shame. I keep asking him when he's coming along to the club one Saturday to try a few ends."

"Eighty-one years young, I tell my friends."

"He's seventy-seven, he is," mutters Mr Huggins.

"Aren't you going to open your prezzies, Gramps?" Posy asks.

They are trying hard, tossing gay balloons of talk across the table like children at a party. But Mr Huggins won't play. He tucks his table napkin more firmly into his collar and asks for the salt. Maud is not cooking with salt these days. She and Manton exchange glances as salt streams from the shaker onto Mr Huggins's eggs. He sits close to his plate and eats the whites first, then pushes the chervil aside and cuts the yolks into strips and when each yellow globe has drizzled over its piece of toast he divides the toast into two, into four, into eight. He always eats his eggs like that. His dentures *tock tock* as he chews.

"Terrible pale yolks, these," he comments. "When your mother and I kept chooks on the farm — " Another look between Manton and Maud stretches the length of the table.

Posy reminds Mr Huggins about his presents. "Aren't you dying to see what they are?"

"I can guess," says Mr Huggins. "Hankies. Slippers. A shirt. Same as always."

A stormy sunrise creeps into Maud's cheeks. "Well Daddy, if you'd *suggest* something — " she begins, but Mr Huggins interrupts. "Who says I want anything different?" He pulls himself to his feet. His gut is beginning to rumble and he's in a hurry to go down the back. He looks around for the newspaper which any other day Manton would have finished with and folded across the back of his chair. "What's happened to today's funnies, Maud? Posy! Where are the funnies?"

After they find the funnies and Mr Huggins has been down the back and washed his hands and dried them carefully because of the cracks in his fingertips, he goes back to his bedroom. In the doorway he pauses. His gut feels good with the result that he feels good all over but all the same he has a feeling something is not as it should be and he looks around the familiar walls and curtains and solid old wardrobe for help. But the bedroom has turned its back on him. His suitcase, fat with his packing, tells him nothing; it is waiting for someone else to carry it. Maud has already stripped his bed and thrown the windows wide open so that even the swirling curtains seem to be trying to elude him.

Only his clock is still ticking away in its accustomed place on the chest of drawers. Good old friend. He and Lottie picked it up at a clearing sale soon after they were married. Whose sale was that? Some poor coot who had clung to his farm till he dropped dead in harness. Mr Huggins blinks, seeing again the dead man's things, shabby and grimed with use, dragged out into the daylight for anyone at all to mull over. He hadn't given it much thought at the time. He was after a couple of milkers, and Lottie wanted a clock for the kitchen.

"This black one, Joe, this'll do just fine. Put in a bid for me, love." "You don't care that it isn't brand new?" ... It is all as close as yesterday, the auctioneer's harsh voice and Lottie's whisper and his reply and then the look she gave him in return — and yet for the life of him he can't remember what it is that has slipped his mind this last half hour. Maud — Maud might know. Hobbling a bit because his right ankle is still playing up, he sets off down the passage to find her.

Maud is in the kitchen, grating breadcrumbs, so he tries not to watch because he knows she is preparing sago plum pudding for a surprise for lunch time. His mouth waters. He always has sago plum pudding on his birthday.

"Ready for your little walk up to the tramstop?" Maud asks.

He shakes his head. "I think I'll stay put this morning."

"But won't your friend Mr Kneebone be waiting for you?"

His friend Mr Kneebone boards with a married couple on the other side of the tramstop, exactly the same number of houses from it as Mr Huggins. Having stopped to pass the time of day there one morning on one of their solitary health-walks, the two old men have got into the habit of meeting at the tramstop each morning for a breather and a bit of old chin-wag. Mr Huggins tells Mr Kneebone about his son Jim who became a country bank manager instead of a farmer, and his son-in-law Manton who does something in the city, and about the old days on the farm before he was forced to sell out because there was no one to carry on. Mr Kneebone who has no family tells Mr Huggins about the larks he got up to when he worked for old Leopold the watchmaker. Mr Kneebone still has his watchmaker's eyeglass which he carries around in his cardigan pocket, and sometimes he puts it into his eye and squints at people walking along the street. Mr Kneebone is always good for a laugh. When there is no one else at the stop he waits until a tram has come almost to a standstill for the two old codgers hunched on the bench, and then he waves it away furiously. Mr Huggins says the conductor will jump down one of these days and tick him off, but Mr Kneebone just cackles.

Mr Huggins shrugs in reply to Maud's query about Mr Kneebone. "I'm going to sit in the front room," he says. Maud looks surprised. Mr Huggins has steered clear of the front room ever since she replaced her nice teak furniture with stuff from fancy second-hand places and then proceeded to fill the room with junk: old-fashioned flat irons for book-ends, old bread crocks full of twigs and dead sticks and yellow everlastings, even a blooming old copper that she spent hours scraping and cleaning and polishing just to fill up with fire-wood! — the sort of stuff, Mr Huggins recalls, that he threw into the wash-away in the back paddock that time he and Lottie let their hair down when wool prices rocketed. "From the front room I'll be able to see Jim's car as soon as it pulls into the drive," he explains.

"But Jim and Jean won't be here for ages, Daddy, not till nearly lunch time. It's a long way, and it's Saturday and they have to drive through all the city traffic."

"All the same . . . " mumbles Mr Huggins.

Maud snaps "Oh dear, we *are* anxious to leave, aren't we?" and immediately looks contrite. She wheels the television set into the front room, brings his suitcase, places his clock on the mantelpiece where he can see it. "Posy and I are right by in the kitchen. You ring as soon as you want your cup of tea," she fusses, giving him the little brass handbell with the elephant handle. "Get away, I don't want that silly thing," he protests, but she clatters on. "Is there anything you'd like right now, dear?"

Mr Huggins is beginning to feel sleepy, but he must not let himself nod off. Something is gnawing at him, chewing at the back of his mind like a mouse in a cupboard. A clock face appears on the television screen and he makes to check the time with his own clock but he can't of course because the television clock is just a funny face with Mickey Mouse ears and popcorn numbers . . . Lottie fancied that clock the minute she — What day was that? Seems only — "Yesterday . . . great eye for a bargain . . . " he murmurs.

"Yes dear," smiles Maud, humouring him. "Now, is there anything . . . ?"

" . . . forgotten," he mutters, as one thick lid and then the other folds over his eyes, shutting out Maud.

He jerks awake as the door chimes jangle and the brass knocker bangs. Are they here already? Has he missed the car in the drive? But no, it is not Jim's voice at the door. "Where is the old sinner today?" he hears. "Hasn't croaked on us, has he?"

"Alf Kneebone, you old scoundrel!" cries Mr Huggins. "Come on in here!"

"What's got into you today, you old heathen?" cries Mr Kneebone, filling the doorway so that Maud has to duck under his arm. And he winks at Mr Huggins, wink wink, to signal his usual greeting — which of course he can't use in front of a lady. "You know how long I've been waiting up at that bum-freezing tramstop?"

"Won't you sit down, Mr Kneebone?" Maud says politely. "We're all topsy-turvy today," she explains. "It's my father's birthday."

"Is it?" says Mr Kneebone. "My commiserations."

"Most people say Many Happy Returns," says Maud.

"I don't," says Mr Kneebone, taking off his overlarge Army Disposals greatcoat and dropping it on the floor. He plonks onto the sofa beside Mr Huggins and stretches out his legs. "Well . . . this is a bit of all right, eh?"

"Yes, eighty-one!" Maud continues gaily, bringing a hanger from the coat cupboard and picking up Mr Kneebone's greatcoat. "Eighty-one years young, I tell everyone."

"Is that a fact?" says Mr Kneebone. "The old reprobate — he ought to be pushing up daisies." And again he winks at Mr Huggins, because they have a private joke at the tramstop about some drop called Daisy.

"I'm seventy-seven," says Mr Huggins. He chuckles as Maud colours up obstinately. "You never were much chop at sums, Maudie."

"Who cares?" says Mr Kneebone. "She's a woman, isn't she?"

"Mr Kneebone!" Maud, nettled, tosses her head and waltzes back to the kitchen.

"Temper! Temper!" says Mr Kneebone, and Mr Huggins laughs outright, big rolling ho-hos that gather and swell and break over Maudie's tizzed-up notions. He is suddenly happy, having old Alf Kneebone come visiting and hearing him voice ideas a cove hardly dare think in this house. Now, Mr Huggins feels, his birthday is really beginning.

"Maud's all right," he wheezes, wiping his eyes.

"What's all this?" asks Mr Kneebone, nodding at Mr Huggins's suitcase with his unwrapped parcels on top. "You're really deserting us, are you?"

Mr Huggins stops laughing. "Yes, Alf. Three months with the girl and three with the boy — might be a ruddy parcel myself!" he adds. And he looks to Mr Kneebone to laugh. Mr Kneebone laughs.

"Bit down today are you, matie?" he asks.

"Something's slipped my mind," Mr Huggins confesses. "I can't bloody think what it is. Been going over everything all morning. Got up . . . packed . . . ate a decent breakfast — I always do, none of this bran and wheatgerm stuff *she* tries to give me — chook food, I call it. Though I must admit when I used to mix the hens' mash of a morning back in the old days it smelt so good I often felt like a bit of nibble myself. You'll be crowing next, Lottie used to say." Again he looks to Mr Kneebone for response. But Mr Kneebone's attention has been caught by something on telly. "Horses! That's a bit of all right, Joe." Mr Kneebone and Mr Huggins lean forward, hands on their knees, staring. Bang! Bang! Mr Kneebone groans as the grey stumbles and the bloke comes a beauty. Mr Huggins laughs at Mr Kneebone. "That poor coot couldn't ride a merry-go-round, Alf."

"Reckon you couldn't either, with your gizzard full of lead."

"Ride! Listen, when my boy Jim was just a bit of a nipper he used to hop on my stock horse Major without saddle or bridle and he'd gallop him up to the top dam for a drink and when Major put his head down the kid'd just about go over his neck into the water and then he'd turn round and gallop back to the house paddock, full gallop downhill without saddle or bridle and the water sloshing around in Major's belly like a runaway drum, and that kid never come off that bloody horse once!"

"Language! Language!" says Mr Kneebone.

A fat man in a chef's puffed cap looks out at Mr Huggins. He has a long fork in one hand and tongs in the other and he is standing over a sizzling barbecue. Grinning like a split sausage he plucks from the coals an enormous tender dribbling steak and thrusts it almost out of the screen —

Underneath Mr Huggins's tongue begins to ache. "Maud's been making sago plum pudding, Alf," he confides. "It's lolloping around in the saucepan right now. Sago plum pudding. D'you think she'll let me have a drop of cream to go with it? Just for special? Eh? What d'you reckon?"

"Whose bloody birthday is it?" roars Mr Kneebone.

Mr Huggins clutches Mr Kneebone's arm. Tears sting his eyeballs and his mouth shakes. "You're the best bloody cobber a bloke could have, Alf!" he says, all choky. "The very best." And he wonders whether Jim would consider taking *two* old men back to the country...

Mr Kneebone pats his friend's shoulder. "I wouldn't say no to a drop of tea," he says gruffly.

Mr Huggins rings the brass handbell furiously. Posy dashes in with teapot and cups on a tray. "Oh so it's come at last, has it?" says Mr Huggins. "This is Maud's girl, Alf. The only filly — Jim's got three boys — Hot! Make sure it's hot, Posy! They've got a thing in this house about drinking tea hot, reckon it's bad for your throat — Not too strong and not too weak, Posy, neither. And three teaspoons... By the living thunder, you've forgotten the milk, girl!"

"But Gramps, it's rosehip tea. Milk would spoil the flavour — "

"D'you hear that, Alf? She knows how I like my tea better than I do!"

"Don't get off your bike, Joe, I'll pick up your pump," soothes Mr Kneebone. He winks at Posy as she flounces back from the kitchen with a jug of milk. "You're going to be a good-looker like your ma, aren't you, girlie?"

"Trust you to stick up for the young ones, Alf," Mr Huggins grumbles, but all the same he feels proud that he has a handsome family. "You wait till you meet my boy Jim," he boasts. Jim... a great boy, that. A man needs a yarn with his son... Daydreaming, Mr Huggins lets a cold skin wrinkle across his tea. Jim would have run the farm as good as me, he muses... but he chose to throw it all away for shining his bum in an office. All that bracken he and Lottie pulled — fences they netted! For what? All Mr Bank Manager Jim could suggest was that Mr Huggins hold off selling for awhile until some rich weekend fun-farmer got wind of it!

His eyes jolt open as Mr Kneebone eases himself off the sofa and goes over to the mantelpiece. Maud has come back into the room and suddenly Mr Kneebone turns on her. "Damned fine clock you've got here, missus, pardon my French."

Maud laughs. "That? Oh that's Daddy's. He's had it forever."

Mr Huggins sits up. "Hardly misses a beat so long as it's wound every day!" he says proudly. "Your mother used to see to that, Maudie, every morning after breakfast."

Maud smiles at him fondly. "I know, I used to live there too."

"Every day, eh?" repeats Mr Kneebone. "Well, that's nothing, Joe — just a little matter of adjustment." His cheekbones are shining with excitement as he turns to Mr Huggins. "Tell you what, let me have a go at her sometime and she'll be an eight-day clock again as soon as whistle."

"No no, I wouldn't want that — " Mr Huggins begins, but before he can say another word, without so much as by your leave the cheeky cow has picked up his clock and carried it over to the window. "Not that I'm taking the back off her today," Mr Kneebone continues. "I haven't got my tools with me today."

"You know something about clocks do you, Mr Kneebone?" Maud asks doubtfully.

Mr Kneebone winks at Mr Huggins. "Clocks were my life once. There's not much I couldn't tell you about the insides of watches and clocks."

"Leopold — he used to work for Leopold," Mr Huggins explains.

Maud looks puzzled. "It's kind of you to bother with Daddy's old clock, Mr Kneebone," she says politely.

Mr Kneebone laughs. "This fellow's a beauty. Genuine antique. Look here, look at this broken arch — "

"Broken? Broken? What's broken?" cries Mr Huggins, trying to push himself up out of the sofa.

"Now that is really something, that is," Mr Kneebone continues. "And the case . . . ebony, I reckon. Late eighteenth century bracket clock . . . English, of course. Think of that, young Posy. Must have come out all that way in some sailing ship and been around ever since, outliving all of its owners, ticking away in living rooms like this one — " Mr Kneebone looks around. "This is a nice room. Homely. Suits a good clock like this."

"Yes, *doesn't* it?" cries Maud. "Daddy — "

Mr Kneebone turns to Mr Huggins. "You're a dark horse, you are. How come you've never let on about this clock?"

"Gramps keeps it stuck away in his bedroom. He won't let a single soul touch it," Posy mutters.

"And quite right too. This chap's a treasure. You have to wind her every day, you reckon? That's probably nothing, the outer hook torn out of the mainspring, maybe. Tell you what, Joe, you leave her with me and I'll give her a good going over for you, take her right to pieces, repair what's needed, clean all the works. Don't look like that, matie, it's your birthday, isn't it? And when you get back from your son's place, I guarantee she'll be going as good as new."

Mr Huggins, thinking about being shunted off to Jim's house without his clock, suddenly remembers what it is that has bothered him all morning like a ruddy bot fly around the legs of a draught horse. The clock — he has forgotten his poor old clock — stood it up — been unfaithful! "Every day — I need to wind it every day!" he protests.

165

"But Mr Kneebone has told us he can easily fix that," Maud reminds him, lightly dropping onto the sofa beside him. "Oh Daddy! — *could* you leave it here this time for Mr Kneebone to overhaul . . . it's only three months . . . would you? A lovely old clock like that deserves to go properly."

"She's right there, Joe," says Mr Kneebone.

A small silence ticks away. Slowly Mr Huggins draws in his breath, slowly releases it. "All right, Maud. Just turn up the telly a bit, would you? . . . Ta."

The door chimes peal. Posy runs in from the entrance hall and looks at the two old men, one with a funny glass in his eye bent over Gramps's old clock and the other drooped on the sofa like a big, flaccid balloon.

"Gramps, they're here — Uncle Jim and Auntie Jean and the boys are here!"

But old Mr Huggins, staring into the convulsing screen, does not bother to look around.

Wayside

When I was very young, a country child, Jessamy my mother spun daydreams as easily as she mixed the turkeys' mash or skimmed a bowl of milk with the slotted spoon. "See that glow of light in the sky behind the ridge?" she would say to me at nightfall before the men got in. "That's it. That's the place. That's where you and me are off to the very minute I've got enough put by in the turkey money tin. Shh! Don't let on to your grandfather or your uncles, huh?"

"You know I wouldn't, Mumma!"

And she would smile that special smile of hers, like a cat stretching in the sun. "I know, Rosa, I know."

She kept the turkey money tin in our bedroom, under the men's longjohns she wore in winter to keep out the cold. My grandfather and my uncles knew all about the turkeys she sold occasionally to Ryan's pub, of course; it was my grandfather himself who had suggested it, first to Mr Ryan the publican who was always on the look-out for fresh poultry — and then to Jessamy. A woman needs a bit of pocket money, my grandfather said. Mr Ryan would send out a message with the man from the butter factory who collected the cream from the farms; "one for Saturday", it might be, or "three for the football dinner", and Jessamy would harness up our horse and gig and drive all the way into the little township with me and the turkey and maybe a list of household needs as well. These were our only outings. We did not call on the other women in the district, nor they on us. "In that other place," she would say to me as we crossed the street in the township, her head held high and her hand on my shoulder — not, I've since realized, to keep me in check but as support for herself — "In that other place there's always to-ing and fro-ing, and telephonings, and afternoon teas, and you leave a little card if you call and find no one at home." I never doubted for an instant that she knew all about how things were done in that other place, the one that flung its brilliance right up into our nightsky, although she herself had never been there, had never even been on the annual Bay trip that every family in the district but ourselves took part in. I tried to ask my grandfather about going to the Bay one year, but he just looked at me, stared down so hard from under his terrible eyebrows that I ran out of his sight with my mouth full of unspoken stones.

My grandfather never asked Jessamy what she did with her turkey money; I suppose if he gave it any thought at all he assumed she spent it on a hair ribbon or a set of combs, or a colouring book for me — "women's fooleries", he called such things. In my grandfather's eyes I fell into that category too, I reckon. But whenever my uncles complained that Jessamy and not my grandfather should by rights pay for my new shoes, or the boys' overalls I wore around the farm, he would shut them up with one of his bristling looks.

My grandfather was known in that district as a just man, hard but just.

After one of my grandfather's silent dressing-downs, my uncles always got crankier with Jessamy, slapping her on the backside, snatching the needles out of her knitting with a dozen mock apologies, shouting at her to send me out to the washhouse to scrub down their backs. Or one of them might grab me by the ears and rub his stubbly chin across my cheek — "Reckon I could do with a shave, girl? Gi's a kiss!" — until I screeched and Jessamy fluttered like a nesting bird. They were terrible teases, my uncles.

"One of these nights when there's a good bright moon," Jessamy would say to me whenever they were being particularly bothersome, "you and me'll climb to the top of the ridge and get a real good look at that place."

Across the nightsky marched a crocodile of schoolgirls, each in a sharply pleated brand new uniform, shiny shoes, white socks stretching to her knees; each marching up to her very own desk to do her lessons at . . . a desk with a real inkwell, not just the end of the kitchen table amongst the ironing and the breakfast crumbs and bits of my uncles' tobacco.

"Maybe from the ridge we'll be able to make out that big grinning mouth that opens onto all the fun in the world," I reminded her.

"Luna Park, do you mean?" Jessamy smiled down indulgently, but I reckon she was as hungry as me for the magic caves and the mirrors and the fun wheels she had told me were inside that big mouth.

My grandfather, overhearing me as he came in, muddy and weary from a long day clearing, or fencing, or ploughing, uttered a sharp bark of laughter that sounded surprised to hear itself. "So long as the buggers don't interfere with us," he said, "they're welcome to their lights. Eh, Rosa?"

At that I hung around him for a few moments as he pulled off his boots, hoping he might have something more to say to me, but he just nodded towards Jessamy. "Go and help your mother, girl." She was, as usual, hurrying to set down the men's dinners that she had been keeping hot in the oven. She and I always ate our evening meal early, before dark. "That's the way they do it in the city," she would tell me. "All the dads home by sunset and everyone sitting down at the table and telling one another the day's doings."

And then she might say to me, over the washing up maybe, "Did I tell you I saw the first robin redbreast this afternoon, Rosa, on that old pine stump out by the little house?"

"Yes you told me." And I would laugh. "Three times now, Mumma."

"Oh well" — drying her hands on my tea-towel — "it doesn't matter. Where's a hairbrush?" And she would unplait her brown silky hair that glinted in sunlight as though she spent hours pouring fresh tea through it. I loved her hair. My uncles, and I suppose my grandfather once, had the same straight brown hair, but without any of the lights. My own hair was like no one else's that I knew of, a tangle of black curls; barbed wire, my uncles called it. And they would thrust their fingers into it and drag them through it with exclamations of mock astonishment. But they did not tease me in my grandfather's hearing. "Leave the child alone!" he would roar if ever he caught them at it. "It's no fault of hers, is it?"

When their chiaking got too much I would go out and talk to the turkeys. "Grow fat!" I would say. "Jessamy needs you fat for the turkey money tin. Come on down out of that tree, damn you, d'you want the thunderstorm to finish you off? Don't die, you brainless thing, don't die on us!"

One cold bright afternoon, when my grandfather and my uncles were away in the truck somewhere, ringbarking scrub on the other side of the ridge, maybe, Jessamy and I went to collect kindling for winter from under the big old manna gums along our boundary fence. The adjoining property had been unoccupied since our nearest neighbour further along the ridge had walked off — stony broke, finished — during the worst of the Depression. Thistles and bracken grew head-high; the boundary fence itself needed tightening up.

That afternoon a fanged wind came rushing down the ridge and gnawed at our fingertips as we struggled to break sticks into fireplace lengths. "Stir your stumps, Rosa!" Jessamy kept urging me. "Keep moving like me or you'll freeze." So when she stopped working I looked up in surprise. She was watching a man on horseback approaching on the other side of the fence.

"Good afternoon!" he called, raising his hat, and dismounting when he reached us. He introduced himself by a name I forgot as soon as I heard it, though I saw Jessamy's lips repeating it silently, as though she liked the taste. "We must be neighbours," he was saying, his voice pretty as daisies. "I expect you may have heard? — I took over this property recently. It's a bit run down but nothing that hard work won't put right so the agent tells me. And he says I adjoin the best farm in the district." We followed his glance from his weed-infested paddocks to our own slopes where cattle grazed fatly. "I expect I'll be glad of all the advice I can get from you people. I'm new at all this."

"Where are you from?" I asked, laughing at him inside me because he wasn't solid and tanned like my uncles, and he carried a plaited leather thong to slap his roan horse with when a fresh green twig would have done just as well.

"From the city," he said. He answered me but he was looking at Jessamy.

"Neighbours?" she was saying wonderingly. "You come from the city? And you're going to live here? As a farmer?"

He nodded. "I hope so. It all depends. For the time-being, anyway. Would your husband be at home just now, Mrs — ? Mrs — ?"

Jessamy shook her head, smiling a slow, stupid smile that made the neighbour smile back, and rest his hands carefully on the top strand of barbed wire, and lean towards her as though she had all the secrets of successful farming to give for the asking.

"Oh well — tomorrow will do," he said. "There's a section of our boundary fence that needs doing up but it'll keep. There's enough bracken here to keep me busy slashing away for weeks." He smiled at her again. "A boyhood dream, all this, you know."

"Oh yes!" Jessamy cried. "We know all about dreams, don't we, Rosa?"

But my ears were beginning to sing with the cold, and I pulled at her arm. "Come on, Mumma. It's time for you to put the men's dinner on. We'll tell my grandfather you're here," I shouted, walking away.

"That was rude, Rosa," Jessamy admonished me as soon as we were out of hearing, but I didn't care because she had come away anyway.

Pleased with myself, I set out to make up. "He has a nice face," I said as we hurried along hugging our bundles of kindling. "He wouldn't scratch like Uncle Ned and Uncle Leo."

Jessamy laughed. "I expect he shaves every day. That's the way they do things — there."

That evening we tried out our news on the men as they were eating their meal. But it came as no surprise; they had heard all about our new neighbour at a cattle sale weeks before.

"He's a doctor turned farmer," said my grandfather. "I don't suppose he knows B from a bull's foot."

"Why's he come here, that's what I'd like to know," said my Uncle Ned.

My uncle Leo leaned across me to the pot and speared another lamb chop with his fork. A dribble of gravy ran down his chin. "Maybe he got caught using an instrument," he said.

"Maybe he just has dreams like the rest of us!" Jessamy retorted, so snappish that everyone looked at her.

"Maybe there'll be children to play with," I put in hopefully. When my grandfather replied "If there's a family, they're staying out of sight in the city", I lost all interest in our neighbour.

But he soon turned up again — the very next afternoon, in fact, when Jessamy and I were getting another load of kindling along the boundary fence. At the crashing of footsteps through the bracken we both looked up, and there he was, carrying a slasher over one shoulder.

"I feel as though I've been at it for a month already!" he exclaimed. "Just look at these blisters!" He held out his hands; they put me in mind of twigs from which the green bark has been stripped.

Jessamy smiled, shaking her head in sympathy. "When you *have* been at it for a month," she said, "your hands'll be just like mine — rough as old stringybark!" And she held her hands beside his until I began to feel all silly inside, and I had to say something, anything, just to make time move again.

"They say you're a doctor," I piped up.

Our neighbour laughed. "News travels fast." He laughed, but he was frowning too; his tone of voice should have guided Jessamy — but because she had so few people to talk to, I suppose, except me and the turkeys, she snatched up my remark and went bounding away like a dog with a stick. "Yes now isn't that something!" she cried. "Only yesterday Rosa here was complaining about aching ears" ("That was the wind, Mumma!" I tried to tell her, but she wasn't listening) "and here we are living right next door to a doctor!" — and she just about forced him to examine my ears, only he couldn't, of course, because he didn't have his torch, so to please her he made me poke out my tongue and peered into my mouth instead, his smooth face close to mine and his breath warm in my mouth so that

I gagged and flung away, hot and angry with both of them.

"Perfectly healthy!" he pronounced, smiling at Jessamy, friendly but laughing at her at the same time. "Do you two collect sticks here every afternoon?" he asked as Jessamy, head bent, went on snapping a twig into pieces. "What other things do you do around the farm? I've heard country women can turn their hands to anything."

So she told him about milking the cows and raising turkeys for Ryan's pub. Although the way she told it didn't make it sound much, our neighbour gave her all his attention. I suppose being a doctor he was used to listening to people. But when she said, darting a shy glance at him, "I reckon you could tell us lots of things about the city" and then, when he did not reply, "The turkeys are for me and Rosa to get to the city", he gave a snorting sort of laugh.

"Oh the city is full of evil and vice, not at all the sort of place for a nice girl like you."

Now Jessamy wasn't used to that sort of teasing; she thought he meant it, and stooped to pick up her kindling to hide her disappointment. And after that, whenever they chanced to meet at the boundary fence she tried to stick to what she thought would interest him. That's the art of talking to men, she once told me. So — the moment he appeared out of the bracken with a cheery "Hello how are you!" — "Oh I felt a bit liverish this morning" she might reply, or more likely "The child's feet are a bit flat, don't you think?" — the child this and the child that until he would look at the child (me) as though he wanted nothing more in the world than to send her off with sixpence to spend at the furthest lolly shop.

Of course, if he got in first with something about farming then Jessamy was forced to stop gabbling. When she was talking about what she felt at home with her face would grow soft and luminous, light on cloud. Both of us would watch her then. Our neighbour had such a lot of things he wanted to know — how to go about choosing a good cow, how many eggs to set under a hen, how soon to sow vegetables. I thought he was a bit stupid sometimes — he would ask the same thing twice. Then somehow his questions would edge around to herself . . . Did she really believe he wasn't too old to learn to milk? How old was she when she had learned? Had she always lived here? Wasn't it hard bringing up the little one on her own, so to speak? And suddenly she would remember, and back the conversation would swing to my health . . . Didn't he think that a double dose of cod liver oil would put a smile back on my face?

"Jessamy!" he protested one afternoon. "You don't have to talk about medical things all the time! . . . It isn't just medicine, is it?" he continued gently, but before the words had flown across the fence Jessamy was exclaiming "Oh now I'm boring you! Oh yes I know how it is you must be missing city life stuck away here in the country we're not much company I'm afraid the menfolk away all day and just me and the child — "

Occasionally he would ask me about my lessons on the kitchen table, or what names I'd given the lengths of stovewood that I had dressed up as dolls. But I would go on sullenly gathering kindling, or collecting smooth white pebbles to construct the grand houses I imagined people lived in in that other place.

"He likes you, Rosa," Jessamy would say to me afterwards. She was asking me something. I refused to reply. We didn't have too much to say to each other those days, Jessamy and I.

One afternoon she made me help her catch a young turkey and then harness the horse into the gig. I thought we must be off to Ryan's pub although I hadn't heard the butter factory man deliver any message that morning. But to my surprise she took me back into the kitchen and sat me down in front of my writing book. At the top of the page she wrote a sentence in her round girlish handwriting that was a model for my own. "The magpie sat on the fence", it said. "I want you to copy that out for practice in your very best writing," she told me. "Right to the bottom of the page. To show Grandfather!" she added, although my grandfather had never taken the slightest interest in my education. I stared at her. Her hair was done into one thick plait wound around itself on top of her head so that her ears gleamed like those chips of old china that turned up sometimes in the garden. She was wearing the good black coat that once had been my grandmother's; on its collar she had pinned a bunch of daphne from the bush by the back door.

She bent down and gave me one of her quick, rare kisses. "Come on now, storm cloud, I'll be back before you've missed me."

"And what if I finish before you get back?" I asked in dismay, rubbing my nose because the scent of all that daphne was bothering me.

"Why, then you copy it all over again on the next page!" she cried — and was gone.

Well, I copied out three pages in all, and just as I was rubbing my poor cramped fingers and wondering whether to start a fourth, my grandfather and my uncles drove back to the house with a half-frozen lambing ewe to warm back to life by the kitchen stove. My uncle Leo had missed spotting her on his rounds of the ewes that morning, and my grandfather was angry.

"Where's your mother? Where's Jessamy?" my uncle Leo blustered as they tramped into the kitchen, their muddy boots making patterns on Jessamy's polished linoleum.

At that moment I noticed that I had let the stove go almost out, a terrible thing to do in our kitchen, so before they had time to rouse on me I sprang out the back door shouting "I'll go and hurry her up!"

I ran along the road, not downhill towards the township but on a hunch in the other direction, further up the ridge. And sure enough, in the distance I spotted the gig and beside it a roan horse and two people standing close together. I stood still. Was she handing the turkey over at that very moment? Giving it to him? For nothing? And if she were, then what had happened to the turkey money tin? Didn't she care any more about the turkey money tin? I jumped up and down and shouted and waved but when she did not move — did not hear me, did not care — I threw myself face down on the rough grass at the road's edge and let my heart break.

After a while, when the ground began to feel as hard and chilly as myself without a heart, I stood up. The horseman was riding away in the direction of his house, and the gig was swaying all over the road towards me. I stepped back into the shelter of a clump of wattles and watched her go by. The reins lay slack in her hands and her hair was tumbling out of her plait and on her face was a light like the nightsky over the ridge.

I took a short cut across our neighbour's paddocks, running and stumbling amongst thistles and rabbit burrows and climbing the fence at a strainer post into our own paddock and so home and indoors again before Jessamy had finished unharnessing the horse.

"Well?" said my grandfather from the kitchen window where he would have seen the gig trotting up our drive. "Been into town, has she?"

I took a deep breath. "No," I said. "She came from the other direction."

All three looked at me then, my grandfather from

under his eyebrows, my uncles from the hearth where they were trying to dribble brandy into the ewe's sulky mouth.

"Well?" said my uncle Leo. "Get on with it, will you?"

My grandfather motioned him into silence. "Tell me, Rosa," he said quietly. "Do you know where your mother has been?"

I opened my eyes wide and shrugged. "Talking to our new neighbour, that's all. Perhaps she's sick," I added hastily.

"Sick? Jessamy sick? She's never sick. What do you mean, talking to our new neighbour?"

I shrugged again. "We often do. When you're not here. He's slashing bracken along the boundary fence and me and her go there to get kindling. And this afternoon she went off in the gig with a turkey." I began to feel frightened as the kitchen grew heavy and still. "And Grandfather, the cold wind makes my ears ache, Grandfather, standing around by the boundary fence," I whined.

"What the hell is she up to this time?" my grandfather muttered.

"What do you reckon?" said my uncle Ned.

"Ask her!" said my uncle Leo in a shrill, urgent voice. "Why hasn't she come inside? Where is she? What about our dinner?"

I rushed over to the window. "She's going straight over to the cowshed, Uncle. I don't suppose she knows you're back so early. Shall I go and tell her you want her, Uncle? Grandfather?"

"She'll be in soon enough," said my grandfather. "You do something about dinner."

" — and look lively!" added my uncle Leo.

Jessamy had already prepared a casserole. I shoved it into the oven and set about scrubbing potatoes.

Just then there was a knock at the front door. The men looked at one another. No one in the country knocked at the front door -- everyone went straight to the back. My grandfather nodded at my uncle Ned. "Go and see who it is, man!"

My uncle Ned came back with our neighbour who walked with his quick light steps into our kitchen, all smiles at everyone, and went to warm himself by the stove. I looked from him to my uncles. He was so slight I reckon one of them could have snapped him in two with a flick of his wrist.

"That *was* a surprise!" he was saying. "I've been busy out at the far end of the property all afternoon, and when I got back to the house a little while ago there on the kitchen table, in a sack with its legs tied together and its head poking out looking at me, was a turkey! She hadn't said a word about it when we said good-day on the road a few minutes before, but I guessed right away that it was from" — he hesitated, looking around the kitchen and then back at my grandfather — "from here."

"From here, that's right," said my grandfather. "From me."

Our neighbour smiled. "Well that's very generous of you, sir. Very generous indeed. They told me country people were generous and friendly and it's certainly true."

"Ned!" said my grandfather. "The whisky from the front room and four glasses."

My uncle Ned came back wiping dust off the whisky decanter with the sleeve of his pullover. My uncle Leo pulled out chairs from the kitchen table. "Here's to success, friend!" said my grandfather, and the three of them raised their glasses while our neighbour grinned and settled one knee more comfortably over the other. They all became engrossed in the usual sort of talk about bulls and clover and the next good rain.

No one offered me anything to drink. I wished I was out with Jessamy, dressed in our milking overalls we kept hanging in the dairy and turning the handle of the cream separator or bailing the next cow. I glanced resentfully at my grandfather and caught him exchanging another of his secret looks with my uncles.

After a moment he leaned forward and tapped our neighbour on the knee. "By the way, there's a matter we might as well take this opportunity to settle — " he began.

"That bit of fencing along the boundary?" said our neighbour eagerly. "I'm not in any particular hurry — "

"No it's not the fencing," replied my grandfather. "It's the lass — no not this little one at the sink here, I mean the other, Jessamy. The lass tells us she's been obliged to consult you about certain medical matters. Don't get me wrong — I'm not asking you to break a confidence, but tell me this, how bad is she this time?"

Our neighbour laughed. "Jessamy's not ill at all. She's — " He broke off, aware for the first time maybe of a certain tension in the three men opposite him. He sat up straighter. "Well yes, she has consulted me a couple of times, I suppose, but they were very minor things."

"A couple of times?" repeated my grandfather, glancing at me. I concentrated hard on cutting the potatoes.

"Well . . . now and again. Nothing, I assure you, to worry about." He frowned. "Is something the matter?"

My grandfather shook his head. "No. No. Only that we owe you something, Doctor, and I'd like to take this opportunity as I said to get it all squared up. Perhaps" — tearing a fresh page from the back of my writing book — "you would be so good as to make out your account while you're here. Ned! — my fountain pen from the dresser, lad."

"Good heavens, I wouldn't dream — " our neighbour began.

"No?" said my grandfather. "Why not? You are a doctor, aren't you? . . . A city man come to learn country ways? Well, believe me we have our ways of doing things. Fencing — that's reciprocal. A turkey — that's a friendly gesture between neighbours. No doubt you'll spare us a cabbage or a bunch of carrots when you get a garden going. But when we call in the vet to a sick cow or the doctor to a sick girl — why then naturally we expect to settle up."

"But — "

My grandfather gave him one of his looks, and he fell silent.

"Now how many times has the lass consulted you, Doctor? Six? Ten? More? Myself and the lads here, we know she needs a lot of care — isn't that right, lads? — she always has done, she's not strong, she's had her fair share of troubles as I daresay you've gathered. We're glad she's been in good hands and now it's only fair that we settle up — we wouldn't want any falling out between neighbours over a debt, would we? Come to that I reckon it's about the last thing the lass herself would want, don't you? That's how we look at it, anyway, and on behalf of the lass we want to thank you for all your attention."

Our neighbour leaned forward to the sheet of paper, wrote, and handed it to my grandfather. "All right then, if that's how you feel about it."

"That's how we feel about it." My grandfather studied the sheet of paper and nodded; then folding it he slipped it into an inside pocket. "Ned! — my cheque book from behind the tea caddy."

Our neighbour left soon after — my uncle Ned took him out through the front door again. Soon Jessamy came in from the cowshed, a bucket of frothy milk for the house in one hand. My grandfather waited until she had strained it into a bowl, then said "Our new neighbour dropped by. He makes quite an impression, doesn't he? He'll get on, I reckon. They've got it all over us poor hayseeds when it comes to business. Oh . . . he left this for you."

She snatched up the folded sheet of paper from my grandfather and hurried into our bedroom. Suddenly we heard a scream, such a scream I thought it was a pig having its throat cut. I made to run after her but my grandfather held me a moment. "Tell your mother we're waiting on dinner," he said.

She was sitting on her bed, the turkey money tin empty beside her and all the money tipped onto the sheet of paper. "Give this to your grandfather," she said. "He'll know what to do with it."

I picked it up. Under the notes and coins I could make out big words, scrawled in an unfamiliar hand. "For Wayside Con-sul-tations" I spelled, and that was followed by the pounds sign, and some figures. I handed it to my grandfather and began to set the table — for once there would be five of us sitting down together.

When Jessamy came out of the bedroom she looked across at my grandfather, a long, appealing, helpless look that I had never seen on her face before. "It's all right, lass," he said gently. "Nothing's gone too far this time. We've stopped it in time." He sighed, and went on even more gently, "There's more than one kind of con man, lassie. Let this be a lesson to you."

As she turned towards the oven her face was so bleak that I ran over and tried to get close to her but she elbowed me aside as she stooped to lift the casserole.

"Will we walk up onto the ridge tonight, Mumma? Will we take a real good look at that place tonight?"

"Just listen to her, will you!" exclaimed Jessamy in a hard, high voice. "She wants to go stumbling around in the dark and there's not even a scrap of moonlight to see our way by! Whatever will she be dreaming up next!"

Very soon after this came the War, and the glow behind the ridge disappeared as in self-defence the lights of the city were blacked out. But Jessamy gave no sign that she missed it. By then however she had come around to my grandfather's opinion of the city and city ways. Only in the hollow where my heart had been there still flickered the memory of those dreams, some hope faint as candleflame that one day if not Jessamy then I would find all a-dazzle that big grinning mouth that opens onto all the fun in the world.

Selling Out

Meg Fanning poked at the wood stove, flicked the dishcloth over the gleaming bench top, poured her husband his fourth cup of tea ... well, two and a half actually if you didn't count what he'd left in the cup after the first few scalding sips; she doubted if he'd get far with this one, either, since the tea by now was as pale as straw.

"Aren't you going to milk the cow before they get here?" she asked again, to fill in the horrible silence when everything in the kitchen — clock, kettle, saucepans, even last year's calendar that they'd kept because they liked the picture — seemed to press against her, clutching, clamping. (Oh those saucepans! She knew by heart every dint, every wobble.) The drip drip drip of the hot water tap crashed in her head; she seized the tap, twisting it until her hand hurt.

Tom Fanning's reply was another grunt, a strangled rumble through closed lips. Then he added "Damn' thing's got out of the house paddock again. She's up on the hill somewhere."

Meg sighed. "I keep saying to you, why don't you fix the catch on the gate? She's not stupid — Daisy's not stupid — "

"I know Daisy's not stupid!" he snapped, scratching at the scab on the back of his hand.

"That thing won't heal if you won't leave it alone," she said. "Not in this weather. Not at your age."

Tom lifted his cup to drink, then changed his mind. "Time she was dried off anyway," he said.

"Then I'll get a bottle of milk in the town this afternoon!" Meg said quickly, snatching up paper and pencil and adding to a list. "I don't know why you've kept old Daisy going all this time when a bottle of milk is so simple," she went on, rubbing her fingers because her arthritis was giving her gyp this morning. "And we've got to get used to bottles of milk sooner or later, the sooner the better, I reckon, now that you've *finally* made up your mind to put the place on the market — " She gave him one of her dry looks. "You've been the despair of that agent, I can tell you, to say nothing of me!"

"You're not the only one that lies awake of a night worrying."

Meg limped across to the breakfast table and shook his arm. "Young Donny Cobb reckons this looker's genuinely interested, Tom."

"He reckons every looker he ever takes anywhere is genuinely interested, Meg."

"What an old wet blanket you are!" She made herself laugh. "The farm is looking its best just now, you say so yourself. And if we put it off for another year prices might have dropped — "

"And fares gone up again," said Tom. "You know how much it costs to go on one of those tours of China? I've been reading it up in those brochures I sent off for." He sat up, his face brightening. "You know, I've always wanted to have a look at the way they do things in China — "

"China!" exclaimed Meg. China was a green patch on a map of the world on the tea caddy. She decided to continue as though Tom hadn't spoken. "Maybe young Cobb's right this time, maybe this looker really is keen. Who wouldn't want this place for a nice little hobby farm, walk in walk out — "

"Hobby farm! Call this a hobby farm!" Tom's cup rattled on its saucer. "After all the years I've put into this place fencing and harrowing and spreading super and going out in all weathers" ("*We*, Tom," she corrected him drily.) "and now a bloke's got to chuck it all in just because he can't get as far as the shed of a morning to milk one poor old cow! I tell you I'm finished, Meg. Sunk. Settled." As he half-closed his eyes and leaned back against his chair Meg felt her head pounding harder than ever; tension, the doctor said it was. Get Tom to retire and in no time they'd both be right as rain again. Get away for a holiday, he told the two of them. Make new plans! Take a trip!

"You're not finished, Tom Fanning," she said firmly. "Not by a long chalk. There's a good few years left in both of us, believe you me! Once we move into the town we'll be right, you'll see. Into our nice new shiny house, not an old barn of a place like this, we've given the best years of our lives to this farm, Tom, and we've earned a bit of a break, I reckon."

"We can't spend all day sitting around in a house," Tom protested.

"Well of course we can't! Sit up for a minute, will you?" She pulled out the cushion from behind him and pummelled it back into shape. "There — comfy? Of course we won't be sitting around," she went on. "I for one intend to be very busy — "

"Gabbing, I suppose," he said.

"Well why not a bit of that too?" (Be a change from listening to everlasting stock prices and rainfall and the rotten deal from the government, she thought.) "I like those women in the town. Alice Whittle's asked me to join the women's bowls. And Marge Brown tells me she's always on the look out for help with the church flowers. And then there's the library — all the years I've been wanting to get into that library, Tom!"

"Come off it! You can get to the library whenever you go into town. And you do. What are you on about?"

"It's not the same from here, Tom. Whenever I go into town I'm in a rush — there's always a shopping list as long as my arm, and you . . . well, you know how funny you get if I'm away from the place very long." Seeing the look on his face she hurried on, "So I dash into the library and never know what to choose, there are all those hundreds of books staring back at me and the librarians look down their noses if you ask for help, so I usually end up grabbing the first thing on the display case that catches my eye — "

Tom began to chuckle. "Yes, that last one you brought home was a bit of a blusher."

"Well isn't that just what I'm saying? If I'd had time to look at it properly . . . When we're living in the town I'm going to spend half my time browsing in the library. And you can go off to bowls every day instead of once a week like now . . . "

"Ah yes," he muttered. "Every Saturday they push old Ernie Howson along in his wheelchair to watch the young'uns bowling."

Meg turned away to wrestle once again with the dripping tap. "In my lovely new kitchen the taps won't leak like this because they'll all be brand new."

Tom heaved himself off his chair. "I've told you, all that tap needs is a new washer. I'll see to it later."

She sighed. She knew what his "later" meant.

"Here they are!" he said from the window, so suddenly that she jumped. Hastily she looked around her, trying to see everything through the eyes of the strange woman from the city. What would she think of it? Would she like it? Meg felt as nervous as a mother on her children's first days at school. And out of the blue remembered how she used to urge them up the steps of the school bus, saying "Go on, you duffers!" — and then run home and have a good cry.

"Two cars," Tom was saying, his voice high and

tremulous. "Donny Cobb's Ford and a big white Merc*ee*des. That's a good sign, a Merc*ee*des. Look."

Meg shrugged, and made a show of one begrudging glance. "I thought it was Merc*ay*des."

Donny Cobb came bustling into the kitchen, big and red and familiar. Meg remembered him when he was just a bit of a kid, blushing under his freckles to the roots of his ginger thatch. "How are we, Tom?" he was saying, all matey — when Tom was old enough to be his father! "Morning, Mrs Fanning. This is Mrs Knox, she's just driven up from the city to look over the property — " Meg smiled to herself at the magnums of respect in his voice as he introduced Mrs Knox. She was a young woman, not a speck of grey yet; she was wearing a short black fur coat, chunky rings on both hands, jeans, high heels — high heels! thought Meg disdainfully, with a glance out the window at the tussocky paddocks.

"Perfect morning to look around the farm," Donny Cobb was gushing. "Though while we're inside maybe you'd like to start with the house, Mrs Knox? Okay with you, Mrs Fanning?"

"Would you care for a cup of tea first, Mrs Knox?" Meg asked stiffly.

"Oh lovely!" cried Mrs Knox to Meg, coming over to the stove to warm her hands. "What a cosy kitchen this is! *Loads* of presence. I felt it the moment I walked in." Her eyes were darting everywhere like a pair of swallows.

"And a slice of Swiss roll," Meg continued, thinking as she flicked a throw-over cloth off the morning tea things that it takes a lot of presence to make a dollar. She heard Donny Cobb laugh. "There, what did I tell you, Mrs Knox? Mrs Fanning's Swiss roll is famous all over the district." So he's been talking about me, has he? thought Meg. As she reached for the boiling kettle she wished she had blacked the top of the stove. It looked naked and grey.

"You actually make sponge cakes in a wood stove oven?" Mrs Knox's eyes were round with admiration. "However do you manage to keep the temperature even?"

Meg smiled. "I've been using this old stove for a long time, Mrs Knox. Looks like it too, doesn't it? Who'd have a wood stove these days? You know what I'm going to have in my new house in the town? A brand new electric stove with two wall ovens and a black glass hotplate and a rotisserie and all you need do to clean it is wipe it over with a damp cloth. I can hardly wait!"

It was Mrs Knox's turn to smile. "Isn't that funny? I find electricity so cold, so — so lacking in personality. I can hardly wait for a real wood fire at weekends."

She went through into the living room where after Donny Cobb's hasty phone call during breakfast Meg had lighted the open fire especially for the looker. "Oh lovely!" she cried, falling to her knees before its blaze. "I can just picture us at weekends! Sitting here in front of a roaring fire reading books and the children drinking cocoa and toasting marshmallows."

"You'd have to watch the amount of wood you put on at one time," Meg warned. "Have it blazing too high and you'd easily set the chimney alight. These old weatherboard houses, they go up in a flash." Mrs Knox stared at her. "And then there's all the mess with the ashes," Meg continued. "And the pieces of firewood dropping bits all over the place. Let alone having to go out in all weathers to get it!"

"Now that *is* something I'm looking forward to, going wooding!" Mrs Knox exclaimed. Nevertheless she cast a wary glance at the fire as she stood up. Taking a step backwards she collided with Meg's old settee, glanced at it, then knelt again to look closely. "This settee," she began, running her hand over its age-darkened grain as though it were a dog or a calf, " . . . the settee goes with the house?" she asked breathlessly. "You aren't planning to take it with you?"

Meg laughed. "Good heavens no! I'm sick of the sight of the old thing. Five bob at a clearing sale years ago. Didn't Mr Cobb make that quite clear? It's walk in walk out, Mrs Knox. We're not taking a stick from here to our new place."

"Ah-*huh!*" cried Mrs Knox, jumping to her feet. She kept giving sideways glances at the settee, and Meg felt the back of her head thump. Was this pampered woman going to reject the entire farm because of an old settee?

Donny Cobb's large ginger-freckled fingers were doing a little dance amongst Meg's treasures, scrunching up the table runner that Grandma Fanning had crocheted, turning the framed photos of the grandchildren this way and that so that she wanted to get the dishcloth right away and wipe them over. "Maybe you'd like to look around outside now, Mrs Knox?" he broke in. He held the kitchen door open for Mrs Knox and Tom, then, as Meg came towards it, half-closed it and huffed at her, "Mrs Fanning, if I were you I'd go easy with your comments. We don't want the client to get the wrong impression, do we?"

Meg did not bother to answer or even look at him, just stared at the door until he opened it again and ushered her out. When they caught up with the others by the back garden gate, Mrs high-jeeled jeans-and-fur Knox was flashing ideas about like the rings on her talkative fingers — a house dam there for her horses (Horses! thought Meg; you can't eat or shear or milk horses!), a new driveway here, a sprinkler system for the garden, white paint everywhere — and Tom was smiling and nodding, the poor fool, the poor darling, putting forward plans to Mrs Knox that he hadn't achieved in a lifetime.

Suddenly Mrs Knox broke off, clapping her hands

and pointing at something in the distance. "Oh look at that lovely cow with sky under its legs!"

They all looked: there on top of the hill, black against the sky, was Daisy the house cow. They looked, and they laughed. In spite of herself Meg felt herself warm to the young woman, because of the funny, poetic way she had of putting things. *She* wouldn't be intimidated by snooty attendants in a library! Tom was saying proudly, "That's Daisy, that's one of the best milkers I've bred on this place. To tell you the truth I was just off to milk her when Donny here rang to say you were on your way out. You're welcome to come over to the cowshed if you're interested in seeing the milking."

"Actually I have to dash now," Mrs Knox replied. "I'm supposed to be meeting a friend for lunch back in the city. Mr and Mrs Fanning — thank you! *Love* your place! Mr Cobb — I'll be in touch. Ciao, everyone!"

"I'll walk out to the car with you," said Donny Cobb. He nodded back at Tom and Meg, thumbs up.

"Well?" said Tom to Meg.

"Well?" said Meg to Tom — and then, as Tom opened the gate, "Tom! Where are you off to?"

Tom's eyes slid around. "Up the hill to get Daisy. Now don't start fussing! Cripes, if a bloke can't manage that bit of a climb — !"

"Don't you want another cup of tea first?"

"What — and leave that poor animal bursting with milk?" He nodded to where Daisy was still grazing up on the hill. "She had a good eye for things, didn't she, that Mrs Knox?" He swung around to Meg, his eyes aglow, his gnarled old hands trembling. "We don't have to sell, Meg. We can ring Cobb and tell him we've changed our minds. We're not finished yet, not by any road. What's all the hurry?"

Meg stared at him. All at once she was aware that her

head had stopped pounding. But all she said was, "So that's your decision, is it? Well you're the husband, be it on your head." And turned away with a half-smile to the comfort of her kitchen.

Solitaire

... and wonders how it is the hitch-hiker is still with them. Because he is, isn't he? She knows he went out for a swim very early because when she was jolted awake by someone crunching on the pebbles at the side of the cottage she pushed aside her curtain and saw him, strong confident shoulders, narrow hips (she has forgotten how narrow men's hips are), no towel or sweater as though he's impervious to pre-dawn chill; saw him drop over the cliff to reappear on the beach and stride towards the flat, stealthy sea until the waiting sun suddenly sprang and man and dazzling morning were one. Half-dozing, prodded into consciousness by Dan's familiar voice in her head harping on about the risks of swimming alone, she must have fallen back into sound sleep the moment she heard returning steps on the pebbles: she didn't hear a thing from the kitchen although the hitch-hiker obviously helped himself to breakfast because when the rest of them got up there were the cereals and the milk and the dirty spoon and plate on the table.

And he's still here, he must be — the sleepout door is shut and his rucksack with the worn pack of cards on top of it is lying where he dropped it last night on the sofa — even though yesterday he said he wanted to be off early, walk around the rocks while the tide was still out, catch up with a couple of mates fishing further on maybe — thanks a lot for the ride down, Linda, and the bunk overnight in the sleepout. Help yourself to breakfast before you go, she told him.

And now it's nearly noon, they've all come back from the beach and he's still here. Maybe he's ill? Or last night did the children say something? Give him to understand — ? Her daughter Diana laughs: Don't be daft, Linda — that hoon! Andrew then or Rex? No Mum, No Mrs Hart, the boys assure her. A look passes amongst them: what's all the hassle? "Oh well!" she says hastily, meaning it's all right, it doesn't matter, he's not exactly a stranger, is he? "Come on, let's go," she says, gathering sunglasses, purse, keys. "What was it the monkey said when he threw the clock out the window, Rex?" she adds, mock-teachery, joking and asserting her position at the same time, and sees Diana and Andrew exchange glances: Mother, the performing pet.

She is going to drive them into the little coastal town where they will all have something to eat together before Andrew and Diana and Rex go off to the carnival, the big attraction, and she will buy fresh fish at the wharf and the paper and come back to the cottage to sunbake and around sunset drive back to collect them. Oh and milk, get more milk, Diana reminds her, since *he* seems to have got through a fair whack already.

Linda rechecks that all switches are off, that the front door is still locked. They come and go by the back door, the one that opens onto the cliff top and below that, the restless, muttering sea. As she is about to fix the back door lock open she hesitates. Shouldn't she leave him a note? "Scott lock door when you leave, I have keys, Linda." Or, since he's sure to be hungry again, "Scott help yr.self to fridge, please lock door . . . " After all he is a sort of guest, *her* guest, since it was she who offered the lift when he breezed into her little office to report on the progress of his week's relief teaching; that's his job, filling in for other people, going from one school to another for a day, two days, a week.

He'd sat on the corner of her desk swinging one leg and when she said something about thank goodness it was nearly Friday, this week had been a killer what with two regular staff away from her department (no reflection meant on him, of course — glancing up quickly) he said Oh you go down to the coast too, do you, doesn't half the city, he was hitching down himself Friday afternoon or Saturday morning —

Hesitating by the back door, she sees again that swinging foot, the long big toe with golden hairs on the knuckle, the bony ankle, worn leather sandals (Scott won't conform to the custom of wearing knee-length socks with sandals and shorts). She hears what Diana would say: Foot fetishist, are we, Linda? — and she smiles to herself, or rather, conspiratorially to Dan: what nonsense children talk, remember the last time you and I were here at the cottage? Her fingers curl at the memory. The doctors had told Dan by then and Dan had told her, and friends they'd confided in had invited the children to stay so that they could have the weekend on their own. Swish of the sea, she hears, swish of sand on the roof, moan of tea-tree against the fibro walls . . . They are lying on their bed, Dan is leaning on his elbows above her and she is memorizing every inch of him, running her hands slowly over that loved body until she comes to where their separate selves join; carefully her fingers explore, marvelling at the simplicity of it, the neat fitting together of the separate parts, partners, the partaking of joy, of joy partaken, the sated reluctance to slide apart, parting ("dividing, breaking, going to pieces") —

She comes back abruptly. Diana is wearing that Indian cotton see-through thing again, no brassiere; Rex's gaze keeps sidling up to it, rearing back. It isn't fair — "Diana, is that what you're wearing?" she asks, pleads.

"Yes," Diana replies innocently, holding her gaze until it is Linda who looks away . . . Tell me what *you* would have done, Dan, she begs silently.

Andrew breaks the tension. "Are you sure you won't come to the carnival, Mum?" he asks, ho ho. "Be beaut fun, Mrs Hart, we'll look after you," Rex adds. She knows they expect her to laugh, refuse; she does so. Then Diana says, with a little showing-off look at Rex as she nods towards the sleepout, "You reckon you're safe left alone with *him*, Linda?" — joking too — everyone's joking again — but concerned nevertheless, it's Diana's way of showing it, saying she's sorry, the good kid, they're all good kids, Dan would be proud of Andrew and Diana, he'd approve of their friends too . . . Linda wants desperately to tell him about them, show off a bit, tell him how well she is managing —

She sees the sleepout door open, Scott is on the porch, he's stepping past her through the bamboo beading; she hears Diana saying "The ones you know are usually the very ones, Linda" so that she has to hush her with urgent clenched eyebrows then turn smiling to Scott. Good morning, did you sleep well, *isn't* the weather marvellous, says Linda's smile.

"Hi!" he says, yawning and stretching and scratching one shoulder. "Bet I was the only one to see the sun rise, huh?"

"Help yourself to the fridge, we're just off into town — can we get you anything?" Linda babbles on brightly, and explains about the carnival.

He shakes his head. "Towns? Carnivals? When there's all that beautiful surf building up right at your door? What's the coming generation coming to, Mrs Hart?" He grins at Diana.

"Well be good then," the girl responds pertly. She slides past Linda through the bamboo beading. "Dear mother is concerned you might rape her."

"Not unless she wants me to," Scott replies mildly, scooping up his pack of cards from his rucksack and going out to the porch where he lays out a game on their picnic table. Diana makes a silly shrugging mouth at Rex, Linda who never slams things pulls the door hard to behind her, and that is the end of that. She decides to say nothing to Diana. But she burns with embarrassment, not for herself but for her child — oh Dan, how *can* she be so clumsy?

In the town, which is inland a little, on the highway, red, yellow and green bunting criss-crosses the main street; flags toss and flap; somewhere in the distance there is a brass band. Linda's heart gives a little tug as she locks the car. Perhaps because she is smiling, expectant, it is to her not the children that two clowns on stilts lean down to hand pamphlets. There's to be a bush band, she reads, with dancing in the street starting around sunset -- and suddenly she is Linda and Dan again, his arms are around her, the thump of the drum is her own frantic heart beat.

But in the end she is left on her own. The others are impatient to get to the action, they'll grab a pie or a hot dog somewhere, they assure her — sure you don't mind, Mother? See you!

See you . . . She stands for a moment looking after them as Diana seizes one hand of each boy and they plunge into the crowd. Courage, Linda! Dan admonishes her . . . She makes herself look for a certain cafe; it used to be The Rosebud when he was alive; now she discovers it's The Ali Baba, with wallpaper like beaten copper and cut into the shape of minarets, on your plate flat bread with a pocket, tiny wide-lipped handleless coffee cups, and overall strange aromas that agitate her palate.

As she glances down the menu she sees Dan's eyebrows rising; Dan was a roast lamb, fruit pie and cream man. Well that's not much use to me now Dan, is it, she chides him, staring at the unfamiliar names while a sallow-skinned girl with black hair and black eyes hovers beside her. "What is this? — and this?" she asks the girl irritably. And is shocked at a violent spurt of anger against Dan that he is not here to help her.

All the way back to the cottage she talks to Scott in her head. She often talks to people in her head: the children, because then they are reasonable; Dan — Dan mostly, telling him things, asking, indulging in private in a quick spring of tears. But Dan is too risky today; already in the cafe she has startled a couple at the next table. Has she been staring? glaring? Have her lips been moving again? So she settles on Scott, familiar enough from his week in her department. She would like to talk about her friend Sasha, also a teacher, who keeps telling Linda she should get out and about, meet people, have some fun —

Could be, says Scott.

Sasha like herself is a single parent — a divorcee with three little children, and two current boyfriends picked up at some group she attends.

Fair enough, says Scott.

But how does she explain them to the children at breakfast? demands Linda. What she really means is, How can she get undressed in front of someone she has only just met? — A good deal of jamming goes on here, she hears Scott say Fair enough, and she hurries on to tell him about The Ali Baba. Chalk it up, Linda, he says. (She reruns that comment a couple of times but can't decide whether he's being caustic.) You can get awfully stuck in your ways, she tells him, especially people of my age. On second thought she leaves out "people of my age" — and remembers that she mustn't forget her henna rinse that Sunday evening; it's a fag but Diana assures her that school kids respond much better to a woman who isn't going grey. A large bottle of henna rinse flourishes itself across her mental screen.

Who'd ever have guessed? Scott says.

Films, she continues . . . going to films alone isn't so bad; Dan never really enjoyed what she liked anyway, and instead of losing herself in the screen she used to find herself on the edge of her seat in a tizz because poor Dan was probably hating it. Now she goes with Diana sometimes. If Diana's going to sneak into "R" films they might as well see them together.

I guess it's tough, she has him say. Oh yes, she agrees, being a single parent's no joke, there are so many things you feel inadequate about, and Diana in particular isn't turning out the way she and Dan had imagined — not that you can ever expect to mould children, of course, but even so — well, bare feet hitched up on the back of the seat in front of you at the pictures when you're with your *mother* for heaven's sake! There are limits . . .

Upon which he laughs, and puts his hand over hers. It's a strong hand, she's had all week to observe it. You don't need to lose any sleep over young Diana, he reassures her. She's a good kid.

And she *is* reassured . . . but is it by the words, or by the hand? Linda doesn't know what to do next with the hand, and nearly swerves off the road. Careful! Dan's alarmed voice interposes. If you roll the car there mightn't be anyone passing this way for hours — it's a very quiet bush road, that's why we chose this area, remember?

Jolted back to common sense, she places herself firmly behind her desk in her office . . . He's a good teacher, keeps his classes in order, not like some relief teachers. Diana doesn't like him but that doesn't count, she just misses her own teacher. Linda on the other hand gives a big plus to people who can make you laugh — poking his head into her office at recess to say You coming for coffee with the hoi polloi today? — a dig at the habit she's got into of working at her desk through recess. He's been to Linda's school on and off many times but not in her department before or not since she's been in charge, anyway. Funny occupation for a man, relief teaching: why doesn't he work fulltime? She's had to since Dan died and now she has risen to a very responsible position, Dan would be surprised — pleased, she means, swinging the car around the cottage and seeing Scott himself. Her foot thumps the brake pedal, gravel sprays.

"Hi," he says, smiling at her wryly as she comes onto the porch. He is still seated at the picnic table, still playing cards. "Thought I'd better pick up my rucksack before I pushed off."

Apprehension is replaced by dismay. "Good heavens — how stupid — did I lock you out? And you've had no lunch — " She is full of apologies.

"Relax, relax," he says. "My fault entirely, I left it inside on the sofa. Never was orderly — " He scoops the cards together, shuffles, deals again.

Linda is so relieved at the explanation that she insists on making lunch for him. She has all that fresh fish from the marina. And immediately begins to worry that she has been importunate, maybe he wants to get going, catch up with his friends — ?

"Lunch will be just fine," he says. He follows her into the kitchen. "Can I give you a hand?"

She casts a glance at those flesh-and-blood hands and almost laughs. "Parsley," she says severely, to dispel any remnants of fantasy. "Parsley by the back step." And as she selects the nicest fillets of fish to cook for him, is suddenly joyful. Try as she will to accept what certain forceful women say about women like herself, she loves the ritual of preparing food, serving it, seeing others take, savour, leave her table replenished. She will give him tiny new jacket potatoes dripping with butter; tossed lettuce, tomato wedges, rings of yellow capsicum.

She puts the potatoes on to boil, dips the fish fillets in flour and egg and breadcrumbs. Her hands, floured and fishy, hover over the pan as a memory surfaces; it isn't much, but it's part of the ritual: Dan, passing his plate for a second helping, joking Why eat out when we've got you, Linda? ... "What?" Scott breaks in, coming inside again and leaning against her work bench. He brings with him sunlight and the green smell of parsley. "What?" he repeats, relaxed, ready to laugh.

And of course she can't drag out Dan, butter and garnish him, serve him up. She hands Scott a heavy knife. "That one's best for chopping."

He shrugs, turns away to the sink; rinses the parsley, dries it on his shirt. Looking around for something to chop on, he picks up the bush dance pamphlet.

"You going?" he asks, knife poised as he reads.

She laughs.

"You should," he says. "Good fun, bush bands."

"Oh..." she says, shrugging, smiling. "You know..."

"No," he says drily. "I don't know. Tell me."

It flashes through her mind that they could go together, Would you like another lift? she could say. But hesitates. He might think — a woman in her situation ... And he's the man, after all, so it's his place to say — But perhaps he thinks she would find that presumptuous, a hitch-hiker latching on. Then again, of course, it's her fault he's still here, first a guest, now a sort of prisoner —

"Your friends — they must be wondering what on earth's happened to you — ?" she begins again.

He shrugs. "They know me."

At his tone of voice she glances at him, and for a moment mourns over a world full of private griefs. Her glance is caught, held: challenged, she realizes, much as she was earlier by Diana over the see-through dress. She feels clumsy, caught staring, and turns away to pour two glasses of riesling. "The tide's still in anyway," she calls over her shoulder as she carries his lunch out to the porch. "That's if you insist on walking around the rocks. You could go along the cliff top, of course, but I wouldn't fancy pushing through the tea-tree myself — too many ticks."

"I don't much fancy scrub-bashing," he says, following her outside. He looks at the single plate. "What about you?" he asks, surprised.

"I ate in the town."

"Oh yes . . . with the kids."

"No, they deserted me," she confesses before she can stop herself, and then, in case he thinks she is looking for pity, "Well it's good practice, anyway, isn't it? I mean, it's important to get out and about, not make career and children one's entire life, get out and meet people — "

Eating by yourself in a restaurant? says his expression.

At his look everything freezes — surf, gulls, the man with a piece of her carefully prepared fish halfway to his mouth. So what would he have her do? — force herself to enjoy that group set up for people in her situation that at Sasha's insistence she attended once and never, never again because she found there nothing but sad lost babblers and hunters on the prowl for a body? No thanks! She would rather sit alone in a hundred restaurants.

Waves crash again, gulls scream, Scott's unspoken question thunders in her ears. "I didn't know you were still here, did I?" she retorts lightly, smiling — sees him smile in return — "Coffee!" she cries, jumping up, still with that fixed smile: Linda, Dan's imperturbable hostess. "You'd like coffee later — before you go? Real coffee beans — I'll dash in and see to it."

When she has ground the beans, measured the water, plugged in the percolator, she goes into her bedroom and quietly closes the door. Undressing in front of her mirror, she plucks a couple of hairs from around her nipples, looks at herself side-on: if she pulls in her stomach muscles, hard, her chest re-appears . . . Dan loved her body, drew from it a hundred responses. Pretending her hands are his, with long sweeps of her fingers she commences stroking her thighs, her belly, her breasts. She clasps herself — her flesh shrieks with hunger. *Never again to have a man put his arms around her* . . . Oh Dan! she rages, throwing herself across the double bed that she can't bring herself to get rid of, Oh Dan, why have you done this to me?

This isn't getting that suntan, Linda, she hears Dan remonstrate. She gets up, scrubs at her eyes, puts on her bikini, gathers together towel, sunhat, sunglasses, headrest, blockout cream for her face, lotion for the rest of her. Then, knotting the tie of her beach robe firm as a resolution, she returns to the kitchen and makes a cheerful clatter with cups, spoons, the bottle of coffee liqueur that Diana gave her for Christmas.

Scott has finished eating and is playing solitaire again. She stands watching, fascinated by the deft, almost careless way he handles the cards — as much part of him as breathing, or scratching his shoulder. He is using a double pack now, and is laying out ten piles of five cards. The object of this particular solitaire, she remembers from childhood holiday games, is to assemble the thirteen cards of each of the eight suits starting with the king — possible, but not easy, she recollects; you needed skills of observation as well as good luck. If you can use up all the cards in a pile, she recalls, you have a space, and into that space you can move a king and build his suit on top of him. Scott looks up and sees her waiting with the tray of coffee things. "Sorry!" he says, sweeping the cards aside to make room. He nods at her beach attire. "All set? Point's working," he goes on, looking down to the headland where waves, deflected, sweep towering towards the beach. "Look's okay for this afternoon."

"Doesn't it!" she agrees. "The point always works with a south-easterly swell." She is quoting Dan. She doesn't let on what a sook she is about surfing, how Dan had to swim with her through the rising waves until they reached calm water, and then even with Dan beside her she was constantly nervous about something — sharks — shadows — returning inshore. "Kahlua in your coffee, Scott?" she says.

And again is beset by misgivings.

He is leaning back in his chair, hands behind his head, long legs stretching under the table. "This is all very nice, Linda," he is saying. "Not another person in sight. The whole beach to yourself. I suppose you come down here pretty often?"

"Oh yes, often — when my husband was alive, I mean. Now — well, the children seem to want to do things with their friends back home most weekends. So — no, I suppose we don't come here all that often. Not as much as I'd like to, anyway." She says suddenly "I don't really spend my time sitting by myself in restaurants, you know."

He looks amused. "You don't?"

"There's my job — I'm pretty involved in that — I've got a very responsible position."

You don't say! says his expression.

"And the children — "

"Out of the nest soon, Linda."

"I'm well aware I mustn't make them my life, of course — but I said that earlier, didn't I?"

"Something like."

"Oh, I could have married again, there was an old friend of my husband's who was transferred temporarily from interstate, but after we'd talked out Dan there didn't seem much left to say." She recalls the many discussions she and Dan held in her head over this; finally they had decided against him. She smiles. "He was so kind — so predictable. Now we exchange cards every Christmas."

Scott laughs. It is a refreshing laugh, and dispels once and for all any lingering guilts she has over refusing that dull worthy man. She refills Scott's cup. "I'm not just babbling, am I? Pouring myself into a sympathetic ear?" He pulls a wry face, twists his little finger in one ear. She laughs, and pours herself an extra dash of Kahlua. "I wouldn't want to turn into one of those babblers."

"What babblers?"

"Oh . . . at some thing I went along to once."

"All babblers, huh?"

"Well . . . not all." She frowns. "Sometimes at gatherings like that you meet a person who impresses you first off as good company, good to talk to — I mean, sometimes I do — did — "

"What went wrong?"

"Oh . . . let's just say, *chacun son goût.*" He raises his eyebrows. "Not my cup of tea," she says.

He looks at her shrewdly. "All he was after was a good lay?"

She feels herself flush, as she always does at coarseness — and also at his sly tribute.

"That's one sort of conversation, Linda."

"Is it?" She looks at him sombrely, recalling the length of time it took her that evening to realize that she was being grossly flattered, angled, lured to the shore of masculine lust. (She is rather proud of that image, and would like to share it with Scott.) "He couldn't see that what he had to say really was interesting, that if he'd bothered to listen maybe I was interesting too, and he might have — might have — "

" — got you?"

She sighs. "Why do men make things sound so crass?"

"So Yvonne used to wonder."

"Yvonne?"

"My wife — ex-wife — "

This is the first time he has mentioned anything of his private affairs. She waits for him to elaborate, but he does not — just scoops up the cards and reshuffles. Cards flick and slap as he builds a new tableau. Linda begins to panic. What is her life but a series of abandonments, first by Dan, now by the children, even by acquaintances such as this hitch-hiker engrossed in a game of chance? She says "You know there's a staff vacancy coming up in third term, don't you?" In fact she has already mentioned it, so casually in the course of that conversation when he sat on her desk making his report that she thinks her reference to it probably didn't register.

"Hmm?"

"Have you considered applying?"

"No." He moves the two, three, four of hearts onto the five.

She sees a three of clubs that he could place on the four of spades. "There can't be all that much for you in relief teaching, surely?"

He shrugs. "Pay's good."

"Yes but — job satisfaction?" she persists. "A few days here and there. Never your own class. Kids out to stir — "

"I switch off. Anyway, what other job is there where I can wake up in the morning, look at the sky and say I'm going to spend the day under a tree by the lake — and know I'll get work again when the phone rings tomorrow?"

"One of the women thinks you must be writing a book. You know, in between these bouts of earning."

(Actually the woman who thinks that is Linda.)

Scott laughs. "No. No book. Sorry."

"Just — relief teaching?"

"That's right."

"But — what are you going to do?"

"Do?"

"For the rest of your life?"

"Do what I'm doing. Okay?"

"Play solitaire?"

"Why not? What's the odds, stacking on an act in some classroom for the next thirty-odd years — or this?"

"Rather you than me, then," she jokes, but it comes out sounding tart, offended even, and she flushes again.

Scott says after a moment, "I said I hadn't considered it, Linda." He throws down his cards, amused, exasperated. "Maybe this very weekend I came down to the coast for a bit of solitary hard thinking about The Rest Of My Life, as you put it."

"Well don't let me keep you!" she snaps, and because that sounds rude, childish, she leans forward over the table; moves the three of clubs onto the four of spades, the king of hearts and his retinue into a space; she needs only the ace of hearts to complete the suit: sees it under a seven of diamonds but can find no eight on which to place the seven. "Oh damn! I thought I had it!" she laughs, throwing herself back in her chair and looking to him to laugh with her.

"Hey!" he is saying. "You've just screwed up my game. The idea is to save those spaces for interchanging cards amongst the piles, not fill them up straightaway. I hang onto those spaces."

Again his tone surprises her; she is immediately apologetic. "Of course, of course, how silly of me, I should have moved the seven of diamonds into the space, *then* I would have had that ace — "

"No. Because that way you would still lose the space. Look — " She is struck by something obsessive in the way he puts back the cards she has moved, squares up each pile, then sets about a complicated manoeuvre that involves moving several small groups of cards and results in the completed hearts suit and as well not one but three spaces. He looks up triumphantly. "You'd never make a solitaire player, Linda. You like everything out first go — solved — neat — "

"No I'll never make a solitaire player," she repeats, and hears her breath catch.

"Hey," he says again, but startled this time, concerned.

Before he can leap for his life, or grab her — whatever a hitch-hiker does when the driver is all over the road — she pulls herself together. "Well this isn't getting a suntan, is it?" she says gaily, swooping up her beach bag. "I'm off! But finish your game," she adds, since his half-raised hands look bewildered. At the cliff top she turns: "You might as well have another swim before you go, the tide's still over the rocks."

Down on the beach, stretched out on her towel, she watches the green belly of wave upon wave draw back, gather itself, then rush towards her to spill foaming and bubbling almost at her feet . . . Coming in? he will say, and she will shake her head, smiling, a settled, lazy smile but firm all the same, dismissive even: Thanks, I'm going to soak up some of this beautiful sun.

Suit yourself, he will say, dumping his rucksack and turning towards the surf. I'll have one quick dip and then I'm off, okay? . . . And, since she is watching herself watch him, she makes him turn back to her: Sure you're not coming in? . . . She sees herself stand up, toss away sunglasses, sunhat, tramp across the squeaking sand and through the shallow, nibbling foam to the rolling green water that plunges and swells; sees herself turn, catch a wave that carries her right in to shore; gasping, laughing, she struggles to her feet: See! she shouts, I did it! I did it! . . . Since it's her own film she is viewing, she runs it again . . . Coming in? She jumps up, runs, dives, turns, is carried with him to shore; hand-in-hand they run laughing back to their things — and now the film speeds up, runs mad, their feet scream across the squeaking sand, her bikini scratches and chafes, it is full of sand and little shells, she snatches it off, Scott tosses his cards to the winds. Who advances on whom? — Linda shuts her eyes at this bit so misses some because when she can bring herself to look again his open mouth is on her in a way Dan never presumed, she is feeding herself to him, herself feasting, grasping, tears stab her eyes with the joy of him, arms and legs jostle, their skin makes little sucking noises like the sea —

And now Scott really is approaching, striding across the sand. "Coming in?" he shouts. She does not answer, staring, Mrs Hart caught bug-eyed at a blue movie. "Linda?" he says, dumping his rucksack and holding out his hand. "Okay? Race you in, huh?"

How is she to respond? *Dan*, she pleads. But Dan tells her nothing. She will have to decide for herself.

Walking the Dog

There was this teacher.

Bobbie Halibut.

Crinkle a piece of red cellophane and there he is. Flick a yo yo and Bobbie Halibut is walking the dog... The first bell might have rung but none of the kids crowded around the performance has made a move towards the classrooms. Just look at them will you — Susie Fisher, Cass Jawkins, Cheryl Whitrod — they're positively drooling. Alvie Skerritt is the only one hurrying towards the maths room because last time she was late old Lamb threatened to write to her father.

It isn't worth a row just to watch Mr Bobbie Halibut. Mr Yo Yo. Mr I Am. "Mr Halibut kept us at practice!" That excuse doesn't wash with Miss Lamb. Look at him, just look at him, Alvie mutters, stopping in spite of herself. For walking the dog he is using two yo yos. They flicker along the corridor in front of him, run towards each other, hesitate. "Grrr!" he barks and one little dog flees, pursued by the other. No kidding. Even Alvie laughs.

Maybe Alvie's dad is right when he says a man like that is a chump. Letting all the kids call him Bobbie. Refusing to join the teachers' union. (Ray Skerritt is strong on unions, he's the shop steward out at the paper mill.) Spending so much time at the swimming pool coaching a bunch of schoolgirls. A man ought to go down to the pub now and then and have a drink with the boys, says Ray Skerritt. But Bobbie Halibut drinks only soft drink. In the milk bar after school with Fisher,

Jawkins, Whitrod and that lot, he'll upend a can of coke and scoff it down in one swallow. No kidding.

The rest of the staff don't like it. Makes everything harder for them, they complain. Bobbie Halibut treats it all as a great joke. "They don't know whether they're Arthur or Martha up there in the staffroom," he confides to the Newts. The Newts are his swimming squad who practise like fiends every morning at six down at the Olympic Pool or jog round and round the oval in the frost. Girls, mostly. Boys usually end up having a row with him. Like Butch Gilbert and Herbie Mason, that time they are fooling around and very nearly succeed in doing Bobbie's trick with the can of coke.

Just wait till he meets someone smarter than he is! says everyone hopefully. But no one is smarter than Bobbie Halibut. All the inter-school swimming cups which the headmaster displays in a glass cabinet outside his office are shining testimony to that. Alvie says getting up before six every morning just to splash around in cold water is a dumb idea. "Suit yourself!" says Bobbie Halibut. He doesn't care.

With Bobbie Halibut you're either in, or you're not in. And if you're in, mind your step. Like that lunch time Cheryl Whitrod tries smoking. She pulls out a tin of Drum and a packet of cigarette papers and starts to roll her own. Bobbie Halibut says nothing, just watches the performance intently, while everyone else looks as though they should have thought of it first. Finally Bobbie Halibut says "You're pretty hopeless at it, aren't you, Whitrod?" And he takes the tobacco and another paper and rolls a perfect cigarette and hands it to her and watches her light up and then he says "Now rack off, Whitrod, anyone who wants to smoke doesn't swim for the Newts."

Strict? You bet he is, when Bobbie Halibut is pulling

the strings. Hear that second bell? You are supposed to be seated in class by now. In spiky heels that make her sound like a typewriter Miss Lamb taps out of the staff room, a pile of assignments across her arm. Kids nudge one another as Bobbie Halibut shuts her up before she can open her mouth. "Just a little demonstration in obedience, Miss Lamb." He gives one of his ear-piercing whistles that echoes around the corridor and at once the little dogs stop dead. They run back along the floor, spin up their strings and jump right into his pocket. The kids goggle. Even Miss Lamb manages to squeeze out a quincey smile.

Now Bobbie Halibut puts on quite a different performance. "Shake a leg!" he bellows. "You! Mason! Gilbert! Beat it!" Everyone scatters — everyone, that is, except Alvie, who is by now so late for Miss Lamb's class that it doesn't matter, and those crawlers Susie Fisher, Cass Jawkins and Cheryl Whitrod. "Gee you're a whizz with a yo yo, Bobbie," they breathe.

"Gee your shirts are awful, Bobbie!" Alvie says loudly. "You look as though you slept in them."

When the other girls utter stifled squawks she does wonder if she has gone too far even with Bobbie Halibut, but he just grins.

"Is that so, Skerritt? Then how about you iron them for me, eh? I'll be around at your place this afternoon right after school with a big basket of ironing."

She can tell by the looks on their faces that Susie Fisher etcetera wish they had thought of it first.

Miss Lamb makes Alvie stay back after school to copy out her assignment correctly. Alvie is in a twitter of apprehension. If Bobbie Halibut is punctual and arrives before her father leaves for afternoon shift out at the paper mill, what on earth will Ray Skerritt have to say about some teacher turning up expecting his daughter to do his ironing? As for her mother . . . Joan

Skerritt is so cranky these days, so droopy and absent since Lurlene was born, she probably hasn't even pushed a broom across the floor or a comb through her hair and Bobbie Halibut will think they live in a slum...

When she finally reaches home she has to shove her way under a line of freshly-ironed shirts on hangers in the kitchen doorway. Her sister Trish, who is pouring her father a cup of tea in one of the best cups from the dining room, hisses at Alvie to shush. Bobbie Halibut is tipped back on two legs of his chair in the middle of some story, and Joan Skerritt is leaning against the ironing board, laughing.

"... never could abide drinking out of anything damaged. So when everyone had gone home I took each one that was chipped or cracked and I dropped it, smash! on the floor. And next day at morning recess, you should have heard the racket: 'Where are all our cups! Has anyone seen our cups? I'm sure we had more cups than this yesterday'..."

Lurlene, propped up against the pillows in her pram, can't take her big blue eyes from Bobbie Halibut's face.

"It's your crew-cut," Joan Skerritt says in her afternoon tea voice. "It must be. Everyone's hair's long these days, or short back and sides like Ray. Alvie said you're a bit of an individualist."

Alvie flashes him the cool mocking smile that she practises in front of her mirror. He begins pulling faces at Lurlene. "Hi, ugly."

Joan Skerritt laughs, all sugary. "Go on. She's the pick of the bunch."

Ray Skerritt winks at Alvie. "Takes after her old man. Well — there's the mill bus. So long, Bobbie, glad we were able to work out something about your ironing. Not much fun for a bloke, this batching caper. We must have you around for a meal sometime."

Alvie looks at her father and marvels. Oh that Bobbie Halibut! ... Mr Con Man himself.

Mr Con Man stands up. "Well, I'm off to Fishers now. I'm helping Susie with her maths."

"Why?" Alvie asks quickly.

Bobbie Halibut grins. "Because she's so stupid, stupid."

As soon as he has gone Alvie bursts out "Have you ever *met* such a nut!"

Her mother laughs. "He's going to bring his ironing around regularly. I'll enjoy that, I could do with a bit of pocket money."

"Teacher's pet, are we?" Cass Jawkins asks silkily, as soon as the words gets around that guess-who cycles home twice a week with that Alvie Skerritt. (Once to deposit the ironing, once to collect.)

Alvie doesn't let on about the ironing arrangement. She plays it very very cool. They think she's in. Okay. So at lunch time she goes along with all the Newts and a few hangers-on who gather around Bobbie Halibut under the clump of gum trees at the far end of the oval. For lunch Bobbie Halibut eats healthy things, a large carton of milk and celery and cheese and nuts and three green apples. Alvie stares fascinated as each apple grows smaller and smaller and the core and the occasional leaf and the last little bits of stalk disappear. It gives her a goosey feeling. Like letting Herbie Mason slide his leg against hers in maths.

Cass Jawkins has heard somewhere that Bobbie Halibut has a wife in Melbourne. Or maybe she makes it up. Anyway, when Susie Fisher puts on her little-girl face and asks him straight out, his raucous laugh makes heads turn all over the oval. "Married! Who? Me?"

The Newts are happy again. Superman never gets married.

"I'm what you might call a fixture," he tells the Skerritts. Joan is fussing around making an apple sponge because he's staying on for dinner; she's got Trish peeling apples, Billy creaming sugar and marge, Ray Skerritt putting ginger beer in the fridge. Only Alvie won't co-operate. She sits hunched over her homework at the kitchen table, right in everyone's road, and she's plotting ways to get the better of Bobbie Halibut, stir him, pay him back. For what? Herbie Mason's pushy thigh? Butch Gilbert's fish-and-chip breath that time in his brother's old panel van? No use asking Alvie. She would only shrug, or look sulky, or kick Trish under the table.

"A fixture," says Bobbie Halibut. "Like a desk, or a timetable. I teach my classes, I coach my swimmers, they grow up, go away, along comes the next batch, young Trish there, for instance" — Trish giggles — "but me, Halibut, I'm a fixture."

"Ho!" Alvie cries. "Where's your sense of adventure? Don't you want to move on?"

"Nope. Why should I?"

"Well *I* do. I'm off to the city as soon as I can." This always annoys her father. She shoots a triumphant look around the room. Bobbie Halibut is the only one taking any notice, and he's grinning. She leans towards him. "You want to know something?"

"No."

"Oho! Yes you do." She has nothing to tell him of course so she tries to look fateful. Mysterious. "You *do*!"

"Rack off, Skerritt," he says, but gently, but laughing. "Get on with your homework, Alvie," says her father. "You teachers — I wouldn't have your job for worlds," coos Joan Skerritt.

It is soon after this that Alvie and Joan have the big row.

It is the beginning of the last week of term, and the school social is coming up. Bobbie Halibut drops in unexpectedly at Skerritts with a parcel wrapped in red cellophane. He says it's for everyone but he hands it to Joan. Inside is an enormous box of chocolates. Ooh! Aah! Give Mr Halibut first choice, Trish. Don't bite one and put it back, silly! How many are we allowda' before dinner, Mum? Do have another one, Bobbie. Joan is laughing too loudly. It's not Bobbie Halibut's usual ironing day so she hasn't swept up the breakfast crumbs or ironed her own blouse but she doesn't care. Alvie glances at Bobbie Halibut. He has that laughing look again, and he's watching her mother. Alvie takes the red cellophane wrapping and begins to smooth it out, slowly, slowly.

"Here, give me that, Alv," cries Joan Skerritt, trying to take it. "I'm going to crinkle it up and put it in the fireplace to look like flames. I've always wanted to do that with a big sheet of red cellophane," she trills, glittering at Bobbie Halibut.

"But Mum — "

"Here — give it to me — " Never mind that summer is over, that any day now they'll be having real fires with briquettes and mill-ends, that they always refold their wrapping paper carefully to use over and over again. Joan is determined. "Alvie, if you want your next pocket money . . . " she begins.

"Get stuffed," says Alvie, and slams out of the room.

The school social is held on the last night of term. You have to buy a ticket beforehand to get in, to keep out hooligans from outside the school, and to pay for the music. Bobbie Halibut organizes everything — hires the band, has a team of kids decorating the school hall, nags people into buying tickets.

"Come on, Skerritt, fork out!" he booms, waving a handful of tickets in her face.

"Can't. I'm broke," Alvie mumbles, then blushes, knowing he'll know why.

"You knucklenuts that forget your money! Here.

Pay me back later — No hurry, kid," he adds, sotto voce.

"Teacher's pet, are we?" Cass Jawkins repeats. She overhears everything. Alvie doesn't care. She's playing it cool. On impulse she hangs around Herbie Mason and Butch Gilbert for most of the social. Bobbie Halibut, monopolized as usual by the Newts, yells at her "Hey! Save a dance for me, Skerritt! . . . Who's walking you home, not those rockapes, I trust?" he murmurs later. Alvie tosses him her mocking smile which she has almost perfected by now.

"I'm cycling, actually."

"Then I'll cycle with you."

Frost glitters in their headlamps. As she pedals hard to catch up to him, the cold air makes her fillings ache. "You're bossy!" she complains. "I could have had a comfy ride home in the Gilberts' old panel van."

"Yeah. That's what I figured."

"What? You just wait!" she shouts. "You think you're so smart!"

"Is that so?" He slows down to ride beside her. "Hey! Remember that crack about my sense of adventure? I'm going to Sydney for this vacation."

"Why Sydney?"

"Why not? I've never been to Sydney."

"Neither have I. We hardly ever get as far as Melbourne. Why don't I come with you?"

"That's a thought. If you weren't so broke. Pity *you* didn't do my ironing."

"For a ride on a Manly Ferry!"

"Luna Park!"

"Kings Cross!"

"Sydney Harbour Bridge!"

"Oh I'd love to see the Harbour Bridge! At night. All lit up." With you, she wants to add. *With you, with you, with you.* "Write to me, Bobbie."

"What — just two weeks vacation and you expect me to sit down and write letters?"

"Oh I do — I do!" She stops riding. Bobbie Halibut circles, draws alongside, leans over and kisses her. All the stars in the Milky Way bubble together, stream in one gulp down her throat and fizz around in her stomach.

"See you, kid."

Two weeks is a very long time. Alvie's thoughts spin around Bobbie Halibut like the little dogs on the yo yos. She will swim fifty laps every day. She will run barefoot in the frost. She will get to do his ironing no matter how many rows she has with her mother. Joan Skerritt seems particularly exasperating these holidays. "What are you drooping around like that for, Alvie?" She says it a dozen times. "You're not getting glandular fever, are you? I hear there's a lot of it about just now. The kissing disease, they call it . . . Oh — I nearly forgot. There's a letter from Sydney for you."

The letter is a postcard with a picture of the Sydney Harbour Bridge. There is no envelope; she supposes that her mother has already had a good look but all the same she hurries to her room to read it.

It takes a few moments to decipher his scrawl . . . "Hi! Things are happening so fast to yours truly I don't know whether I'm Arthur or Martha (Well go and have a look as the little old lady didn't say to the bishop — ha ha) Luv, B." . . .

She rereads it a couple of times, then tosses it into a drawer.

When school resumes he isn't there. Some woman has taken his place. All through his lesson the Newts fix the woman with eyes like stones. Alvie stares out the window.

At recess time they collect in the old spot, under the gum trees at the far end of the oval. Lemony sunshine trickles through the mist.

"Look what I've got," Alvie says and hands the postcard around.

Cass Jawkins smirks. "Look what *I've* got." She produces a cutting from a Sydney newspaper.

Susie Fisher takes one look and shrieks "He's never! He said he'd never! He *promised!*"

Cass Jawkins snaps "Well it just goes to show someone else was a lot smarter than he was, doesn't it?"

Susie Fisher wails "I think I'm getting a migraine. I'm going up to the sick bay. Oh . . . Oh!"

"Wish it was me," Cheryl Whitrod sighs, rereading the cutting.

"Let's send him a present — a telegram — a card — "

Susie Fisher dabs at her eyes. "Strychnine," she hisses.

The girls laugh. The bell rings. They jump up at once and hurry to their lockers. No excuse now to say "Mr Halibut kept us at training down on the oval."

Alvie lingers, staring at the cutting. "Madeleine and Robert," she reads . . . *Bobbie and Alvie* . . . "Robert recently resigned from his teaching post in a Victorian country town in order to travel with his bride on an extended honeymoon . . . "

When the girls are out of sight she hurries to the edge of the oval, drops into the storm water drain and runs along it until she is well away from the school.

At home, Joan has just finished bathing Lurlene on the kitchen table. She is patting her dry with a big towel, a special one that's been used for all the babies. The edges are fraying, Alvie notices, crowding close to the table. Lurlene's mouth opens in a fat, crooked smile when she catches sight of Alvie.

"What's up with you?" her mother asks, patting and powdering.

Alvie hands her the cutting. "He said he'd never get married."

"That's what people *say*." Joan studies the cutting. "So. No more ironing, then."

The kitchen clock ticks loudly. Lurlene, neglected, begins to grizzle.

"What's up with *you?*" Alvie asks.

Joan scoops up Lurlene and tosses her to her shoulder. "Ah well . . . it just goes to show us, doesn't it, girls?" She holds the baby over her head and shakes her. "Men like to play with fire" — the little girl shrieks with laughter — "so long as it's only
                       coloured
                                     cellophane!"